P9-EDE-756

WITHDRAWN
UTSA LIBRARIES

MANHATTAN
PRIMITIVE

MANHATTAN PRIMITIVE

A NOVEL BY ROBERT A. CARTER

STEIN AND DAY/*Publishers*/New York

First published in 1971
Copyright © 1971 by Robert A. Carter
Library of Congress Catalog No. 75-122428
All rights reserved
Published simultaneously in Canada by Saunders of Toronto, Ltd.
Designed by Bernard Schleifer
Printed in the United States of America
Stein and Day/*Publishers*/7 East 48 Street, New York, N.Y. 10017
SBN 8128-1381-2

Line quoted from Wallace Stevens reprinted with permission of Alfred A. Knopf, Inc. from *The Collected Poems of Wallace Stevens*. Copyright 1923 and renewed 1951 by Wallace Stevens.

Lines from "Sailing to Byzantium" reprinted with permission of The Macmillan Company from *Collected Poems* by William Butler Yeats. Copyright 1928 by The Macmillan Company, renewed 1956 by Georgie Yeats.

Lines from "Whole Love" by Robert Graves reprinted by permission of Collins-Knowlton-Wing, Inc. Copyright © 1966 by Robert Graves.

LIBRARY
The University of Texas
At San   io

FOR
MARJORIE

*   *   *

I have visited many museums, and worked in one famous museum. The Museum in this book is what is called in art a work of assemblage—a kind of architectural collage. The people in these pages—artists, curators, trustees, patrons—are what one would expect to find in an imaginary museum—wholly fictional beings.

ACKNOWLEDGMENTS

I should like to express my appreciation to my publishers, Sol Stein and Pat Day, and to my editor, Renni Browne, for support and encouragement beyond that an author may ordinarily expect. Thanks also to the following, for reading the manuscript and offering various technical suggestions: Aldis Browne of Associated American Artists, Inc., Herbert H. Lyons, Robert E. Banker, and Robert Anderson—as well as to those persons who helped me without ever being aware of it.

No such place as The Museum exists; I know, because I have been there.

That is no country for old men. The young
In one another's arms, birds in the trees
—Those dying generations—at their song
The salmon-falls, the mackerel-crowded seas,
Fish, flesh, or fowl, commend all summer long
Whatever is begotten, born, and dies.
Caught in that sensual music all neglect
Monuments of unageing intellect.

   —From "SAILING TO BYZANTIUM,"
  William Butler Yeats

We have no art. We try to do everything
as well as we can.

     —Javanese saying

We aren't going to spend a kopeck
on this dog shit.

   —Premier Nikita Khrushchev

1

THE LAST CHANCE SALOON in Bottleneck was jammed with cowboys, ranchers, and local businessmen having a round or two of redeye to lay the Kansas dust silted in their throats. At one of the tables a grimly silent poker game was in progress. There was Mischa Auer clutching his cards in front of his brocaded vest—hope, passionate but unfounded, shining in his limpid Slavic eyes. And look: wasn't that Charles Winninger playing Walsh, the old barfly? Now Marlene Dietrich stepped upon the bar in a black knee-length dress fringed with gleaming sequins. With a smile, she flicked off her characterization of Frenchy, the lady no better than she should be, and put on her own mythic persona. Then she sang, in that smoky Berliner contralto:

> See what the boys in the back-room will have
> And tell them I'm having the same. . . .

And the telephone rang clamorously.

Groaning softly, Lloyd Thatcher turned down the volume on his television set and picked up the phone. He swung himself to a sitting position on the studio couch, tucking the phone under his ear.

"Hello?" His voice, normally low and resonant, now suggested the slumbering bear aroused in his cave. "Thatcher speaking."

"This is Martha Crane, Lloyd."

"Oh—Martha. How are you?" He spoke now in a lighter, almost festive tone. He liked Martha Crane, whose column was required breakfast reading for him as for anyone in the art field. Moreover, after three long exclusive interviews, one of them over *sôle bonne femme* and a great deal of Montrachet at La Côte Basque, he felt at ease with her.

"Lloyd—I'm sorry to disturb your Thanksgiving . . ."

"I don't mind," he said, and his voice carried conviction. At the same time, his eyes strayed toward the mute television set, where two tiny gray figures—Marlene and Una Merkel, wasn't it?—struggled ferociously in the saloon. Locked in combat over the hapless Mischa. And there came Jimmy Stewart as Destry, the Gandhian deputy sheriff, breaking up the savage catfight with a bucket of water. It was like watching a silent movie. Trying to watch one, rather.

"I tried to reach the Museum offices first, but there's no one there."

"Not on a holiday," Thatcher said.

"Yes. Well—I called to pass on a warning. About an hour ago, I think it was, Abe Zachary phoned the city desk . . ."

"Zachary?"

"He said he was showing up at the Museum at four o'clock sharp—photographers please note—to personally protest . . ."

"Oh *no.*"

"To call attention to the many injustices committed against artists in the name of art. I'm quoting."

"Yes?"

"I think he meant the words 'art' and 'artists' to be capitalized. As in Capitalism. What he said was taken down in detail, of course."

"Did he sound serious?"

"Why else would he call?"

"I'm not always sure when Zach is serious and when he isn't," Thatcher said. "He broods a lot if he's not painting, and then when he does sound off, he's like some Old Testament prophet of the Babylonian Exile."

"Anyhow, I'm curious enough myself to pay your Museum a visit this afternoon. Even though it will shoot my plans all to hell."

"Not to mention my own plans," thought Thatcher. Through the open door of his bedroom he could catch the pungent fragrance of turkey roasting in the oven downstairs. During the next station break he'd intended to fix vodka Negronis for his sister and himself. And Susan had challenged him to a game of backgammon. He sighed.

"Zachary might not show, Martha."

"And then again, he might."

Thatcher took the phone away from his ear, massaged it with his free hand, then spoke with a scowl which was virtually audible.

"I wouldn't worry too much if I were you, Martha."

"Would you call me if anything nasty happened?"

"Well . . ."

"That's why I think I'd better stop by personally. Happy Thanksgiving, Lloyd."

Thatcher hung up the phone. Damn! He was wearing old slacks, a sweater, and socks—now he'd have to shave and dress quickly. Lorraine would have to turn her oven down, and she wasn't going to like it, not at all, nor would his daughter. He'd promised them faithfully to spend the day at home; now he was going to disappoint them for the ninety-ninth time—if anyone was keeping count. Glancing down at the television screen he saw that the black-and-white beauty of *Destry Rides Again* had given way to a pastel commercial for anti-perspirants. Disgusted, he switched off the set. Marlene Dietrich had always been his star of stars, more dazzling even than Garbo, because more accessible somehow—electrically beautiful but still one of the guys—and with that appealing strain of good-natured contempt for the whole mystique of movie-stardom. Moreover, though he hadn't seen it in years, this 1939 Dietrich film had always been one of Thatcher's favorites. He'd looked forward to viewing it all day. Now, he would have to watch the television pages for it to turn up again.

Stripping off his shirt, humming the *Moritat* under his breath, Lloyd Thatcher went into the bathroom and reached for his cordless shaver.

Some seventy blocks downtown from Thatcher's co-op apartment, in the shadow of the Williamsburg Bridge, stood a tenement building which had so far been overlooked by the task forces of urban renewal. The building—at the foot of Monroe Street, deep in Little Italy—was black with a grime that must have sifted down on the bricks in the days of coal-burning stoves and steam locomotives; narrow and weather-worn and solitary in the center of a lot strewn with rubble and the rusting fragments of an abandoned automobile.

At about three o'clock that Thanksgiving afternoon, two young men approached the building's entrance. They were appropriately dressed for the neighborhood, from their heavy boots and baggy corduroys to army-surplus jackets, their collars turned high over masses of hair. The taller of the pair tipped his head back to take in the entire scene: the crennelated rooftop bristling with smoke-blackened TV antennas, the cold blue sky splashed with cirrus clouds —the sun almost as warm on his face as in late summer.

"This it?"

His companion nodded his head.

"The great man's home." He stroked his sideburns reflectively.

"Our leader lives here?" said the first young man, who was clean-shaven and terribly pale. "Well, now. I'm ready to follow him *anywhere.*"

"So are we all," the other agreed. "A fine figure of a man, don't you think?"

"Oh yes. The grand old man of the arts."

"Shall we storm his den?"

"Let's."

They entered the hall, whose plaster and tile were moldering. They looked closely at the mailboxes until they found one which was both intact and labeled. A. *Zachary*, read the yellowed fragment of paper. Underneath the name was a scribble: *Don't ring, Bell busted.*

Up they went—six flights up, feeling their way carefully along the ruined steps, skirting a suspicious-looking puddle on one landing, and a fine rain of plaster dust on another—following their noses, for the higher they climbed, the stronger were the cooking odors, until they'd reached the sixth and ultimate floor and stood, breathing hard, in a hallway grossly redolent of meat and garlic.

"Knock knock," the tall man said.

The other slid forward and rapped sharply on the scarred metal door. After a moment it swung open. A young woman stared impassively out at them.

"Yes?" She had the face of a madonna—soft, full, beautiful in its calm—and a body so fat that it seemed grotesque. Her bulk filled the doorway and spilled out into the hall, the large thighs and arms straining against the fabric of her housecoat.

"Is Abe Zachary here?"

"Sure," she said. She turned and called out: "Abe? Company!"

She stepped back out of the way, moving with surprising grace. She smiled encouragingly.

"Friends of Abe?" The tall one nodded.

"Painters or sculptors?"

"Mixed-media men."

"Well fine," she said, and shrugged. "So, don't just stand out there. Come on."

She led them through a living room whose walls were almost completely covered with paintings, though the room was rather bare of furniture: a few thick cushions covered with monk's cloth, a low coffee table, and more stacks of canvases. The floor had been painted black, the walls a hospital white. Past the living room was the kitchen, huge and shabby. On the kitchen table lay the remains of the lasagna they had smelled in the stairwell, along with ragged scraps of dark Italian bread, a half-full bottle of wine, a white cheese with a pocket knife thrust deep into it.

In the far corner of the kitchen Abe Zachary leaned over a bathtub, his broad, powerful back turned to the door, his shaggy head bent over the tub, arms moving rhythmically back and forth. Water flecked the kitchen wall.

"Ina," Zachary said without turning his head. "Bring me a towel."

Only when his wife had handed him a long, thick bath towel, draping it over his shoulder since his hands were still immersed in water, did Zachary turn to greet his guests.

In his hands he held a naked baby, flushed and squirming; held it high as though to show it off for everyone's admiration. The baby cried out lustily—a loud peal of defiance.

"Meet Siegfried," Zachary said, happily wrapping the child with the towel until only its face was visible. "*Ecce puer.*"

"Man, look at that," said the tall man. "That's some kid for you."

"Charismatic," his friend chimed in.

"And I mean *tiny*. Must have been born the day before yesterday."

"Six weeks old," Zachary said. "Beautiful, isn't he?" He handed the child along to Ina, patting it on its way. "My fifth kid," he continued, putting an arm around each of his visitors and drawing them toward the kitchen table. "Ina is my third wife—the best of them

17

all." He lowered his voice to a hoarse whisper. "Built to have babies. I may have a whole new family by the time I draw social security. Sit down, boys."

"Isn't it getting kinda late? We gotta get to the Museum by four."

Ina Zachary, still holding the child swathed in her huge arms, raised her lovely head.

"You going to the Museum, Abe?"

"Yeah, I never get tired of the place," he said. "Where's my jacket?" He stood up and ran his hands through his grizzled mane of hair—as close as he ever came to combing it. Then he clamped a Basque beret on his head—an odd, old-fashioned touch for an artist of this decade.

They had nearly reached the front door when Zachary stopped.

"Forgot something," he said, and headed back for the kitchen. He leaned over the kitchen table, pulled the jackknife out of the wedge of cheese, and folded it shut.

"What do you need that for?" Ina asked.

"Oh," he said. "Well, you never know. I might come across a big smoked salami. You need a knife if you're gonna eat a slice of salami."

Ina nodded thoughtfully. "Sure, Abe. Well—hurry back."

"I will. I got work to do." He put the knife in his pocket.

"Coming, Abe? We still got to pick up the others."

"Yeah, right away." Abe Zachary leaned over and embraced his wife and son, stroking his chunky hand down the spongy shelf of Ina's back and saluting her lightly on the rump.

"*Shalom*," he said, and then hurried out the door.

Thatcher asked the cab driver to drop him off on the corner nearest the Museum, and set off the rest of the way on foot. He walked with a light, springing step, striding along as though he were crossing an open meadow early in the morning instead of threading his way through midtown traffic.

Four high-school girls walking along arm in arm smiled at him with the slightly parted lips of near-recognition. Thatcher was not quite a celebrity yet, but he'd been on television half a dozen times in the past few months: twice on educational programs which regularly dealt with the arts at hours when not even housewives or the bedfast were watching; he'd also had three network interviews and one late-night talk show.

Thatcher stepped past the four girls and smiled back at them. One of the girls pulled a scarf off her hair and then burst into giggles.

The crowd in front of the Museum was spread out along the wall; Thatcher had to stand and wait before he could enter. He had not been with the Museum long enough to tire of looking at its façade: panels of light green glass alternating with peach-toned Vermont marble, the solid blocks relieved by flowing sculptures. The main entrance doors led through a three-story glass wall to an indoor garden roofed by skylights.

Moving along with the crowd, Thatcher stepped into the subtropical lobby, which always reminded him of Gauguin backgrounds. Peperomia and quicksilver covered the earth and draped the sides of free-form planting areas. He noted with pleasure that the scarlet antherium had burst into bloom near the avenue side, spreading their livid petals between tall poinsettia bushes. On his left, bordering a raised terrace which fanned out to connect the lobby with the Museum's restaurant, bookstore, and office wing, glossy-leaved camellia bushes grew among feathery birds'-nest ferns, framing the fountain and its recirculating pool.

Thatcher stopped to look at the thermograph hanging from a branch of the nearest red-twigged dogwood tree—72 degrees, he noted—then continued on his way through the lobby, breathing in the odors of green leaves, musky earth, and flowers. The fragrance lingered until he passed the ticket booth and the turnstiles, where he nodded matter-of-factly to the cashier and the guards, but caught the attention of the ticket taker.

"Had any problems this afternoon?"

"Just the big crowds."

"Well, keep your eyes open for possible trouble."

Thatcher headed straight for the private elevator to the office wing of the Museum. Everywhere there were crowds—rustling, shuffling, fanning out from the white granite foyer to the first-floor galleries and to the staircases. Crowds in an art museum, he thought, had a rhythm, almost a pulse—slowing down, then speeding up; coming to a stop, then moving quickly again.

He did not realize that he had been leading a small crowd of his own until the elevator door closed, shutting him off from several startled faces just behind him.

He looked at his watch. Four o'clock—he would have to alert the security guard quickly.

Thatcher sat in the white captain's chair behind his desk, his back to the office window, which took up an entire wall. The glass was tinted amber to cut the direct glare of sunlight in the morning.

It was out of this window that Thatcher could look over the Museum's outdoor sculpture garden, a splendid sight now that the linden trees were displaying autumn foliage. Fallen leaves drifted across the pool of the shining fountain; visitors flowed over the bridges and along the terraces. The marble steps, too, were crowded with human traffic.

He picked up the telephone receiver, then returned it to its cradle. If only he could predict what Abe Zachary had it in his mind to do.

Thanksgiving was the second busiest day of the Museum's year. Though he had always considered it a family holiday, now that he thought of it, most of his own Thanksgivings had been spent anywhere but at home. In football stadiums, in bars, in the libraries of the University of Chicago and the Sorbonne—and once, when he was six or seven, on a noisy sound stage where his mother was dancing in the chorus of a musical. And now, in the city, it seemed that nobody stayed home on Thanksgiving. Nor, apparently, did they go to church. The one time Thatcher tried *that*, the empty sanctuary had so depressed him that he quickly got up and left.

What a large percentage of New Yorkers did do on Thanksgiving, it seemed, was drop in at the Museum, straining the capacity of its galleries to the limit.

It was one hell of a day for trouble to happen.

Of course, it was just like Abe Zachary to choose a day when he would have a large audience. In one-to-one engagements Abe usually came off badly—he was too intense, stood too close, breathed too hard, spoke too loud. It was less tiring to stand in a group and watch him from a distance.

Thatcher picked up the phone and dialed his chief security officer.

Martha Crane had phoned ahead to her city editor and asked for a photographer; Howie Preston, his scuffed-up Rollei and light meter dangling around his neck, was waiting for her in the Museum lobby.

"What is it this time, Martha?"

"Some kind of rumpus, I hope."

"No fine-art shots?"

"Don't waste your film, Howie."

It occurred to Martha that any disturbance would probably break out in the sculpture garden; so long as the weather wasn't too cold, it was the ideal place in the Museum to attract a throng. She and Howie took up their stations near a massive Henry Moore figure and waited.

"Now then," said Dolan, leaning against the edge of Thatcher's desk. "Is this fellow dangerous, do you think?"

The chief security officer carried his short, chunky body on surprisingly thin legs. He had a snub Celtic nose; otherwise his features were fine and regular, making him look younger than his forty-eight years. He was wearing a navy-blue blazer and a pale yellow ascot—to let the world know, Thatcher surmised, that he was working on his day off.

"As far as I know," Thatcher said, choosing his words carefully, "Abe has never done harm to anyone but himself."

"A man who will do violence to himself will usually do it to others as well."

"I wouldn't say so. Abe gets carried away, but it's mostly bombast."

Dolan frowned. "Well anyway, we can't allow a demonstration inside the Museum. Have to look out for the property."

"Let's not provoke him into doing anything rash," said Thatcher.

"I'll alert the police to stand by, just in case."

"No police."

Dolan seemed startled.

"We have enough uniforms around as it is. Our own guards should be able to handle whatever comes up."

In the six months he'd been director of the Museum, Thatcher had often wished that he could get rid of all but a handful of the security guards and replace them with young women who would smile and talk politely, and know at least as much about art as airline stewardesses know about airplanes.

"The guards are fine, Lloyd, but nothing discourages bad behavior like a cop standing in plain sight."

Thatcher dialed Garvey's unlisted number.

"Dr. Garvey's residence."

As usual, Thatcher played the game of trying to identify the various accents of Ira Garvey's collection of servants. This one sounded Viennese. Or was she from Munich? There were grace notes in her voice which reminded Thatcher of Wolfsberg, where he'd gone skiing with Jeanne during his only sabbatical, years ago. He was sorry when the cool music of the girl's speech gave way to Ira Garvey's dry, clipped voice.

"Garvey speaking."

"Lloyd Thatcher, sir."

"Yes, Lloyd. Mrs. Garvey and I are expecting you for dinner tomorrow evening—have you marked the date on your calendar?"

"Of course," he lied. How could Lise have forgotten to tell him? Or was it Lorraine who'd been called at home? Damn.

Why was it, Thatcher wondered, that when he spoke to Ira Garvey he so often felt like a schoolboy? He did not react that way to any of the other trustees, though many of them were years older than Garvey. Garvey, of course, was chairman of the board, and Thatcher necessarily was more in his company than anyone else's except the members of his personal staff. He wanted to feel easy and natural with the doctor, but the tension in his voice, or the restless movements of his hands, were forever betraying him.

"Ira, we may be in for some trouble down here, and I thought you'd better know about it." How should he put it? A demonstration is forming outside our walls? An angry old veteran of the aesthetic wars is planning an invasion? We don't know how many troops he has, or what he means to do? Thatcher sighed and repeated Martha Crane's warning. As he spoke, the demonstration seemed more remote and unlikely than ever, as did Abe himself: a vague figure from Thatcher's past, an old acquaintance who'd refused to grow up, a warrior who just wouldn't turn in his armor. Unfortunately, there wasn't any way he could describe Zachary to Ira Garvey without making him sound like some kind of lunatic.

"You've taken all possible precautions?"

"I believe we have."

"Fine. We must protect the Museum's reputation at all costs."

Odd how they were concerned for such different things, Thatcher thought. Dolan for property; Garvey for the Museum's reputation;

himself for the art. And nobody could guess what Abe Zachary might be concerned about.

At four-fifteen, twilight was already spreading its cobalt shadows across the stone pavings of the garden. The last pale rays of sun, more silver than gold, gleamed softly on the leaves of the plane trees brushing the Museum's outer wall. The crowd had thinned out somewhat. In the restaurant the lights had been turned on.

Thatcher thought of his first visit to the Museum with Jeanne— almost twenty years ago. It had also been their first trip to New York. Like any tourists, they'd persuaded a passerby to snap a picture of them in the garden: the image of their eager faces floated into his reverie, and he saw again the self-conscious, possessive way they'd stood so close to each other. . . .

Thatcher checked his watch again, and felt relieved. It looked as though this Zachary threat was a false alarm. The Museum would close at five-thirty. If Abe got there much after five, any protest he might make would be lost in the surge of visitors homeward.

Still, he was hardly surprised when the phone rang: Dolan, telling him that Abe Zachary had arrived, and that he was not alone.

There were six of them in all. Four, including Zachary, showed their artists' passes at the door. The first three went in, but the guard at the ticket box motioned Zachary aside and pointed at his pass.

"Sorry," he said. "Can't let you in."

Zachary's eyes narrowed. "Why not?" His voice rang out through the lobby.

"Well," the ticket taker said, "this pass has expired. You see, it says good until April this year. You better apply for a renewal at the office."

"Bullshit!" The sharply outlined veins at Zachary's temples throbbed. "You mean I can't come in," he said, lowering his voice only slightly, "because of *this?*" He waggled the pass in front of the guard's face.

The man shook his head. "Not unless you pay."

"Read that name," the painter commanded, and then read it to him, his voice booming again. " 'Abraham Zachary.' I was an artist before I got this pass, I was an artist when it expired. Do you think this pass is what *makes* me an artist?"

The ticket taker looked around him uncomfortably.

"You're wasting time. Let me in."

The ticket taker looked around again for someone to help him, or to take the burden of decision from him.

Zachary waited no longer. Leaving his pass in the ticket taker's hand, he swept by into the Museum and caught up with the three artists who had preceded him.

The fifth artist stopped at the window to buy an admission ticket, while the sixth chose to hunker down in the outer lobby, gripping a crudely lettered sign between his legs:

> THIS MUSEUM IS A MUSEUM PIECE
> LIVING ART HAS NO PLACE
> IN A MAUSOLEUM

Occasionally he waved the sign to call attention to it, or smiled nastily at passersby. At one point he lifted his head and hawked ostentatiously, ready to spit. A guard nearby shook his head and pointed toward the exit.

That was how it started.

2

THE DEMONSTRATORS, Dolan thought, might have been chosen to serve as some cross section of modern art—one was black, one was brown, and another looked queer. In his view, the only odd thing about the appearance of the group was that two of them, a young woman and one of the men, were quite neatly dressed.

All of them marched with Zachary into the Museum.

At the entrance to the garden Zachary was stopped again, this time by Dolan's assistant. Jaimez, a strapping security officer in plain clothes, was a Puerto Rican, soft-spoken and gentle in manner. He stood fast before Zachary, his hand out, palm forward.

When Zachary started past, Jaimez reached out and placed his hand on the older man's arm.

"Please," he said. "Do not make trouble in our garden."

Zachary stiffened, jerked his head up, and roared: "Take your hand off my body!"

"*Por dios*," Jaimez murmured in astonishment. "I don't intend to harm you."

"I won't be touched!"

"I'm sorry," Jaimez said. "But no trouble."

Zachary stared straight back at him.

"We are nonviolent," he said.

"Here they come," said Martha Crane.

"Jesus," the photographer said, "what a raunchy-looking contingent." He raised his Rollei and began shooting. "I could round up a better crew of hungry artists in Washington Square any day of the week."

From his office window Thatcher saw Abe Zachary and his three companions pass into the garden. Zachary took up a position at the base of the marble steps leading to the lower level, mounting a balustrade so that he towered above the crowd. Thatcher watched him begin to speak—a dumb show of waving hands and outstretched arms, his thick white hair moving in the wind that had suddenly come up. Some of the bystanders raised their coat collars, hugging themselves.

Below Zachary, the demonstrators formed a tight semicircle. They carried signs, coarsely made and lettered, the largest reading:

BLACK ART
TECH ART
SEX ART
THERE IS NO
ART FOR ART'S SAKE.

Slipping on his tweed jacket, Thatcher left the office and headed for the elevator. There was, as usual, half a cigarette's worth of waiting for the car to reach his floor. Nor did it help to punch the button more than once, though he jabbed at it anyhow.

When he reached the garden Dolan was there with six or seven of his guards, his attention on Zachary. In the center of a crowd of perhaps forty or fifty, Thatcher spotted two of his younger curators and the head of the Department of Painting and Sculpture. Martha Crane and Howie Preston were overlooking the garden and the demonstrators from the terrace. The reporter recognized Thatcher and waved gaily at him. As Thatcher watched, Jaimez entered the garden from the lower level, came up the steps, and stood behind and to the left of Zachary, his arms neatly folded, waiting.

"Who dictates what the public is going to see in our galleries and museums?" Zachary was shouting. "The rich, the corrupt, and the power-mad! But who hears the lonely voice of the artist? Nobody!"

Thatcher stepped forward and moved well into the garden. He heard a few jeers and catcalls; the crowd seemed to be losing interest, and many were shivering as the wind took the temperature steadily down.

"Artists . . . shamelessly exploited . . . victims of a conspiracy!" Zachary's voice rose and broke hoarsely in the force of the wind.

One of the bystanders pushed up close to the balustrade and shouted something at Zachary.

"Hear me out, friend—I have a right to speak in this place," the artist said. "I have a painting in this Museum right now worth sixty-five thousand dollars. Maybe it's worth seventy-five thousand or more. Who knows? But I'll tell you what I got for it five years ago—fifteen thousand dollars. And did I get any part of the resale price? You bet I didn't!"

Thatcher moved even closer to Zachary. Out of the corner of his eye, he saw Martha Crane bearing down on him. He tried to keep some of the crowd between himself and the reporter, but she pushed on through to his side.

"So that's the man who painted *Dallas*," she said. "Where's he been lately?"

"Oh, Abe's been active," Thatcher said, annoyed. Granted that Abe Zachary was no longer fashionable, seldom mentioned in *Artforum* or any of the other journals. Granted too that the critics now considered him cranky and intractable—against their best advice, he'd given up painting and started working with metal and then with neon lighting. He spoke of creating an art which would combine common artist's materials—paint and paper and clay—with natural materials, grass and earth, organic and inorganic compounds. Still . . .

"Overnight fame and then nothing," Martha Crane said. "A one-painting painter."

"Maybe," Thatcher said. "Maybe not. We have to wait and see. *Dallas* is painting on a heroic scale—there's not much of it around."

A *triumphant synthesis*, one critic had written, *of several contemporary styles: expressionism, surrealism, and neo-realism, grounded on a solid mastery of cubist principles. . . .* Possibly so. At the same time *Dallas* was a lasting lament for a martyred President, so powerful it reduced many who came to see it to tears.

"It has had a life of its own, hasn't it?" Martha said. She stared up at Zachary intently, as though she could not quite believe that this posturing creature had produced one of the century's most famous paintings.

". . . but do I have any voice in how or where my painting is to be hung? God forbid, say the Museum authorities! You're only the artist!

27

I wanted my painting put where anybody who wanted to could see it free of charge! Now people have to pay to get at it—"

"Is that true?" Martha Crane asked.

"More or less. Abe wanted to give *Dallas* to the government, but before the transfer could be completed we were off and running in Vietnam, and Abe disowned the whole affair."

". . . not in the permanent collection, where it can be appreciated for its own merits, but in a silly, so-called historical exhibition—" Thatcher winced. "—hanging with paintings that cheapen and detract—"

The old man's heckler had moved nearer. "If you're such a great painter," he called out, "whyn't you go paint instead of shooting off your mouth?"

Zachary smiled a gentle forgiving smile, and addressed the crowd again. "We ask your support. In the cause of the exploited artist!"

The heckler snorted and made an obscene gesture with his fingers.

"Like an animal!" one of the demonstrators called out.

The heckler stepped forward and pushed him back into the crowd. "You're the one belongs in a zoo with that hairy face!"

"We demand consideration!" Zachary protested. "Your respectful attention is the least we have a right to ask. *Listen* to what we have to say!"

A crackling, jittery wave of laughter started somewhere in the crowd and moved swiftly through the cluster of spectators. It was the laughter of embarrassment, not amusement, but no less harsh for that.

Zachary stopped abruptly and dropped down from the balustrade—with surprising agility, Thatcher thought, for a man nearly sixty.

Now the guards began to move forward. Lester Dolan looked sharply around, then motioned to Jaimez. Several persons in the crowd backed away from Zachary. An elderly woman—pushed, or stepped on—screamed.

Zachary raised his massive head and looked straight out at Thatcher, in desperation.

"I'm through talking!" he cried.

He broke and ran for the door of the galleries, so quickly that neither Dolan nor any of the guards had the opportunity to head him off.

Thatcher saw Dolan signaling frantically to his guards. When he spotted Thatcher, he headed his way. Ignoring him, Thatcher turned and ran into the lobby, toward the nearest stairway. Close behind him came Martha Crane, and after her the photographer, his camera bobbing as he ran.

Thatcher was sure he knew where Zachary meant to go.

Don't do it, Zach, he thought as he raced up the steps two at a time. Breathing hard, he threaded his way through the bewildered crowds like a broken-field runner. *For the love of Christ, don't do it.*

3

ABE ZACHARY SPRINTED up the gallery stairs. Reaching the landing, he slowed to a dogtrot. Even so, he jostled an elderly man with a cane who was hobbling toward an elevator.

"What's this?" the old man cried out.

Zachary looked stricken. "Oh God—I'm sorry," he said. "You all right?"

He did not wait for an answer. He was moving again, racing toward the galleries. A quartet of women approaching him split apart, all four shying away from Zachary. They could hear his rasping breath as he charged by.

Straight ahead lay the entrance to the exhibition. A catalog desk stood at one side of the doorway; above it hung a long glass panel, boldly lettered: "THE PASSIONATE MYTHMAKERS: FROM CAVE PAINTINGS TO GHETTO MURALS."

Zachary stopped, turned, looked down the hall behind him. Only a few people moved along it. Then one of the Museum's docent lecturers appeared from an adjoining corridor, in his wake a group of gallerygoers, listening attentively as they walked.

"Catalog, sir?" asked the girl at the desk.

Zachary shook his head and hurried past the entrance. Inside the exhibition gallery he turned right, changed his mind, and trotted straight ahead along the main corridor.

In an alcove off the central passage, he found *Dallas*. Two spotlights at the foot of the facing wall shone steadily on the huge canvas.

A young couple holding hands stood in front of the painting, silent and absorbed, as though mesmerized by the urgent flow of the composition from one end to the other; watching them, Zachary had the odd feeling that he was seeing his own painting as a spectator might. No matter where one chose to look, the eye was drawn instantly to the center of the work, to that troubling image of the empty rocking chair, foreboding as a gallows; and then forced away into a whirlpool of other images: an open car moving as though it were trapped on film, yet hurtling toward the helpless bystanders; the flat burnished Texas sky; the massive jetliner circling ponderously overhead. Yet all these images, some of them dark, others so brightly acrylic one could hardly bear to gaze directly at them—all were transformed on the canvas into brooding, spectral presences rather than literal images.

Beside *Dallas* stood one of the Museum's guards, hands laced behind his back, his gaze fixed on the middle distance.

Abe Zachary stepped around the corner of the alcove and flattened himself against the wall.

When Thatcher reached the exhibition gallery he found his progress blocked by the twenty or so visitors clustered around the docent.

". . . in this work we see clearly how Cézanne prefigured the Cubists in his handling of the flat planes in the landscape . . ."

"Let me through, will you?" Thatcher tried to clear a path around the outer edges of the group; they held fast.

"Stop pushing!" somebody called out.

"Sorry," Thatcher said. "Emergency."

He felt completely surrounded, outnumbered by nuns and schoolchildren and matrons with high-pitched voices. He stood motionless and seething for an instant, then squeezed by, hugging the wall. Once he'd broken free, he ran straight past the catalog desk and into the exhibition hall.

"What's wrong?" It was a cry of alarm behind him; Thatcher did not turn around. "My God—it's not a fire, is it?"

When Thatcher reached *Dallas* the alcove was empty. The guard had just started his regular patrol up the corridor leading to the west wing. Thatcher caught up with him and seized his arm.

"Have you seen a man about sixty—white hair, leather jacket, and corduroy pants?" Thatcher was perspiring freely. "Stocky fellow—about so high?"

The guard shook his head.

"We've got to find him—fast," Thatcher said. "You take one way, I'll take the other."

He turned back toward the alcove.

"We have to catch up," said Martha Crane.

"Damned if I'm gonna run," said Howie Preston. "I'm too fat for this sort of thing."

Martha started off in search of Thatcher. In the first room off the main corridor of the exhibition galleries she found a young woman, alone, seated on a bench in front of an enormous Picasso. The still, white room with a glorious riot of color on one wall seemed an island of tranquil reverie in the middle of confusion.

Meanwhile Howie Preston sank down gratefully on a padded bench in the corridor, stretched out his legs, and checked the lens and shutter openings on his Rollei.

Howie didn't know it, but he had a ringside seat.

At the sound of receding footsteps, Abe Zachary moved back along the wall toward the alcove. The guard was gone. No one else was in view. Zachary did not see Howie Preston back in the hallway, but the photographer saw him and raised his Rollei.

Zachary pulled the jackknife from his trouser pocket. He snapped the blade open.

Just then Thatcher came around the other side of the alcove.

"Wait, Zach!"

Zachary looked up and uttered one strangled cry, then began to saw hastily away at the lower right-hand corner of the canvas with the mottled, broken point of his knife. To Thatcher the sound of metal punching through cloth was like a scream of pain. It must have sounded like that to Zachary, too: he hesitated before thrusting again —before drawing the knife upward in the long, slashing stroke that would rip the painting wide open.

"Jesus H. Christ!" Howie Preston snapped and cranked and snapped again, as fast as he could.

Thatcher reached out and grasped Zachary's left shoulder, then lunged awkwardly for Zachary's right arm as he saw the knife. When Zachary feinted with the right hand, Thatcher slipped and fell to one knee.

32

"Stop it, Zach!"

"Lemme alone!" Zachary jabbed the canvas viciously a second time.

Thatcher got to his feet and tried for a purchase on Zachary's wrist; instead, he got hold of the knife blade. A stab of pain darted up his wrist and arm from the palm of his hand, but he had no choice now except to hang on.

When Zachary saw a tiny stream of blood running along the blade, he groaned and released the knife. It clattered to the floor. Thatcher tightened his fist to stop the flow of blood from the cut.

At first Zachary looked as though he meant to turn his attention to Thatcher's hand. Then he swung back to the painting. Raising his powerful arms, he grasped the frame by both hands, tugging with all his strength.

"That's *enough*," Thatcher said. "For God's sake, Zach!"

The painting tipped crazily on the wall. Thatcher drew back his bleeding fist, taking careful aim at Zachary's jaw. The painter was oblivious of everything except his struggle to bring *Dallas* down. One corner of the frame came crashing to the floor, and a ridge of twisted canvas appeared in the face of the painting. Thatcher swung and drove Zachary several steps sideways. The painter staggered, shook his head blindly.

Now the guard appeared in the alcove. He came boiling into action, pinning Zachary's arms together in a bear hug. The artist went suddenly slack. His head slumped forward.

"You crazy old buzzard," Thatcher said. "You're about as infuriating as they come." He rubbed his knuckles ruefully. "I haven't had to hit anybody for years."

Zachary lifted his head. "But I didn't go down, did I?"

"No, I couldn't deck you," said Thatcher. Then: "Just look at this mess."

"Lloyd. I'm sorry," Zachary said quietly.

"I hope so."

"About that cut on your hand, I mean. Are you all right?"

Thatcher looked down at his hand. It was beginning to throb, but the cut itself, he could see, was trivial. He knotted a handkerchief around it, then turned to the guard.

"Let's get Mr. Zachary to my office."

Another guard appeared with a walkie-talkie in his hand. Thatcher instructed him to stand watch beside the painting until he was re-

lieved. As far as he could see, none of Zachary's crowd were anywhere in sight. Still . . .

"Zach, can you give me your word that none of your buddies
will try a stunt like this?"

The artist looked at him in bewilderment. "How would they
dare?" he demanded. "It's *my* painting."

"It's all over here, people," Thatcher told the bystanders, now
crowding the gallery dangerously full. "Please now—everybody move
along."

"What happened?" demanded a heavily rouged lady in a sealskin
coat, disappointed at having arrived too late to see the incident.

"An outburst of artistic temperament," Thatcher said.

As unobtrusively as possible, he reached down and picked up
Zachary's knife. On the side of its well-worn handle he noticed, as
he stowed it in his pocket, the fleur-de-lis emblem of the Boy Scouts
of America.

4

"SONOFABITCH," Martha Crane said softly. "Just my luck."

She had searched the entire gallery for Thatcher and Zachary, arriving back at the *Dallas* alcove just after the drama was over. What was more exasperating, the principals had now disappeared.

"I got it all here," Howie said smugly, tapping the black case of his Rollei.

"Well, I'm glad of that, anyway." Martha pulled out a cigarette, remembered where she was, and put it away again.

"You know where they went?" she asked.

"Yeah, to Thatcher's office."

"Then I'll go there. Why don't you try the lobby? Maybe you can get some good shots of the other demonstrators."

"Okay, doll." Martha winced and turned away as Howie sauntered toward the stairs.

Waiting for an elevator, she ran into a *New York Times* photographer and a stringer from *Newsweek*. They had missed most of the action, and their second-hand information was fragmentary.

"*My* story," Martha thought.

All they knew was that Thatcher had been cast in a hero's role of sorts. And it was rumored that Abe Zachary was under arrest.

The demonstrator who had occupied the Museum store left after buying a catalog and a handful of picture postcards of works from the permanent collection. So far as the bookstore clerk could tell, he hadn't liberated any of the stock illegally, and his money was genuine. The clerk did not feel it necessary to summon a guard.

The two who had come uptown with Zachary were still in the sculpture garden, sitting on the marble stairs. As it grew colder and darker, they shivered and huddled together for warmth. The crowds thinned out; no one paid them the slightest attention. At last they stood up, planted their signs in a bed of ground ivy under one of the sourgum trees, and headed for the outer lobby. There they lingered, watching the streams of people moving homeward, until the galleries had emptied out.

"This place ticks me off," said one.

"Yeah. Ask me, the whole thing's been a fizzle. Screw Zachary."

"Screw this museum, too. I think . . ."

"What?"

"I feel a protest coming on."

"Whatcha gonna do?"

For an answer, he opened his fly and sent a thin jet of urine arching across the lobby.

His companion followed suit, playing his own amber stream as the other was spent.

None of the few witnesses to this scene quite believed it—except for Howie Preston, who was busy with his Rollei, smiling all the while. They may not be printable, he thought. But I certainly got 'em.

Abe Zachary sat on the divan in Thatcher's office, staring down at his gnarled hands, clasped together in his lap as though they were manacled.

"All right," Thatcher said. "Have it your way."

"What I did speaks for itself," Zachary said.

"By no means. But we'll leave that aside. . . . What about the rest of your gang?"

Zachary stiffened.

"I don't mean to put them down, Zach, but I didn't recognize any of them."

"So?"

"Who are they?"

"Artists. All of them."

"Surely I'm not so cut off from what's going on that I wouldn't know at least *one* of them."

"That's your problem," Zachary said, smiling for the first time since he'd let himself be frog-marched into Thatcher's office. "I know them."

"What do they have in mind?"

"They want the same things I want."

"And what the hell is that?" Thatcher persisted. When Zachary did not answer, he shrugged and walked toward the window, turning his back on the artist.

"I wish I knew why you planned this whole thing." He snapped his head toward Zachary. "You did plan it, didn't you?"

Abe made an odd snuffling sound, midway between amusement and scorn.

Thatcher sat down and drummed with his fingers on the polished surface of his desk like an actor waiting for his cue. "It's too bad we couldn't have picked a more pleasant occasion for a reunion, Zach."

"I'm agreeable."

Thatcher shook his head. "There isn't any back way out of here, Zach," he said. "I'm sorry."

"That's all right."

"I just wish you'd tell me your real reasons. There are reporters waiting out there who are just as curious as I am—and much less patient."

"That's a beautiful desk," Zachary said.

"What? Come *on*, Zach. . ."

The painter thrust his finger this way and that. "And such works of art for decoration—masterpieces! Imagine being able to sit and work right under a priceless Matisse—"

"That's enough, I get your point."

"Well—who can say you don't deserve all this? You're a man of stature now. But I say you're in prison, my friend. And the look on your face is the look of the prisoner—haunted and oppressed."

Thatcher, who had been searching his desk for a pack of cigarettes, raised his head. "Dammit, Abe, right now the only one oppressing me is you."

"Please—you don't have to agree with me," Zachary said with great dignity. "But you want to know why I did what I did? I'll tell you. So I can be free, Lloyd. Free of the dead weight of the past."

Thatcher sighed. "All right, Zach," he said. "No more rhetoric, please. Just let me remind you that those reporters are here in large part because you asked them to come. So I hope you have a statement to make, Zach, since I'm going to call them in now—and *I* sure as hell don't have one."

"Did you really mean to destroy your painting?" Martha Crane demanded. "Or was it only a gesture?"

Abe Zachary bowed his shaggy head and went into conference somewhere deep inside his skull. Or so it seemed to Thatcher.

The press conference had been going on in Thatcher's office for nearly twenty minutes. The first questions had been directed toward bringing out the details of what had happened in the exhibition gallery; only now had the reporters begun to consider *why* it had happened. And Thatcher, from his customary post behind his desk, could tell from the looks on their faces that they were more than eager to help Abe Zachary write his own indictment.

"Well?" Martha Crane said.

Watching Zachary, Thatcher suspected that he was struggling to conceal what must have been the first signs of alarm about his predicament. Now and then he shot a troubled glance in Thatcher's direction, almost as though hoping for guidance. Thatcher had stood impassive, his face masklike, through all the early questioning. His heart, though, was still pumping blood for battle stations.

"I consider the painting better off destroyed," Zachary said finally, "than hung as it now is in this museum."

The reporters started talking at once.

"Please try to understand," Zachary said, interrupting them impatiently, wearily, "that I regard the painting as mine."

"But you sold it to the Getchell family," said the stringer from *Newsweek.* "And then it was sold by Getchell's widow to Austin Vanderhanks and given to the Museum. Right?"

"That painting is my work," Zachary said stubbornly. "I made it—not just with canvas and paint but with my heart and my brain and whatever skill I could bring out of *my* hands. What's a so-called property right compared to that kind of possession?"

"Nevertheless you were paid for it," another reporter said. "You took the money—it was a perfectly legal business transaction. Don't you admit that?"

"And I spent the money to support my family," the painter said. "Would you begrudge them their food because their father is an artist?"

"Hell, a sale is a sale, whether the money is gone or not."

"Everybody got what they wanted," said Zachary. "The first buyer got his name in the newspapers. His widow got the money back, and then some. The Vanderhanks got a fat tax deduction when they turned the painting over to the Museum."

"And what about us, Zach?"

It was Thatcher, breaking his silence for the first time. "What about the Museum's rights?"

"You paid nothing whatever," Zachary said quietly. "Yet you exploited the painting most of all. You put it into one of your shows without my permission—for the sake of your insatiable box office. And then you hung me just the way Christ was crucified—between two thieves."

"Come off it, Zach."

Zachary ignored him. "The inventor earns royalties on his patents, and no matter who manufactures or sells it, the invention is considered his. Authors and composers can determine what use will be made of their work and are paid royalties for that use. Why should artists have to sell theirs outright and have no voice in what is done with it?"

"But artists *do* sell their work outright," Martha Crane said. "And often enough for a hell of a lot of money. *Dallas*, for example—"

"I didn't make the system what it is," Zachary argued. "Neither did any other artist. We're the victims of the system more often than its beneficiaries. At the beginning of our careers we're usually not paid enough by anybody to keep alive. When we're successful, the galleries and museums set the values on our work, and if our pieces are ever put on the open market again, all the money they bring goes to the tradesmen—the buyers and sellers, the moneymen and moneylenders—not to us. I spit on the moneymen!"

"Mr. Zachary," a young woman in the corner called out, "don't you feel differently about the museums, as opposed to the private collectors? I mean—don't you *want* your work in museums?"

"I wanted *Dallas* where everyone could see it as easily as possible," Zachary answered. "This museum charges admission, it's not a public institution. You can walk into a dealer's gallery, maybe—if you look as if you have a checkbook in your pocket. But you have to *pay* to get in here.

"I also wanted my painting to be seen on its own merits, to speak to people with its own voice. Instead it's been hung in an exhibition with other paintings it bears no relationship to, near the works of men whose motives and credos I repudiate. Painters like Arnold Burgess—that little fascist! Did anyone ask me if I wanted to be put in his company? What's worse, I not only have to compete with second-rate talents, but with overhead projectors and mounted photographic enlargements and other such mechanical gimmicks, right in the same room—all the junk and intellectual corruption of the electronic age. Was I asked my opinion about that, either? I was *not*. Well, I claim that my rights in these matters are greater and more binding than the rights of any collector or museum. I also maintain that these rights have been violated. So why should it matter if the painting itself is violated too?" The flow of words stopped, and for a long moment the office was completely silent.

"Just one more question," Martha Crane said. "Are you willing to buy back the painting yourself? And wouldn't that be the only fair thing to do—before you ruin it?"

"I've already answered *that* question," Zachary said. "But yes, I am prepared to buy it back."

Several reporters stopped writing to look up at Zachary.

"I estimate," Zachary continued, "that I used forty-two dollars' worth of canvas, two dollars' worth of fir stripping, and about six dollars and eighty-five cents' worth of oil paints. I'm therefore prepared to pay the sum of fifty dollars and eighty-five cents for *Dallas*. No matter what anyone thinks he bought, that's all he got."

The press conference was over, and except for Martha, the reporters had all gone their separate ways. At Thatcher's request, Zachary had remained behind in the office. But the anteroom outside was nearly as crowded by now as one of the galleries.

Dolan was the dominant figure in the tableau, though he was almost dwarfed by a city patrolman, one of the biggest men Thatcher had ever seen in a uniform. The two guards who had been in the exhibition gallery with Thatcher earlier were still standing by, along with two of the Museum's maintenance men. Several strangers whose identity he couldn't even guess at turned out to be bystanders Dolan wanted to keep as witnesses to the vandalism.

"Vandalism of the worst sort," Dolan said. "Attempted destruction of a priceless work of art."

"Malicious mischief is the charge," the patrolman added. "And possibly trespassing."

"He came in on a pass," Thatcher reminded them.

"An expired pass."

"Yes, we've been all over that, too."

"Then let's have this fellow Zachary taken in and booked, shall we?" Dolan said.

"I think we should wait," Thatcher said. "We'll decide whether to prefer charges later."

"Suppose Zachary tries this again?"

"I should think you and your men are alert enough to handle him."

"Well—"

"And I don't think he'll come back."

The door opened and Alexander Gibbs walked in.

"Hello, Lloyd," he said. "Is everything under control?"

"I think so, despite appearances. If we could just clear out the militia—and anyone else who doesn't belong here."

Gibbs turned to Dolan. "Well, Les?"

"Lloyd doesn't think we should prefer charges."

Thatcher turned and looked hard at Dolan, who had been specifically told not to call in the deputy director. Yet here he was—fresh from the banquet table, in dinner jacket and black tie, a chesterfield coat draped over his shoulders. Any stranger might have taken him for the director of the Museum.

"Really, Lloyd?" Gibbs said. His nostrils flared in distaste. "Do you know what happened just now in the lobby?" Glancing at Martha Crane, he leaned closer and whispered: "Somebody has *pissed* on the floor."

It was news to Thatcher. "Well, now, we can't hold Zachary responsible for everything that happened today," he said.

Gibbs shifted ground. "I'm sure you want to consult with Dr. Garvey before taking any other action. . ."

"I did say I would give him a full report, yes."

"All right, Les," Gibbs said to Dolan.

Thatcher smiled at the two of them—a smile tight with pride under checkrein. Or was it vanity?

Martha Crane joined them and nodded politely to Gibbs, whom she vaguely remembered having met somewhere. She took Thatcher's arm gently and, with no resistance on his part, drew him away from the group.

"What do you intend doing about the painting itself?"

"Making whatever repairs are necessary."

"Will you put it back on display as soon as it's been repaired?"

"We'll consider it."

"In other words," Martha persisted, "you think there may be some merit to Mr. Zachary's complaint?"

Thatcher smiled. "That depends on which complaint you mean of Mr. Zachary's numerous complaints."

"Aren't you being just a bit legalistic, Lloyd? He objects to having his painting in your exhibition, right?"

"Certainly there is merit in some of the points Zachary raises," Thatcher said politely. "They'll all be discussed in detail at the appropriate time. We've considered many of these problems here at the Museum too, of course. Long before this happened."

That was a lie, but not by much. Both he and his curators were far too busy to give much thought to the vexations of artists. Artists were hardly a chorus singing the blues in unison—only a straggle of solitary voices. Thatcher had listened, all right, but never enough. For who wanted, or needed, another quarrelsome minority?

Abe Zachary appeared in the doorway of Thatcher's office, looking haggard. When he saw that Thatcher was not alone, he straightened up.

"I'm going now," he said, and Thatcher felt the question in his voice.

"Go ahead, Zach."

Zachary moved in a deliberate swagger toward the door, then turned.

"I'm sorry about your hand, Lloyd." Thatcher looked down at it, still wrapped in his stained handkerchief.

"Forget it."

42

"No, I really am. I didn't mean to hurt you."

"Zach—"

The artist turned again. "Yeah?"

"What you did to your painting hurt a good deal more."

Zachary blinked. He worked at a smile that didn't quite make it, then shrugged instead and went out the door.

5

THE WIND HAD shifted direction and gathered force, and was carrying the weather of Canada with it by the time Thatcher reached his apartment building that evening. In Central Park the sycamore leaves, usually the last to fall, were whipping off one by one into the violet dusk. A few minutes more and it would be as dark as it ever gets along Fifth Avenue. Within a few weeks the city would be fixed in winter.

Like most Southern Californians, Thatcher was never really prepared for December's ambush of snow and ice. He preferred to imagine that the snowstorms would not come, that the Ice Age was still receding, that Manhattan might even one day become a lush tropical jungle as green and mysterious as any imagined by the Douanier Rousseau.

"Good evening, Mr. Thatcher," said the doorman.

"Good evening, Eric."

"A quiet evening, sir."

It was certainly that, Thatcher agreed. The city's incessant clamor had died down, and the streets were now almost empty. It was as though the entire Upper East Side had paused to take a deep breath before the uproar resumed. Thatcher's aborted Thanksgiving was about to be given a second chance.

"Good evening, Mr. Thatcher," the elevator operator said. "Special-delivery letter for you."

"Thank you, Johnny."

A stranger might have taken the writing for a young girl's—loose and looping and joyous. But Thatcher instantly recognized the childishly shaped letters and erratic alignment of his mother's script. He didn't want to read it until he had to.

"Just heard from my son, Mr. Thatcher."

Thatcher shoved the letter into his pocket.

"What does he have to say?"

"His time is almost up. They'll be sending him home right after Christmas. Now if he'll just take it easy this month and not try for a medal—"

This endless war, Thatcher thought for the hundredth time. This endless, vicious, hopeless war that we do not want to fight and can't win. Thatcher was glad he had no son to sacrifice to it.

The elevator door slid open into the foyer of Thatcher's apartment. The soft overhead light bathed a towering *diffenbachia* plant in the corner (a housewarming gift from the Garveys), a series of framed posters on the wall (*Du* . . . *Dubon* . . . *Dubonnet*), and a card with Thatcher's name chastely engraved on it under the doorbell. No other doors led off the foyer; every floor in the building was completely private.

As he let himself in Thatcher heard the rattle of dishes far back in the kitchen.

"Is that you, Daddy?"

"Yeah, I'm here, honey."

Thatcher paused for a moment in the hallway. This was the largest apartment he had ever lived in—ten rooms on two floors, and all for a family of three. The first floor began on the Fifth Avenue side of the building with a cathedral living room, and ended half a block later with a maid's room and a bath which his sister Lorraine used as her study and sewing room.

The apartment was still being remodeled. The plaster was gleaming new; many of the rooms were unfurnished, unpainted. Though the hallway wall had been scraped down and spackled, it was still awaiting an enamel undercoat. Drop cloths, paint cans, and dried brushes formed an obstacle course all along the hall.

Still, with all its disorder it was a place of wonder to Lloyd Thatcher. He might have dreamed this apartment years ago in Balboa, California, under the spell of his own dazzling future.

The trustees of the Museum had had nothing so elaborate as this in mind when they agreed to provide him a Manhattan apartment. But when the retiring director, Robert Saint-Simon, asked him early in the negotiations what terms he would accept to become the new director, Thatcher was surprised to find himself insisting on "a suitable apartment in the city" in addition to the high salary and generous expense account that went with the job.

"Lloyd, it's hard to imagine the trustees accepting those terms." Saint-Simon sighed. "Of course the job is worth what you're asking, nobody knows that better than I do. It's what I should have been getting for some time." He shrugged. *"Autres temps, autres moeurs. I just came along too early.* No—I don't really believe that. We both came at the right time, you just happened to come along in a rampant inflation."

In the end, the trustees agreed to forty thousand dollars a year with a five-thousand-dollar increase at the end of the first year; five weeks' annual leave; an expense allowance up to ten thousand dollars a year; and an apartment. Because the Museum could not own an apartment in its own right, the trustees proposed to lend Thatcher the money, without interest, to buy a cooperative apartment in his own name. Thatcher was to pay the monthly maintenance, which came to about seven hundred dollars. The full purchase price was one hundred and twenty-five thousand dollars, a figure Thatcher liked to recall whenever he tripped over scaffolding or paint cans.

Susan did not understand how anybody could *buy* an apartment; Lorraine was shocked at what she thought was a grotesquely inflated price to pay—and not for a real house with grass and a sidewalk, but for a fraction of a building. At the same time, her regard for her brother's new eminence was visibly enhanced. This was what senators and college presidents and the chief executives of smaller corporations were being given to tempt them away from wherever they happened to be. Lorraine insisted that Thatcher have a physical examination, including an electrocardiogram, as soon as possible. He was now forty, she reminded him, and the pressures on any man in his position would be considerable.

She was right, he felt. He had just turned a youthful forty, and the world, in all its commonplace glory, lay at his feet. When the internist at Life Extension Institute who gave him the checkup told him he had the physical tone of a thirty-year-old, he went out immediately and bought a new aluminum tennis racket at Abercrombie and Fitch.

Thatcher bent down, picked up a brush, and dipped it into a can of white paint. On the stained and spackled wall, in three sweeping strokes, he painted the letters L T.

"Hi, Daddy."

"Happy Thanksgiving, Susie."

"Yah. . .Thanksgiving," she said, almost in a whisper. "Well anyway, they closed the snob factory for a couple of days. Here, let me hang up your topcoat."

"I can manage."

She insisted, and he yielded, as he always did, to her desire to please him. As she was hanging up the coat, she pressed the camel's-hair sleeve against her cheek hopefully.

"It's dry," she said.

"Sorry, pet." California-born Susie was waiting for snow, looking for it to fall every evening as the weather got colder, looking every morning for white streets and ice-covered trees. She was beginning to find New York City a more and more frustrating place.

Susan had been meeting Thatcher at the door when he came home ever since her mother's death eleven years ago. It occurred to him that she had, increasingly, the kind of intuition a wife should envy—she knew when he needed a drink and when he wanted a nap first; when to be silent and when he would appreciate chatter. And there was always this one unchanging response: the moment of greeting, their best time of day together.

"Daddy—your hand!"

Thatcher put the bandaged hand back into his pocket.

"What happened?"

"A scratch. Everything's under control."

"We were worried," she said. "It was on the radio, Mr. Zachary and the Artists' Round Table."

"The *what?*" Abe Zachary had never been inclined to formal associations.

Lorraine came in from the kitchen while Susan made Thatcher a drink. She held her cheek pressed against his long enough for him to catch the sweet odors of roasted meat and herbs in her hair,

47

mingled with the fragrance of *Ma Griffe* still clinging to her throat.

"I hope this delay doesn't spoil your dinner."

"I don't know what we'll do with a ten-pound turkey anyway," she said. "Just the three of us." When she broke away from his embrace, he could also smell the gin and tobacco on her breath—the odors of a long wait.

Lorraine Thatcher just missed being beautiful. She was perhaps two inches too tall and ten pounds too light for even dress designers to feel comfortable with her figure. She was thin where nature was expected to be bountiful, with a cast in one eye which spoiled an otherwise direct gaze of great sweetness and warmth. Even so, wearing a bright red sheath, her pale hair crisply styled, she made a handsome sight. Sister, consort, surrogate mother, hostess—and in between she'd somehow managed to fit two husbands. Birds of passage, they'd come and gone so quickly Thatcher couldn't quite remember either of them clearly. All this had happened to her—much of it trouble—without much disturbing the quality of her composure.

They were a close but not a closed corporation, someone had said of the Thatchers.

Thatcher headed back toward the brightly lit kitchen; so long as the painters and plasterers were still around, it was virtually the only room in which they could be comfortable together. Well, there was something cheerfully early-American about sitting around the stove—even an electronic wonder like this one, all steel and chrome and infrared baking.

"I wish I knew how long it would be," he said. Lorraine lit a cigarette and drew deeply on it, discovering a moment later with some confusion that she had left one burning in an ashtray above the stove.

"When the contractor was here yesterday, he told me they'd finish for sure next week. He swore it."

Thatcher muttered something about the first of October; Lorraine mentioned the painters' strike. It was a ritual between them.

"And there's *always* a strike anyway," Thatcher concluded. "Carpenters, electricians—they take turns, the quarrelsome bastards. It's a conspiracy."

"It'll be so beautiful when it's done." They hadn't said it aloud, this time.

48

"Will we have a housewarming?" Susan asked, handing her father a martini in a huge brandy snifter. He looked at the shining balloon glass gratefully, and at her in the same fashion.

"Certainly. And we'll invite the entire board of trustees."

His daughter's face fell so eloquently that Thatcher rushed to reassure her.

"Don't worry, Susie—we'll have fun among ourselves, too."

"Who else do we know to invite?" she asked.

Lorraine looked concerned. "It isn't as though this apartment were just ours," she said to Susan. "We will have to entertain a lot of Museum people here, too."

Thatcher stared into the depths of his glass, swirling the contents. *I promise you both, this will be our home in fact as well as in name. It will not be open to the public, it will not become an annex to the Museum. So help me.*

"I hope it's ready for Christmas," Susan said, unnecessarily.

Tired of talking about the apartment, his mood gone sour, Thatcher pulled the special-delivery letter out of his pocket.

Lorraine reached out eagerly for it. "What does she say?"

"I haven't read it yet." He passed the slightly rumpled envelope along to his sister, and went to the sideboard of the pantry to mix himself another drink. Susan stood at his side while he fussed with the bottles and the ice tray.

"Listen!" Lorraine's voice was unusually high pitched. "Let me read you what she says. After saying she hopes we're all well, and happy, then she says—"

"Could we see the letter if you've finished reading it?" asked Thatcher.

Lorraine went on stubbornly, holding the letter tightly in both hands. " 'A cat came into my room last week. The tiny little thing was starving. I don't understand how she could have gotten in through so many closed doors. I decided to keep her and feed her. I named her Angela, isn't that a nice name for a kitten with wicked bright orange eyes? But a nurse found her and now she has been put outside the walls. I wish she could climb back in again. I think of all of you often. How is George's Chevrolet agency doing?' "

"George?" Susan asked her father.

"Your aunt's first husband. Before your time, honey."

" 'Tell Lloyd to work hard and do well. . .in his studies.' "

49

She let the letter fall to the table as she got up. It was written on lined notebook paper torn from a spiral binder. On the back of the sheet, facing upward, was a sketch of an animal, apparently meant to be a cat—but a savage twist of the pencil had turned it into something brutal and beaked, like a bird of prey.

For several minutes Lorraine busied herself with her pots and pans, treating them without mercy. When she turned around, she was smiling as though her brother had just then walked through the door.

"Shall we eat?"

Thatcher held chairs for them both, poured out a half-bottle of Sauvignon into the wineglasses, carved, and served with concentration.

"What were you two up to while I was out this afternoon?" he asked finally.

"We walked over to the park," Susan said.

"Yes, it was nice for a while," Lorraine said. "For about ten minutes. Then a dog attacked Susie. A big, slobbering beast, with breeding but no training—"

"He didn't really *attack* me, Aunt Lorraine."

"He didn't break the skin if that's what you mean, but he certainly did intend to bite you. Anyway, Lloyd, I screamed and he ran off, but no one was there to discipline him. No one punished him at all, it's no wonder he's wild. I have never seen a place so full of demented animals as this city! Many of them wearing clothes, too. . . ."

She trailed off, shaking her head theatrically.

"They say if you're not afraid of dogs," Susan said, "they won't hurt you. I just told myself over and over—I'm not scared. I'm not."

"We have guard dogs in the Museum now at night," Thatcher observed. "A pair of boxers, quite well trained. Still, I wouldn't want to walk around the galleries alone late at night unless they were leashed."

The telephone rang.

"Shall I get it?" Susan asked.

But Thatcher was already up. He knew who was calling.

". . . How are you, Ira?"

Garvey's thin nasal voice rattled at the other end of the wire, carrying all the way to the kitchen table.

"Yes, of course I intended to call you," Thatcher said. "Just as soon as I'd finished dinner."

"You're still dining?" Garvey did not mean this to sound like an apology for his interruption, nor did it.

"I don't mind," Thatcher said. "It's usually pretty late by the time we have dinner. I must still be on California time."

This remark was received in silence. Thatcher regretted it instantly. Then: "Thatcher, I've been called by a newspaper reporter."

"I'm not surprised. What did they want to know?"

"Whether the Museum intends to press charges aagainst this artist —what was his name? Zachary? Of course, I didn't have the necessary information. . . ."

Thatcher sighed. "What *did* you say, Ira?"

"That if any law had been broken we would certainly want it enforced."

"I would rather you'd withheld comment altogether until after we'd talked."

"So would I."

"You see, the situation isn't completely clear yet, Ira."

"Oh?" Garvey said. "Then perhaps I'd better wait to read the newspapers tomorrow morning."

"But things are well in hand."

"Good. I'm glad. I'm sure you've handled the matter competently. And that you'll make sure there are no sequels to this episode. It may be that making an example of this unfortunate man will save us considerable trouble later on."

"Perhaps."

"Well, good night, Lloyd. I'll see you tomorrow."

"I'll be there."

"I'm so sorry," Lorraine said as he hung up the phone. "I don't know what happened—my mind just works like a sieve sometimes. . . ."

Thatcher looked blank.

"Dr. Garvey's dinner tomorrow. Didn't Lise mention it? I'm sure I must have told her."

"Don't worry about it," Thatcher said. "Just another social evening."

He was thinking of Abe Zachary, whose knife still weighted down his coat pocket.

6

THATCHER ARRIVED at the Museum the next morning at ten o'clock, only half an hour before it opened to the public. He usually came to work around nine, but he'd passed a white night—sudden, convulsive awakenings and the kind of vertigo that comes when the sleeper falls headlong into a stream of confused dreams. He marked the passage of the night with fleeting glimpses of the glowing clock dial on his night table: three o'clock . . . five . . . six-thirty. By then he thought he might as well get up. And so, of course, he dozed off and overslept.

Inside the main lobby of the Museum, its floor washed by the sunlight pouring down through the skylights, the guards and elevator men—all in dark blue uniforms with gold piping—were lined up in reasonably even formation. Twenty-five of them were standing there: some with their hands clasped behind their backs; one or two shifting comfortably back and forth on his heels and talking.

A low murmur traveled raggedly down the line, and then they fell silent as Lester Dolan stepped out in front. Wearing his cream-colored Bogie coat, Thatcher observed.

Dolan leaned closer to various guards as he passed along the line, exchanged a confidential remark or two, adjusted one man's lapels. At length the last man finished buttoning his uniform coat, and Dolan appeared satisfied. He had returned to a position in front of the formation when he spotted Thatcher.

"Morning, Lloyd," he said. Thatcher acknowledged the greeting and looked inquisitively toward the men, now dispersing.

"Gave them a bit of a special briefing today," Dolan said. "After yesterday's incident I want them all on the alert, ready for whatever comes."

"I doubt we'll be bothered again today. Still, you're right to be prepared."

"You saw the morning papers?" Dolan asked. "Big back-cover picture in the *News*."

"Not exactly the kind of publicity we like," Thatcher said. He pointed toward a stocky, middle-aged guard with spiky black hair who was staring at the entrance to the main gallery. "Which man is that?"

"Birnberg," Dolan said. "Five years here."

"Yesterday he provoked one of the demonstrators out in the garden," Thatcher said. "His remarks were out of line—he said troublemakers would probably have the hell kicked out of them in any museum but this one."

"Birnberg said that?" Dolan shook his head. "Hard to believe. Of course you're right, and I'll talk to him. But try to understand how any of the guards might feel about those demonstrators barging in with their dirty clothes and paint under their fingernails . . . and *pissing* on the floor! Even a reasonable man might be provoked."

"Jaimez conducted himself properly even when Zachary defied him."

Dolan went right on. "And then, afterwards, when he sees that a demonstrator has broken the law and had no charges brought against him. . . ."

"We'll see whether charges should be preferred after a full investigation has been made," Thatcher said calmly. "Meantime, keep the security force ready—but even-tempered."

"The next time," Dolan promised, "we'll have reinforcements in reserve, you can count on me for that."

Yet as he watched Dolan follow after his men, Thatcher felt anything but reassured. What we need here, he thought, is Wallace Stevens' "heavenly labials in a world of gutturals." Or is my approach all wrong?

Instead of going directly to his office, Thatcher took a detour to the Restoration Lab. One of the waking dreams that had haunted him the night before was the image of a masterpiece hanging on the blank white wall of his bedroom, its canvas surface striped with slashes, its frame crushed.

The Restoration Lab was set in a remote corner of the Museum—on the top floor, far above the galleries.

The Lab looked to Thatcher like an operating room, its long worktables scrubbed clean until they shone like old ivory; a twelve-foot rack of tools hung on the wall where you might expect to find, in a hospital, a cabinet of sterilized surgical instruments. Here were hammers and mallets, saws of a dozen sizes and lengths, a balanced series of gleaming drills, awls and rasps and files in a precise row: everything carefully mounted on a red pegboard ten feet long.

In one corner stood the varnishing compartment, a large metal cabinet from which a white aluminum vent spiraled up to the ceiling and on out to the Museum's roof. Inside it were easels on which paintings were mounted when they were ready to have varnish applied—at which point one of the Restoration staff would slide the metal door of the cabinet shut, switch on the powerful motors of the ventilating system, and turn on the tap of the compressed-air tank which fed the spray gun.

In the other corner along the same wall were three deep racks in which paintings were stacked side by side.

And in the center of the room, on the largest and longest of the worktables, lay Abe Zachary's *Dallas*.

At one end of the painting Rudi Lovbörg, the manager of the Restoration Department, leaned so close to its surface that it seemed he must surely lose his balance and topple directly onto the canvas. Lovbörg, a tall and bony man, seemed permanently bent over. When Thatcher walked through the door, Lovbörg ignored him for several moments. Only a slight twitching of his ears and a stiffening of his back showed that he was aware someone had entered the room. One of his two female assistants stood nearby and at right angles to him; the other was across the room, carefully running an electric iron over the back of a canvas, pressing liquid wax into the fabric.

When Lovbörg finally looked up at Thatcher, the worried frown on his broad, thickly veined forehead ebbed slowly away, to be replaced by a thin but unmistakably sweet smile.

"Ah," he said. "Here it is, Mr. Thatcher."

At heart an articulate and enthusiastic man, Rudi Lovbörg had grown used to having people interrupt him or turn their attention elsewhere whenever he tried to explain his work or point out the physical deficiencies of some work of art. As a consequence he now talked so seldom that he had the reputation of being grouchy and ungracious. But Lovbörg had sensed at their first meeting that Thatcher was genuinely interested in restoration work; that, moreover, he knew something about it himself and wanted to learn more.

"How bad is it, Rudi?"

Lovbörg straightened up and walked over to Thatcher, rubbing his hands on a piece of cheesecloth. He was wearing a long white laboratory coat, starched and immaculate this early in the day.

"I am encouraged," he said. "You realize I've made only a quick preliminary examination."

"I know how thorough your quick examinations are, Rudi."

Lovbörg acknowledged the compliment with another smile. He beckoned Thatcher toward the painting.

"Look," he said. "I show you."

They looked down at the canvas in silence for a moment or two. Thatcher had examined the painting closely perhaps a dozen times, most recently when he was planning how it was to be hung in the exhibition. Also he'd seen it reproduced in magazines, on post-cards, in anthologies of contemporary art—it must be a source of bitter amusement to Abe Zachary to know that his work was on so many coffee tables at which he himself would not be welcomed.

As they looked, Thatcher was filled again with admiration for the breathtaking technique of Zachary's achievement. To him the painting always seemed to have been conceived and executed in one intense burst of energy, with a thousand brushstrokes carried head-long over the canvas as though they were a single stroke, and without hesitation or uncertainty.

Thatcher's eye traveled down to the lower right-hand corner, where the wound was. Though it was only a small tear on the canvas, perhaps eight inches or so, it became, by virtue of its harsh intrusive-ness, the dominating element in the composition—true violence on a violent field, a stubborn knot of pain made visible.

Lovörg snaked his right hand into a white plastic glove and traced the edges of the cut with his index finger.

"Not a neat cut," he remarked. "A rip."

"The knife was dull," Thatcher said.

"Evidently."

"I've never had to deal with a slash before," Thatcher said. "What do you do—sew up the canvas first?"

"No. We first make the tear into a hole and then we patch that. Here, I show you."

He drew Thatcher over to an American primitive painting lying half shrouded in a plastic cover. The painting was a portrait of a child of the early nineteenth century. One of the child's eyes was gone entirely from the canvas; in its place was an oval patch of some dead-white material.

"Gesso," Lovbörg explained. "After you've got the canvas backed up with masonite, and the slash cut into a hole of the size you need, you fill it with gesso. You know, plaster of paris. Then you put the proper coloring on the gesso."

"Oil paint?"

Lovbörg shook his head and carefully drew the cover back over the primitive. With his bony left hand he picked up a small jar of some soft blue substance.

"This is a plastic coloring," he explained. "Oil changes color when it dries, and so it wouldn't match the rest of the painting. But with this material we get a perfect color match. You see?"

"How about the broken frame?"

"Oh well," Rudi said lightly, "that is nothing." Then he looked at Thatcher's face and quickly added: "Thanks to you, Mr. Zachary was stopped before he did any really serious damage. The canvas was not torn. As for the frame—well, that is simply carpentry. Anybody with training in woodwork could do it."

"Rudi," Thatcher said. "You make me feel a lot better about the whole thing."

"Fine!" Lovörg smiled happily.

"The patient will recover quickly."

"Oh, well, there was never any doubt. Not bad damage at all. When you see some of these other paintings—then you want to cry."

Thatcher accompanied Lovörg to the storage racks on the opposite side of the lab.

"This one, for example," Lovörg said, "was almost half destroyed by fire. We talked to the artist and he asks us to cut it down, saving whatever we can, and build a new frame for it." He shoved the work back into its slot on the rack. "He had a bad studio fire, with many things completely lost. But it is a good thing he's a drip painter,

nobody will know what we have done. . . . You remember the Boccioni landscape that was damaged in a fire?"

Thatcher nodded.

"Well," Lovbörg said, "we restored about eighteen inches of
the painting right here in this room."

"In fact," he continued, as he walked with Thatcher to the door,
"you should put a wall label up next to that painting: 'This landscape two-thirds by Boccioni, one-third by Lovbörg.' Okay?"

The last thing Thatcher saw as he closed the door of the Restoration Lab behind him was Rudi Lovbörg's smile—not fading, but
stronger and brighter than ever.

By the time Thatcher reached his office, his secretary looked as
distraught as she ever did. Lise had one telephone call on "hold,"
was talking to someone else on another extension, and was trying to
carry on some kind of serial conversation with Malcolm Crawford,
the Museum's press director—all at the same time. Crawford was
perched on the edge of her desk—a thin little man with unfashionably
short hair and the voice of a carnival barker. Alongside Lise, Mal
seemed even shorter, which may have been why he preferred to sit
on top of her desk. It wasn't concern for his masculine image; he
made no secret of his homosexuality, though he was not so obviously
effeminate that even the most conservative members of the board
could find him disagreeable. One thought of Mal's sex life as a
hobby, like collecting antique coins or butterflies.

As for Lise, she found Mal Crawford amusing but was not taken
in by his small and exquisitely fabricated intrigues. She was amazed
that he found time for so many kinds of politics despite the pressure
of his work, which he did with casual skill and apparent satisfaction.

"Good morning," Thatcher said, dividing his salutation impartially
between Lise and Mal. He dropped his coat on one of the chairs
near Lise's desk and headed for his own office. Mal slid from the
desk and planted himself in Thatcher's path.

"Coffee inside," Lise said, muzzling the telephone mouthpiece
and reaching for a pencil with her free hand. "I have Mr. Stringfellow on five twenty-four, Mrs. Lord on five twenty-six. And Alex
Gibbs has asked to see you as soon as you're free."

"How about you, Mal?" Thatcher asked.

"Please—try to squeeze me in before Alex."

"All right." He turned to Lise. "Mrs. Lord first, then I'll call Mr. Stringfellow back when I can. I should be free to see Alex Gibbs at eleven—do I have a lunch date?"

"No, but you asked me to remind you to get a haircut today."

"Actually I should get a wig, it would save time. Well, see what you can set up at Bergdorf's. Who was the man there—the one that George Trueblood recommended?"

"His name was Hector. I forgot his last name, but he's Cuban."

"A genius," Mal Crawford said.

"Hector, then," Thatcher said. "If he's good enough for George. . . ."

He smiled broadly at Mal. George Trueblood, chief curator of the Museum, was brilliant, a prima donna among art historians, an infallible guide to restaurants, stores, and all the essential male requirements. Of all the Museum's curators, he was the most flamboyant: worth keeping if for no other reason than to show how exotic the species might be. He and Mal Crawford were rumored to have been lovers years ago. Thatcher thought it possible, since they now maintained such an elaborately polite dislike for each other.

Thatcher closed the door to his office firmly. Serena Lord's voice on the telephone was warm and friendly, with just a touch of impatience at being kept on "hold" for so long.

"I'm sorry," Thatcher said. "You should have let me call you back."

"I know you're busy, Lloyd—and I'm really not, you know. Well, only half."

"I thought you kept on the go all day long. Isn't that why you have a social secretary?"

"She just quit. May I steal that lovely Brünnhilde of yours?"

"Lise? No you may not, though I wish I could help you. . . ."

Mrs. Ashbrook Lord had let Thatcher know in a variety of deft and quiet ways that she would enjoy much more of his company than her trusteeship required. He was both flattered and pleased. Pleased because she was, at forty, a beautiful woman. Of course she could afford to work at it, but she'd been born to beauty as to money, and on the same generous scale. Flattered because she was one of the Social Register "Married Maidens": her name was entered along with her club (Colony), her school (Briarcliff), and her address (668 Park Avenue).

As for Thatcher, his interest—or was it curiosity—grew each time

58

he saw her. And then, he had the impression, so gratifying to his self-esteem, that he could keep her in a state of agreeable "hold" indefinitely.

"Did you read the *Times* this morning, too?" he asked her.

"Not yet. I'll tell you why I called," Serena said, speaking more rapidly. "I want you to meet Aaron Redburn, Lloyd. He could mean a lot to the Museum."

"A lot of money, I assume."

"Several millions, if he wished to. He's almost as rich as Vanderhanks. Moreover, he earned it."

"I always thought it was considered in poor taste to talk about where money comes from."

"Talking about money, my dear, is one of the very best kinds of gossip. Art and money are part of the same thing."

And what thing is that, Thatcher wondered. Power? Property? Distinction?

"That's the first lesson they teach us in Museum Director's Basic Training, Serena," Thatcher said. Personally he detested fundraising, but a flair for it was part of his reputation.

"Aaron could also be a good stalking horse for other business money," Serena continued cheerfully. "If you don't mind the comparison."

"Not if he doesn't."

"An exceptional man, and you'll like him, I know."

"Say when."

"He's taking me to an opening this afternoon. Why don't you join us there?"

Thatcher agreed and hung up. He wished he'd been able to tell Serena about Abe Zachary. He would rather she had his version of the incident first, not the melodramatic newspaper reports of it. Anyone reading Martha Crane's column would have thought Thatcher was entitled to a Purple Heart, and that Abe was some kind of Zach the Ripper.

Mal Crawford started talking before Thatcher cleared the doorway.

"Lloyd, we've simply got to issue some statement today, or there will be all kinds of misunderstanding."

Thatcher walked around him and crossed the room to the coffee table, where Lise had left a tray with a stainless steel percolator and a supply of white cups and saucers. He poured himself a cup of coffee, dropped in a saccharin tablet, took a sip, and acknowledged Mal Crawford.

"I'm not sure I know what you mean by misunderstanding, Mal."

"The way you were quoted in the newspapers this morning, you sounded positively sympathetic."

"You wouldn't suggest I sound unsympathetic to artists, would you?"

"No, no, certainly not, but you know what I mean. I'm a bit concerned about what the trustees might think."

"And how about the public? The museum-going, newspaper-reading segment?"

A pout formed on Mal's lips. He sat down, crossing one leg over the other and swinging it briskly.

"Now you're being facetious."

"The hell I am," Thatcher said. "It's pretty hard to predict what anybody will think about demonstrations these days. But it's a safe bet that much of the public already classifies artists as either hopelessly spoiled children or as misfits, outcasts. And the very successful few resemble privately held corporations. It's getting hard to find anybody anywhere who honestly *likes* artists—why should we add to the public's resentment?"

"But we have to say *some*thing."

"No, we need not say anything. Hasn't that possibility occurred to you?"

Mal had no answer.

"Look, why don't you go ahead and draft a release," Thatcher said.

"Along what tack?"

"Say the Museum believes its interests are sympathetic to the artist as well as to the public. And that—try it this way—we are always willing to talk to any individual artist, or any group of artists, but in a peaceful atmosphere which will encourage discussion. You might add that we're planning to appoint a committee—"

"We are?"

"An ad hoc committee of distinguished figures from the field of art and from other areas of public life. To study the problems of the artist in our society."

60

"Sounds like a lot to bite off," Mal said.

"If we do all that," Thatcher said, turning his chair so he could look out over the garden, "we won't have done anything at all. We'll only have stopped to think."

"All right. I'll be back when I have a release ready." He paused at the door and turned, his hand on the knob. "By the way, one of the independents wants to use the Museum for location shots."

"When?"

"Around Christmas."

Every so often movie producers asked to use the Museum, usually the sculpture garden, as a setting. Like a public park or a Middle-European village square, it attracted a gallimaufry of picturesque idlers, from old men sitting and counting their hours to artists sizing up the competition and taking the measure of their own ambitions; mock-artists, students, girls with short skirts and long legs, tourists. Everything always stopped dead around the camera crews except the life the actors simulated; this made film crews a bloody nuisance, in Thatcher's opinion.

Thatcher sighed. "What do we charge them?"

"Eight hundred dollars a day."

"Is that enough, do you think?"

Mal Crawford looked startled, and before he could answer, Thatcher added: "Or is it too much?"

"So it costs us," Mal said. "We have to hire extra guards, pay the regular shift overtime. And it means more custodial help for the technical parts. Just to move art across the room calls for a union man. . . ."

"I was only wondering," Thatcher said, "whether we knew for sure why we're charging what we've been charging."

"Well now," Mal said. "Maybe we better look into that. I'll talk to Alex Gibbs and his numbers people."

The minute he had gone, Lise was at Thatcher again with messages. "Mr. Stringfellow wants to talk to you, Alex Gibbs and Les Dolan are both waiting, Dr. Garvey wants to confirm dinner for tonight, black tie. Mrs. Lord rang up again to say that she and Mr. Redburn will meet you at the Walker Gallery at four-thirty and would you please be prompt—Mr. Redburn is attending another opening at the Benlow." She stopped to take a breath. "And Hector can take you at one o'clock unless you also want a shampoo."

Thatcher nodded, almost a bow. "How do we begin?" he asked. "In chronological order, or in order of urgency?"

"That would be Mr. Stringfellow any way you look at it," Lise said. "Oh, I almost forgot! Martha Crane would like an in-depth interview."

"When?"

"This afternoon. She wants to talk about your plans for the Museum—and your friendship with Abraham Zachary."

Thatcher nodded, shut his door, and waited at his desk for Lise to ring Manley Stringfellow.

Friendship with Abe? They had been teacher and student, if anything. But the memories of those years in California came now like light from another galaxy, arriving years after departure. As distant, as hard to recognize, as the eighteen-year-old Thatcher himself, he thought—passionate, desperately ambitious, and absolutely honest.

7

GALLERY-GOERS AT openings are divided into two distinct breeds, those who head first for the bar and those who head for the walls.

Not that it was easy for Thatcher to reach the paintings at the Walker Gallery that afternoon. He'd entered the building fifteen minutes earlier than his four-thirty appointment, glanced around quickly to see if Serena had arrived, and then proceeded toward the exhibition. On his way through the lobby he was stopped twice—by Clarence Walker, and by a critic for *New Horizons Magazine*, anxious to learn what Thatcher might think about the paintings he had not yet seen. Thatcher just smiled, squeezed a hand which he found not only soft but damp, and turned to thread his way through the eddies of brightly plumed young people—and a few older men quietly draped in banker's gray—who are most in attendance at such *vernissages*.

Thatcher preferred the French word for openings; "varnishings" were what they usually turned out to be. In New York City there were over four hundred art dealers like Clarence Walker. Perhaps a thousand paintings were sold at retail and wholesale levels each week during the gallery season, from October through May. In November, buying and selling was at its height, so Thatcher was not surprised to see the gallery crowded.

He quickly decided he did not care much for the work on display: imitations of American avant-garde painting of four or five years ago, but done by Polish and Rumanian artists who did not have the advantage of novelty—not in these surroundings—and who had the great disadvantage of practicing a form of art long unwelcome to their governments. Thatcher gave only fleeting attention to the outsized constructions in sheet metal and terra-cotta, the grotesque paintings of what looked like overblown kidney stones and purple gallbladders. But near them were a number of lithographs—prints of striking originality and technical proficiency. One lithograph in particular fascinated him. Titled *The Beach*, it was a representation of a shoreline where dark, lace-edged waves broke harshly against a beach composed entirely of human beings—bodies propped up in every variety of posture and attitude: coiled and twisted, gaunt, haggard, pale, naked forms.

Thatcher looked closely at the name of the artist, but even as he turned away from the wall label the name slipped out of his mind, weighted down by its ballast of consonants.

Fame, it occurred to him, was hard to achieve if one's name were something like Czilczsynciwicz. You needed one or two tight syllables —*Arp*, or *Miró*, or a longer, more plangent combination of sounds like *Picasso* or *Motherwell*.

The owner of the gallery hove into view again, this time accompanied by two women, one on each arm, both tall enough to dwarf him. Far from minding the contrast, Clarence Walker seemed to relish it. He hugged them both close to him. One was obviously his wife; the other was so unqualifiedly handsome that Thatcher's curiosity was aroused immediately.

The woman introduced as Mrs. Walker had fair hair drawn into a heavy, shining bun, one of those celebrated English complexions, and a smile of youthful brilliance.

"Mr. Thatcher," she said, just touching his hand. "The bright new hope of the art world."

Thatcher looked at her in dismay, without answering.

"Everybody says so," Mrs. Walker continued. She gave him an even brighter smile. "And some of us believe it."

As Thatcher laughed gratefully, she reached out and pressed his arm, a gesture that seemed both graceful and understanding.

"I can imagine, Mr. Thatcher, what it's like to be the young new director of a museum so full of its past glories. And its past heroes too. But there is *so* much that needs to be done. Really, museums are out of step now with the world we live in, wouldn't you say?"

Clarence Walker smiled indulgently at his wife. "Do you expect Mr. Thatcher to agree to that, Margaret?"

"Maybe I do," Thatcher said. "Perhaps that's why the Museum hired me."

"Take the young people," Mrs. Walker rushed on. "Years ago one had a job persuading anyone that cinema and photography belonged in museums. Now the difficulty lies in convincing the young that painting and sculpture are art forms."

"It's not that bad," Clarence Walker protested.

But his wife had moved to another subject. "Of course, Robert Saint-Simon was the most marvelous man, but really, it's true, he was *ready* to step aside. Trying to run that place any longer would have killed him, if the accident hadn't."

"I know how deeply everyone felt about him," Thatcher said uncomfortably.

"Loved him."

"Yes, that's the right word."

"Remember," she said, leaning closer, "not to make the mistake of trying to be like him."

"Margaret," Clarence Walker reminded her, "Mr. Thatcher wants to see the paintings. Let me give him Alexandra here so he can resume his tour."

Alexandra Kozlowkda, as she was introduced, took Thatcher lightly by the arm. Her touch was disarmingly polite, with just a tiny bit more pressure in her fingers than seemed necessary. This was not the way she would guide a much older man, it was clear, or a child, but beyond that, he must draw his own conclusions.

Thatcher looked at her as long and appreciatively as he had at any of the paintings in the exhibition. As he stared, she smiled at him without a trace of self-consciousness.

She was wearing a black and gold hostess gown which turned into a pants suit when she started walking. Her left breast, unencumbered under the gown's soft fabric, brushed against Thatcher's arm as she piloted him through the vestibule and back into the gallery he had just left. She had dark, loose hair, and skin which Thatcher thought looked too pale, almost translucent, as though she had once suffered from a long illness. But it was an intelligent face, and he found the liveliness in it instantly appealing.

"May I tell you something about these artists?" Alexandra said. She had a low, theatrical voice, the kind that seemed to hold reserves of laughter—or, should it be required, a cutting edge.

"I've taken a look at the work already," Thatcher said, "but I'll admit it was only once over lightly."

"You don't like them much, do you?"

"You're right, I don't. I think they're dull."

Alexandra did not seem to mind this frank admission, and Thatcher was glad he had not tried to dissemble his feelings about the paintings. Sometimes he believed he could not really look at any piece of art clearly until he had isolated his own opinion about it, and put that opinion out where he could look at it objectively. Then it was as though the painting carried a label: "UNTITLED. Acrylic on beaver board. 13 x 24 inches. 1965. From the collection of Mr. and Mrs. Austin Vanderhanks. Disliked on principle by Lloyd Thatcher." From that point forward, he could begin to see the painting for what it was.

Alexandra released Thatcher's arm and moved gracefully over to a corner of the gallery.

"When these were done," she said softly, "there was no gallery or museum they could be hung in. But there's a park near the center of Krakow, near a bridge across the river. Everyone goes to the park on Sundays. Lovers used to come there and lie on the grass, and the artists would set up their easels under the trees and paint. When someone was ready to show a painting, and maybe hoped to sell it, he would bring it to the bridge and lean it against the railing. So on Sunday there would always be a line of paintings and drawings along the bridge, and sculpture, too—even prints mounted on poster board. The work all together looked beautiful with the river running fast underneath, and there was a marvelous strong feeling of life about everything, not only the colors but also noises and smells— exhaust fumes, fresh vegetables and flowers on the market trucks, even the smells of ourselves. Fresh paint, turpentine, food and wine. . . . And when it rained suddenly, we would have to scoop up our paintings and sculptures and run into the park with them to keep them dry under the trees."

She broke off abruptly.

"I don't blame you for saying that the work looks dull," she said. "We have nothing to teach the Americans. But it didn't look dull on the bridge—maybe it belongs there and not in a gallery at all?"

"We can't bring that bridge here," Thatcher said, unsure of how seriously he was answering her question. "Maybe the artists aren't even in the park any longer, though I hope they are. But art belongs wherever people are. Including your bridge, Alexandra."

"Well, now," she said, with a slight curtsy, "what else can I tell you about the painters of my youth?"

They stopped again; the room was filling up rapidly. Thatcher heard someone say: "Lloyd Thatcher? Who else is here?" and winced. "As far as I'm concerned, they're still commies even if they paint like Picasso." "But Picasso's a communist, too. . . ." And one particularly sharp voice: "How like Clarence Walker to get in on the ground floor! Do you suppose we'll have a Balkan vogue?" "I'm not buying paintings, darling, not in a bull market—only nucleonics and pharmaceuticals. . . ."

"Let's have a drink," Thatcher said to Alexandra.

Alexandra stood in the practiced cocktail-party stance: left hip thrust slightly forward, weight concentrated on the right foot. She declined a cigarette and sipped her Dubonnet slowly, making small, satisfied faces. Thatcher found her moodiness provocative.

"Lloyd! Here you are, dear."

He turned to face Serena Lord, towing a tall, heavy-set man about Thatcher's age. From his perfectly groomed auburn hair, just edged with gray, to his highly polished boots, he looked like a model for the Gentleman of Substance and Cultivation. Thatcher did not need to be told his name.

"Aaron Redburn," Thatcher said.

"That's right."

They shook hands and turned to Serena. There was something more than beauty in her appearance today, Thatcher thought: in her cameo-clean profile, in the flowing pleated lines of her burnt-almond chiffon dress—most of all in the fine, slightly curved plane of her back and shoulders.

"I've finally got you two together," she said in the voice which was the youngest of her youthful features—light and warm and full of lazy laughter. "I hope I haven't put you off each other doing it."

"Hell, I don't see why we shouldn't get along, Serena," Redburn said slowly. His drawl seemed a jarring contrast to his looks—an Oklahoman, Thatcher guessed.

"This isn't supposed to be a blind date anyway, is it?" Thatcher said, smiling.

"The people I like," Serena announced, "don't always like the other people I like."

"Why should they?" Redburn said. "Why's it got to always be kiss me, kiss my cow?" Somehow he got an extra syllable, the Southwestern one, into "cow." Thatcher decided he liked Redburn's accent. It wasn't the raw western leather; it had been nicely polished without losing its strength.

"Mr. Redburn," Thatcher said. "I agree, but—"

"Make it Aaron if you don't mind."

"—but if we don't get along we'll still have to answer to Serena for our imperfections."

"I do, I already do," Redburn said. Were they lovers? Thatcher wondered. They seemed so well suited to each other: a matched pair in money, looks, vitality.

"You're getting a lot of art today, aren't you Aaron?" Thatcher said.

"That's what I mean," he said. "Serena here is exposing me to as much of it as I can possibly take in. It wasn't so long ago I didn't know much excepting Charlie Russell or maybe Frederic Remington. When I was feeling like serious art, Grant Wood and Thomas Hart Benton were it." He turned to Serena—"But she's the best teacher a man could have." Then to Thatcher—"Lloyd, you probably know we're on our way to another show. . . ."

"Yes, Serena told me."

"So we can't talk much now. I barely had one drink here to hold me to the next party and now we have to rush off, but I'd be most grateful if you'd come along with us."

Thatcher looked at Serena. Almost imperceptibly, she nodded.

"You see," Redburn continued, "sometimes Serena and I don't agree about what we see, and it would be handy to have you along with us to keep the peace."

68

"All right," Thatcher said.

"Now don't bring up anything too serious," Serena protested. "You can always arrange a lunch date later."

When Redburn left to get Serena's wrap, Thatcher bent over her: "You're throwing us at each other, you know."

"Trust me," she said. "You won't be sorry."

Spotting Alexandra near the door, Thatcher suddenly realized how rude he'd been to her. He excused himself briefly from Serena and hurried over.

"If you'll forgive me first," he said, "I'd like to thank you."

"But whatever for?"

"For helping me to see your artists more clearly."

She seemed uninterested. "Call me," she said. "I'm in the directory."

"A lovely girl," Serena said when Thatcher rejoined her at the bar. "Polish?"

Thatcher nodded.

"I see I must keep my eye on you." Her smile was only partly facetious.

"It's the other way around," he heard himself say. It was the sort of foolish remark he hated, but Serena went right on.

"I'm surprised Aaron didn't pay more attention to her—you must have made quite an impression on him."

So they weren't lovers, then, after all. . . .

At last Redburn joined them with Serena's wrap on his arm, deprecating the poor service in the checkroom and the crowds between it and the second floor. How could anyone enjoy art, or even drinking, in such a mob scene? Well, Serena observed, by the time they got to the next opening, it should have thinned out.

As they descended the spiral marble staircase toward the front entrance of the gallery, Thatcher saw Alexandra standing near the checkroom—her chin held very high, a slender young man in a fur coat beside her, helping her with her wrap. She looked straight at Thatcher, her smile a sunburst on the white mask of her face. Then the smile was gone as quickly as it had appeared, leaving an expression both wise and sorrowing, tinged with regret. Did she fancy herself a Justine, Thatcher wondered, amused at her theatricalism and yet affected by it. Some evening soon he would accept the invitation.

On the way uptown Serena said to Thatcher: "A command performance tonight at Garvey's."

"Certainly for me," Thatcher said.

"For me, too," she said. "Ira was quite insistent—I got the impression he wouldn't *give* the party unless he was assured of perfect attendance. Though I must say, he didn't give a clue as to what it's all about."

"Maybe it's just a partying party," Redburn volunteered.

"Somehow I doubt that," Serena said. Then she fell silent.

Thatcher stared moodily out of the cab window. The cobbled courtyard of the Archdiocese of New York slipped by, then a stream of brightly lit shops, most of them wearing their holiday best. Thatcher rubbed his forehead and rolled down the window an inch or so to let a stream of cold air flow over it.

A surprise party, he thought, wondering without really caring what the surprise would be, and who it had been prepared for.

8

IRA GARVEY's town house was too small to impress the casual passerby
—one expected something grander as the residence of New York's
wealthiest surgeon. In actual fact, the house was perfect for the
Garvey family: Ira Garvey was a small man, barely five feet six inches
tall; his wife was only five feet, and their three children were constructed on a scale closer to hers than to his. Even the servants seemed
to have been selected so they would not tower over their employers.

All the same, Thatcher considered the Garvey house one of the
most beautiful he had seen in the city. It's façade was kept a glowing
cream color, where many neighboring houses had turned a morbid
gray. The shutters and grilles on the building's face were not permitted to lose their black enamel sheen. Near the curb, a thriving
plane tree faced the door, providing Garvey's visitors with an elegant
green shelter. If a Garvey servant saw a dog on leash approaching this
tree, the alarm went out, the door opened, and the dog and its owner
were politely directed away from the tree.

Thatcher was ten minutes late, a more than acceptable margin,
he thought, since the invitation called for cocktails at seven-thirty.
Even so, the other guests had already arrived.

Trustees to the right of me, trustees to the left of me, trustees to
the front of me, he noted as he stepped into the sitting room. There
was a formal, almost stagey atmosphere in the room—an air of
expectancy—as though they had all been invited to take part in some
mysterious ceremony.

Austin Vanderhanks, past president of the board, stood in front of the marble fireplace, sipping a glass of sherry. Marcus Hammer was installed in a corner, chatting with Professor Oscar Wood of Columbia. Dexter Llewellyn, the only artist on the board, shared a love seat with Serena, who looked as though she'd changed not only her gown but also her hair style since Thatcher had accompanied her and Aaron Redburn to the Benlow Gallery just two hours ago. These five, with Ira Garvey, made up the trustee contingent—unless you also counted Manley Stringfellow, who was standing before one of Josef Albers' opulent homages to the square, his bony white hands splayed out behind his hips, his shoulders slumped wearily forward. One of Thatcher's predecessors, Stringfellow was officially retired, but continued to serve the board as an adviser. He sometimes worked in a section of the Museum he himself called the Geriatric Ward; he showed up at parties and trustee meetings, but never without an invitation.

A youngish, epicene man whom Thatcher did not immediately recognize hovered near the love seat. He decided it must be Briggs, Winthrop Briggs. Though he wrote on art for one of the women's service magazines, Briggs's primary responsibility, reportedly, was to keep Dexter Llewellyn feeling youthful and well loved.

Thatcher spotted George Trueblood near the service bar. Thank God George was here—the party couldn't be completely stuffy so long as he was around.

Moving past the charmed circle, Thatcher waved to Serena, who blew him a restrained kiss. As soon as he had greeted the Garveys, he made his way to Trueblood's side.

The Museum's chief curator was wearing a midnight-blue velvet smoking jacket with a white stock and a waistcoat that seemed to be at least fourteen-carat gold. His mirror-black pumps were surprisingly tiny for a man so pudgy. Over his vaulted bald crown he had drawn a few strands of black hair, in the nature of a caricature, Thatcher assumed—as a few charcoal lines in a drawing might represent an entire landscape. Round-faced and jowly, George looked, it had been said, like Queen Victoria. Certainly no hint of self-doubt or irresolution ever crossed that pink countenance. The eyes opened so wide they might have seemed sad except that their gray pupils most often glimmered with affection, or high spirits, or with plain joy in the gossip George Trueblood loved.

"Listen, my dear," he said to Thatcher urgently, "I've got the most delicious news for you."

"Yes?" Thatcher's spirits brightened. Maybe George knew what was going on tonight.

"The deWitts are *divorcing*,"

"And that's good, George?" Thatcher was faintly puzzled. It wasn't like George to take pleasure in anyone's bad luck.

"When they make the settlement," Trueblood continued, "the collection will go to her, she's already set her lawyer straight on that."

"So?"

"Don't be obtuse, Lloyd. He's a trustee of that *other* museum, and she's a former student of mine at Barnard. I gave her a C-plus and she's revered my judgment ever since. She will not only give to us right now some of that magnificent collection, but she will also write us into her will, along with her budgerigars, her dalmatians, and her favorite charities."

"Beautiful," Thatcher murmured. He was only half-listening now. Across the room, Marcus Hammer had both his hands on Serena's shoulders; as Thatcher watched, Serena moved gracefully out of the financier's grasp.

Leaving Trueblood to his champagne cocktail, Thatcher headed for the garden room, where, before long, he found himself sipping a martini with Manley Stringfellow.

"How's the book coming?" Thatcher asked. The two men were standing at the window wall overlooking Garvey's terrace and garden, now empty and still in a bitterly cold moonlight.

At Thatcher's question, Stringfellow's white head came down in a ducking motion toward his concave chest. The posture of his thin body suddenly inspired Thatcher to look at the Giacometti wire sculpture the Garveys had placed in the corner of the room; it seemed to have the same air of tormented concentration.

"Excuse my taking so much time to answer you," Stringfellow finally said in a near whisper. "Speaking these days, Lloyd—" He paused and took a deep breath. "—is almost as hard for me as writing."

"I'm sorry to hear you haven't been well, Manley," Thatcher said.

"I suppose I shouldn't complain," he replied. "Lucky to be a survivor."

Manley Stringfellow was seventy at most, perhaps a few years younger, but a combination of liver disorders and mild strokes had aged him another decade. And it was said that only the massive reference book on the last century of art history which he'd been writing since 1944 still sustained him—because to finish it would also be a kind of death.

"Mind if we join you?"

The voice was pleasant, the accent transatlantic. Dexter Llewellyn came originally from Chicago, where his family had made its fortune in refining and smelting iron, but he'd spent a large part of his life in England. Like Henry James, he preferred the view of his native land from the other side.

"Dexter. . . . You're always welcome," Stringfellow whispered. He made a small face when he saw Winthrop Briggs standing next to Llewellyn, like a younger, more willowy reproduction; then he smiled and nodded.

Thatcher suspected the old man was wondering whether a peacock like Briggs could actually have enough brains in his skull to write knowledgeably about art. The answer, of course, was yes; the cocktail groves of Manhattan were full of brainy peacocks.

"Lloyd," Llewellyn said, "how the hell are you?" Instead of adopting Britishisms, Dexter Llewellyn preferred to speak his own Midwestern idioms in an Oxford accent. The effect was somewhat startling: he sounded like an Englishman trying to ape a Chicago businessman.

"Happy and busy," Thatcher said. "Busy and happy."

"Good for you," Llewellyn said, his tone all but snappish. It was well known that Dexter Llewellyn only painted when he felt like it, and that he felt like it less and less often. His reputation, though, was secure; his early work, when he put it on the market, brought higher and higher prices.

"Are you entering a new period, Dexter?' Stringfellow asked.

"I always paint better in Surrey than in Duchess County," Llewellyn said. He turned to Thatcher. "You've settled into our Museum then, Lloyd?"

"It's the most unsettling—by which I mean fascinating—place I've ever known," Thatcher said.

"You've been around. Aren't museums much the same?"

"Nothing half so Byzantine as this one." Thatcher thought he'd better smile in case Manley Stringfellow might take offense, but the old man nodded as though it were the exact word he would have chosen himself. Briggs uttered a short laugh.

Only Dexter Llewellyn was slow to smile. "You must mean us," he said.

"I was thinking of the staff," Thatcher said. "Are the trustees also Byzantine?"

This time Llewellyn laughed first, and loudly. "Especially so," he said. He squeezed Thatcher's arm like an old friend who takes much for granted. Thatcher drew away.

"All trustees, without exception," Llewellyn continued. "All are devious."

"Speak for yourself, Dexter," Austin Vanderhanks said, moving from the edge to the center of the conversational group. "As for me, I'm cast in the Puritan mold. In fact," he went on in his flat voice, "I've always had a sneaking suspicion that collecting art was sinful—a lustful indulgence of the eye. That must be why I enjoy it so damn much."

Everyone but Thatcher and Llewellyn laughed far too energetically. Watching Win Briggs flutter around Vanderhanks, it occurred to Thatcher that one of his duties was to do Dexter Llewellyn's fawning for him, the painter being either too preoccupied or too arrogant to do it himself.

"Oh balls, Austin," Llewellyn said. "You're the most complex and subtle of us all."

"Then would you paint my portrait in the cubist manner, Dexter?" Vanderhanks asked. "If you were to paint it?"

"Is that a commission, Austin?"

"No, certainly not. I'm much too busy nowadays to sit. . . ."

"And I'm much too busy to paint."

Garvey's butler appeared at Vanderhanks' elbow. "Washington calling you, sir," he said. "Will you take it in the study?"

"If you please," the financier said, and followed him into the hallway.

"His brother Otis, no doubt," Llewellyn murmured to Thatcher. "Have you met the Vice-President yet?"

"No, I haven't."

An older brother, Thatcher knew, was a retired five-star general. A third, the youngest son, was reputed to own half the state of

75

Hawaii. Even his sister Geraldine had distinguished herself on the Broadway stage. In short, a legendary tribe.

"The family gets together only once a year—at Christmas," Llewellyn said. "They spend the holiday with Austin's mother. The old girl is eighty-seven now . . . eighty-eight."

"I don't know where he got his taste for art," Manley Stringfellow said, "but it was certainly not from his mother. She collected only Sèvres china and diamonds of large carat."

"I suspect Austin of arranging these intrusive phone calls on purpose," Llewellyn said. "He has a telephone in every room of his house, and a closed-circuit television set in his limousine connected with the Exchange. When they invent one, he will carry a telephone in his coat pocket. And it will *always* be busy."

Vanderhanks rejoined them. "Sorry," he said. "Have you seen Ira's new Pollock?"

Apparently they all had except Thatcher, who thus found himself away from the group and more or less alone with Vanderhanks.

"Well, Lloyd," he said affably, "what do you think of the plans?"

Thatcher stared directly, and blankly, at Vanderhanks. "I haven't seen them."

"No? I was sure you'd have looked at them before tonight."

Thatcher regarded the financier even more closely. Was there a note of irony in Vanderhanks' voice?

"Could you tell me about them?"

"They're Ira's, but I don't see why not." He set his empty glass on the mantel. "Let's go into the study. . . ."

Garvey's major-domo beat softly on a set of throbbing chimes, summoning them into the dining room.

"Oh my," Vanderhanks said. "It's time."

Thatcher blessed his good fortune: Serena Lord on his right, Mrs. Oscar Wood on his left. Professor Wood's wife could be counted on to be amusing; she was fond of ticking off the trustees one by one, sparing only her art-historian husband, whom she adored, and excusing him for the company he kept by pointing out that he was the only one on the board who *really* knew a damn thing about art. That was why he was kept on, she insisted, "because he's obviously as poor as a grasshopper."

Yet Professor Wood had an art collection too, Thatcher knew—

76

made up of gifts from his students, pieces bought before the artist had any market, and some things acquired by swap or barter. There wasn't anyone in this room, he reflected, who didn't have the incurable urge to collect.

"Mr. Thatcher," Edith Wood said to him in a stage whisper, "can you tell me the purpose of this little get-together?"

Thatcher shook his head. "Do you know, Mrs. Wood?"

"No, but whenever Scrooge and Marley assemble—" She pointed toward Ira Garvey and Austin Vanderhanks. "—with the ghost of Christmas past—" A gesture toward Manley Stringfellow. "—I feel certain some major pronouncement of policy is in the works. I thought you would know what it was."

He shook his head again. Mrs. Wood was amusing, but she was also right. He pushed away his consommé untasted.

He turned his attention to the other guests. They were twelve at a long, narrow table, servants moving among them, swiftly reclaiming the consommé cups and delivering the entrées. A Marisol plaster sculpture and a Mondrian oil hung at one end of the room; at the other, one of the joyous collages of leaping nudes which Henri Matisse had shaped with scissors and multicolored paper at the close of his long life.

"Aren't you hungry, Lloyd?" Serena Lord asked.

"Not especially." An impeccably rare slice of roast beef lay before him, untouched. "Must have spoiled my appetite eating prawns. You have to watch out for prawns."

"Why don't we eat lightly here and have supper together afterward?"

"Fine."

"I *would* like some more of the burgundy."

Two courses later, Ira Garvey rose and struck his wineglass sharply with the tines of his fork.

"May I have your attention, my friends?" Conversation stopped almost instantly.

Garvey stood at the head of the table. His string tie and gold watch chain gave his evening clothes a démodé fussiness. He lifted one hand for tranquillity, peered through his Franklin spectacles at his guests, and then looked over the lenses as he spoke.

"As friends of the Museum," he said, "you will all surely be pleased with our announcement tonight. It concerns a desire dear to my heart and even dearer to our past president." He bowed slightly to his immediate left, where Austin Vanderhanks sat with his chin on his hand.

"Austin and I share a deep concern about the Museum's financial future, particularly in the inflationary spiral in which we find ourselves now. How will this museum, as a private institution, survive? On the gifts of its friends, such as ourselves? On the generosity of private donors—artists and foundations? And what other choices are there? Contributions from business? Our new director hopes so, as did our previous directors, but right now it's a hard fact that business does not give a fraction of one percent of its profits to the arts.

"As for the government? Well—" He paused for effect. "—we all have a good idea of what *that* would mean. I think I can safely assume that none of us wants Congressman So-and-So or Senator Such-and-Such—" Here he smiled apologetically at Vanderhanks. "—telling us what we can do—or not do. No, our aim must be to use private means to serve our public purpose.

"But to get to the point. . . ." he said.

George Trueblood, catching Thatcher's eye, made an almost imperceptible "V" sign with the fingers of his right hand.

"It is our intention, which will soon be officially announced, to launch a fund-raising drive whose purpose will be to give us a new Museum for the seventies.

"Ten years ago, we raised thirty-five million dollars for structural improvements in the old Museum, and for endowment funds. This year—" He paused dramatically again. "—We will raise the sum of *sixty* million dollars!"

A small sigh spread around the table: a corporate intake and exhalation of breath followed by a respectful spattering of applause.

"My God, that is a lot of money," Serena Lord breathed in Thatcher's ear.

"Moreover," Garvey continued, "I'm happy to announce that we begin our fund-raising drive with two firm pledges in hand. The first, and largest, is a pledge by Austin Vanderhanks for five million dollars."

Louder applause and one cheer, which Thatcher thought came from either Winthrop Briggs or George Trueblood.

78

"The second pledge, a more modest amount, is for one million five hundred thousand dollars. It is my own."

More applause, while Dexter Llewellyn frowned, deep in thought. Was he perhaps calculating how much of the sixty million he would be expected to contribute?

"We expect these two contributions to be followed by many more—not only from our trustees but from friends of the Museum everywhere. We will go to business, we will go to the foundations— we will go wherever there are men and women who love art.

"We have asked one of our trustees, Mr. Marcus Hammer, to take charge of the fund-raising drive. You all know him—let us show our appreciation of his willingness to undertake this challenge. Marcus Hammer!"

As they clapped, Thatcher studied Marcus Hammer, who had risen to his feet. He was a political fund-raiser without equal—a director of conglomerates, of merged companies picked up at fire-sale prices. A genius of his kind, Thatcher knew, and yet he looked like a Baptist deacon whose stomach was bothering him. . . .

"I'm not going to waste your time," Hammer said, "by going into all the details of how we intend to raise the money, or what it will be spent on. That comes later." Thatcher stiffened.

"But I thought you would want to know that at least half that sixty million dollars is for endowment. Ten million in cash to be invested in growth securities, and twenty million dollars in income-producing real estate.

"We intend to build a tower over the present Museum building, using the Museum's air rights. This tower will be rented as prime office space to corporations hungry for Midtown Manhattan offices."

He gestured clumsily with his hands.

"We estimate the tower will produce the same revenue for the Museum as twenty million dollars of securities. Moreover, it will be a hedge against inflation, since real estate values have generally increased more rapidly than any other form of investment. Ladies and gentlemen, I give you—Museum Tower!"

At this cue, a servant entered, bearing what might have been a birthday cake—dazzlingly white, resting in solitary splendor on a great silver tray. It was an architectural model. One white square, perhaps a tenth of the whole construction, represented the present

Museum. Sitting on top of it, like a brooding hen, was a two-foot model of the proposed tower. Along with the museum and tower, models of all its neighbors had been constructed—a solid block of buildings, all of different sizes and shapes. Thatcher could almost imagine the hazy sky overhead, the roaring traffic below, the tower itself densely packed with office workers.

It was, he had to admit, a hell of a show.

The applause was no longer scattered as they all clapped and cheered.

All except Thatcher, who sat now in a stunned silence.

And Manley Stringfellow, who dozed on until the noise built and woke him.

"What is it?" he cried out faintly. "What *is* it?"

They had all been in the library for some time, and Thatcher had not yet had a chance to talk privately with his host. What made him angriest of all was that Garvey's choice of setting for the revelation, his own home, made it extraordinarily difficult for Thatcher to speak freely. How could he oppose Garvey's insane scheme in Garvey's own library? Why hadn't the man waited for—or called—a board meeting to discuss these plans? And most of all, why hadn't he warned Thatcher of what he intended to say? He felt like a damned fool.

Thatcher extended his brandy snifter when the Armagnac came riding by on a salver. He felt dangerously like getting drunk.

He had carefully installed himself at one end of a long sofa, his legs politely crossed, his pose aloof.

"Don't let it get you down, Lloyd," Serena whispered as she passed by the sofa. She bent down and pressed his shoulder gently with her hand; no one saw the gesture. Then she went on into the living room with Mrs. Garvey and Edith Wood.

Finally Garvey plumped down on the sofa next to Thatcher.

"What do you think of our plans?" the doctor asked.

"I was rather surprised."

"Oh? But you've known for some time of our need for a fund-raising program. I know Robert discussed it with you, and I've mentioned it—"

"Of course it's been discussed. But not as though it was already decided. I thought we were still in the planning stage. As for the amount—"

"Don't you believe we should raise enough money so that we won't have to come back in a few years with our hats in our hands?"

"Yes, I believe that. But don't we need a new program first? How are we going to persuade people to give us sixty million dollars unless something exciting is being done?"

"It could all be raised," Garvey said, almost as though he hadn't heard Thatcher, "with contributions from only forty or fifty persons. If they are the right persons."

"I still think we should plan our program and then think about raising whatever money we need for it."

"Now Lloyd," Garvey said, "why don't you and your curators worry about the program, while the trustees and I worry about the fund-raising? Don't you see that we want to make it possible for you to have the most exciting museum anywhere in the world?"

Austin Vanderhanks suddenly materialized in front of Thatcher and Garvey.

"Sixty million dollars," he said, "might be just enough."

Thatcher said nothing.

"What's wrong, Lloyd?" Serena asked. They had stopped at The Sign of the Dove for supper, and at Elaine's for a nightcap. Now she sat huddled in her coat, leaning against her side of the cab. On the opposite side Thatcher was staring out of the window.

"I don't like being caught off guard," he said.

"Ira's a very determined man."

"So am I."

Serena put her hand gently on Thatcher's arm. "Lloyd, believe me —the worst thing you could do would be to get into a power struggle with Ira Garvey."

He tried to express some of the frustration that was boiling away in the pit of his stomach, but the words wouldn't easily come. He shifted to his most recent contretemps with Garvey—Abe Zachary had been served with a summons. And as little as he told her, Thatcher had the feeling he might be saying too much. She was a trustee, after all, however friendly.

"I've known Ira Garvey for ten years now," she said. "He's a man of honor—old-fashioned as that sounds."

"I'm sure he is," Thatcher said.

"On the other hand—"

"I'm new," he supplied. "An unknown quantity."

"You must be patient," she said. "That's all. It shouldn't take long."

"This is it," said the cab driver over his shoulder.

"Thank you for the lift, my dear," Serena said. "You'd better hold the cab."

"No, I won't need it."

She looked at him with a questioning smile.

"I feel like walking home," he said. He paid the fare and joined her on the sidewalk in front of her house.

"Another night," she said, "perhaps you'll join me for a drink." She leaned forward and printed a cool dry kiss on his cheekbone. "Good night, Lloyd."

"Good night, Serena." He watched her go through the door, waiting until a light shone out from the hallway before setting off down the street.

He walked at first without any particular destination, just to fill his lungs with different, colder air. He walked past low buildings shrouded in darkness and the shadows of towering bare trees; past the Museum, grand and solemn in the weakening darkness. Looking up, he tried to imagine Museum Tower thrusting forty stories above the street—a giant block of white granite and glass. He could think only of the Pan Am Building and the General Motors Building—and felt mildly sick to his stomach.

The fountain in front of the Plaza was still occupied by mottled flocks of pigeons, twitching and comatose. Figures were dimly visible through half-lit restaurant windows, filling up coffee urns and putting out table settings. News delivery trucks unloaded their bulldog editions, and a few newsstands hopefully raised their flaps, to the accompaniment of banging trash cans and the hideous growling of a garbage truck.

All the way home Thatcher carried with him that echoing, breathless feeling of the city just before dawn, when the life and resolution of the evening die underfoot. As he entered his apartment building, aching for sleep, a piercingly cold mist drifted over the black waters of the East River, curling into the lobby.

9

APPROACHING THE Manhattan Criminal Courts Building, Thatcher found it ugly, narrow, and mean in its proportions. The epigraphs chiseled along the granite steps—"Only the just man enjoys peace of mind" and "Be just and fear not"—served only to sharpen his concern over Abe's chances of getting a fair hearing.

Once inside, Thatcher had to admit that the building did have its own powerful sense of community. It was a world within the city— vivid and loud, bursting with vitality. Dirty, unswept, the air heavy with stale cigarette smoke and the sweat of anxiety, its hallways were crowded with people: policemen, clerks in shirtsleeves, guards in Sam Browne belts, lawyers clutching their briefcases or their clients, and the ranks of the indicted.

Abraham T. Zachary was charged with malicious mischief, a misdemeanor, returnable at Criminal Courts Building, Room 317, Part C22C.

"Is this what they call Magistrate's Court?" Thatcher asked Alex Gibbs.

"Not any more," he said. "When the courts were reorganized a couple of years ago they dropped the name. It's just referred to now as a misdemeanor court."

"Alex—what do you think Abe will get?"

"Maybe a fine . . . or a short jail sentence."

"That would be too bad."

"I suppose so," said Gibbs. "But the man *must* have known."

"I'm worried we might be overreacting. Some of Abe's friends may want us to come on strong, and if we do, we'll be playing right into their hands."

"We have to keep this kind of thing from happening again," Gibbs said. "Garvey's made the right decision, I'm convinced of it. An example must be made of this man."

"I didn't agree with Garvey, you know."

"I know," Gibbs said.

Room 317, Part C22C was crowded, so crowded that Thatcher didn't see how an orderly trial could possibly be held in it. At the front of the room, on a bench along one side, sat eight women—all blacks, all dressed to the nines, all young. Prostitutes, Thatcher guessed. At the same time, his lips formed a silent apology for jumping so quickly to the obvious conclusion. How pleasant it would be to be proved wrong—to learn that the girls were all secretaries or sales clerks charged with shoplifting.

The first row of seats in the courtroom was filled with bored-looking police officers. Through two doors at the front of the room a series of court attendants and policemen came and went. The doors were seldom closed, and beyond them Thatcher saw a staircase leading, he presumed, to a cell block. The back of the courtroom was also filling up. Out of the corner of his eye Thatcher saw one or two familiar faces, artists he remembered from the demonstration. He nudged Gibbs.

"Looks like some of Zachary's friends are here."

Now there were four or five of them, then a sixth and a seventh. Eight. Then Zachary himself.

They were dressed with somewhat more restraint than at the Museum; there were sportcoats in evidence, and one business suit. But the artist in the suit, a tall black sculptor named Bolo Van Buren, had forgone wearing a shirt for a bright violet-and-gold silk scarf knotted around his neck.

Abe Zachary sat on one of the benches, staring straight ahead.

The bench at the front of the room was empty. An American flag stood on a staff behind the judge's chair and to one side, and on the wall overhead was the inscription "IN GOD WE TRUST" with the letter "I" missing.

Thatcher thought the inscription a curious anachronism in view of the Supreme Court's various rulings about prayer. Perhaps instead of taking the legend down, they were simply going to let it fall down, letter by letter.

"Hear ye, hear ye," the bailiff chanted. "All persons having business before this court step forward and ye shall be heard. Part C22C now in session, Judge Arthur Fein presiding."

Judge Fein was a tall, round-shouldered man with thinning hair and glasees—indistinguishable from the middle-aged lawyers in the room. Thatcher heard him speak to one of them—he had a deep, melodious voice, pitched so softly that Thatcher could catch nothing of what he was saying. The bailiff, on the other hand, used a microphone.

"Is Abraham Zachary in the courtroom? Abraham Zachary?"

"Here." Abe got up and lumbered forward.

When he reached the dock, a brown oak lectern about the height of his waist, Abe leaned forward and rested both hands on it.

"I am Abraham Zachary."

"Are you represented by counsel?" Fein asked.

"No, your honor. I will represent myself."

Looking at the summons, the judge leaned over and spoke into the bailiff's ear.

"I beg your pardon, sir. I can't hear," Zachary said.

The judge looked up.

"Wasn't talking to you," he said. He spoke again, inaudibly, to the bailiff, who raised his microphone.

"Anyone else having part in the case of the City of New York against Abraham Zachary, please step forward."

Thatcher and Gibbs walked to the front of the room and identified themselves, then stood next to Zachary at the dock. When Thatcher whispered a greeting to the artist, Abe refused to look at him. Nevertheless, he stayed close to Zachary, keeping several feet between himself and Gibbs, as though Gibbs were the prosecutor and he and Abe both defendants.

The judge read through the charge rapidly.

"Are the details correct?" he asked.

"They are correct," Gibbs said.

"How do you plead, Mr. Zachary?"

"Not guilty, your honor."

The judge's eyebrows went up slightly. "You came here without counsel, yet intend to plead not guilty?" He sighed. "Are you quite sure you don't want me to appoint an attorney for you, Mr. Zachary? You're entitled to one, you know."

"I know. I'll plead my own case."

"Very well. You also understand that, in this particular case, you will not have a jury."

"I know that, too."

"All right then." The judge leaned back and folded his hands in his lap. "We'll proceed. Do you deny the sequence of events described in the reading of the charge?"

"No, sir."

"You did indeed attack the painting named *Dallas*, first with a pocket knife and then with your bare hands, with the apparent intent to destroy it?"

"That's right."

The judge turned to Gibbs. "Is there any physical evidence in the case, Mr. Gibbs?"

"Yes, your honor. These photographs of the incident were taken by a newspaperman named Howard Preston." He placed a sheaf of photographs on the lectern. The bailiff picked them up and passed them along to the judge, who examined them closely. "You will undoubtedly recognize Mr. Zachary as the subject of these pictures, your honor."

The judge peered over his glasses at Zachary. "There is a more than passing resemblance," he said. "What about the knife?"

"We couldn't find it. I assume the defendant has it," Gibbs said.

Zachary shook his head slowly from side to side.

And Thatcher, who still had the knife at home, remained silent.

"Mr. Zachary," the judge said, "on what possible grounds do you plead not guilty? Were you perhaps mentally unbalanced—emotionally disturbed—when this episode took place?"

"No, your honor. I was not and am not insane. I plead my case under the ancient principles of *jus usata et abusata*."

By now there was so much noise in the back of the room that

Thatcher was having trouble hearing the judge. Several more of Abe's followers had come in, along with a small group of women now gossiping in the back, as though they were in a laundromat or a supermarket. It was the damnedest babble for a courtroom, he thought, the way courts must have been in the Middle Ages when they were theaters, sports arenas, and cockpits all in one, with the spectators eating, drinking, brawling, or nursing their young while some poor creature was being sentenced to lose his nose or his ears.

"Be quiet back there and take seats, or else get out of the courtroom," the bailiff said. He walked back to scold the offenders.

"What was that you said?" Judge Fein asked Zachary.

"*Jus usata et abusata*," the artist repeated.

The courtroom clerk who was transcribing the proceedings squinted up at Zachary.

"The law of use and abuse," Gibbs murmured.

Judge Fein leaned back, clasped his hands behind his head, and rocked gently back and forth in his huge brown chair.

"May I ask," the judge inquired, "what relevance you think this ancient principle of property has to the Museum's complaint against you?"

"That principle," Zachary said, "drawn from the Roman codex, has passed through English common law, and is not without relevance in our own judicial system, although it has been circumscribed by the *jus civitas*."

The judge leaned forward. "Mr. Zachary, would you mind very much skipping the legal lecture and confining yourself to the matter at hand?"

"I shall. Briefly, your honor, this property right gives the owner of something complete disposition over it, including the right to destroy it if he chooses."

"Within reason, that is true," the judge said. "Of course, it does not give the owner the right to damage property not his own in the course of destroying his own."

"No one has accused me of destroying or damaging anything except my own painting, Judge."

"You maintain the painting *Dallas* is yours?"

"I do. I painted it—whatever merits it has flow out of the work of my hands. Who has a better property right to it than me?"

The judge turned away from Zachary. "Mr. Gibbs," he asked, "what is the precise status of the painting so far as the Museum is concerned?"

Gibbs cleared his throat.

"It's a promised gift, your honor."

"A *promised* gift? And what kind of a gift is that, Mr. Gibbs?"

"It means that the donor has agreed to leave us the painting in his will."

"But you already have possession of it."

"Yes. On a form of extended loan."

"I see." The judge leaned forward again, all his attention now focused on Gibbs.

"It's not likely the donor will want it back again—either to sell to somebody else, or hang in his living room, or give to another museum?"

"Not likely, no."

"But possible?"

"It *has* happened—codicils can be added to wills. Minds have been changed even on the deathbed."

"In other words, Mr. Gibbs, the ownership of this work can be said to be uncertain?"

"Not at all, Judge. That is, we certainly know that this man Zachary doesn't own it. He sold it long ago."

"To whom?"

"Mr. Austin Vanderhanks."

"Is he your donor?"

"Yes."

"I see. You have a distinguished patron, Mr. Zachary."

"He's no patron of mine," Zachary said. "And I didn't sell the painting to him. He got it from some other parasite."

"I think, Mr. Gibbs," the judge continued, "that it would be more logical if Mr. Vanderhanks were represented here today rather than the Museum. More logical if Mr. Vanderhanks had filed this complaint against Mr. Zachary, not the Museum. Don't you agree?"

"It might be more logical," Gibbs admitted, "but Mr. Vanderhanks is an enormously busy man."

"So are we all, Mr. Gibbs.

"Your honor," Gibbs began, "I fail to see—"

88

The judge began to cough—at first, perhaps, to call the room to attention—but he continued to cough and hack, more and more loudly. At last the paroxysm subsided. He blew his nose definitively.

"Mr. Zachary," he said, dabbing his eyes with the sleeve of his gown, "the ownership of this painting is clouded enough so that there are unquestioned irregularities in your summons. And in the Museum's handling of the charge. However—"

Thatcher felt a surge of relief.

"—I wouldn't want you to think that because of any ambiguities of ownership you have the right to do what you please in a place like the Museum. I therefore have no choice but to find you guilty as charged and to sentence you to thirty days in the city jail." Scattered hisses and catcalls broke out in the rear of the courtroom. The judge frowned. "But in view of the fact that you have no known criminal record, I'm suspending the sentence. Just don't let me see you here again. Case closed."

He brought his gavel down on the top of the bar, then noticed Gibbs's expression.

"I take it you would not be so lenient, Mr. Gibbs?"

"No, your honor, I wouldn't. I foresee future outbreaks of this kind."

"Well, you have the right to take any additional civil action you wish. I believe it would also be within your province to deny Mr. Zachary admission to the Museum until you feel he can be trusted."

Gibbs looked at Thatcher, whose lips shaped a No.

"I don't think we would ever want a situation," Thatcher said, "in which an artist was refused admission to the Museum."

A spattering of applause came from the back of the room. Gibbs turned and glared at the claque of artists.

"We may wish we'd come to it," he said.

Thatcher, seeing the expressions of the artists' faces, could share some of Gibbs's dismay. There *was* something sinister about the congregation.

"That'll be enough," said the bailiff loudly.

The artists stared at him in silence, still gathered in a sullen, restless circle. He stood his ground—and so did they. After a few moments they broke apart and drifted out into the corridor to wait for Zachary.

"I'm glad you won't have to go to jail, Zach," Thatcher said.

"I spoke my piece," Zachary said. "What I did was what I had to say. And *Dallas* is a more honest work of art now than it was before." He turned and walked away.

Thatcher was startled. A more honest work—with the canvas slashed and broken? Apparently Abe saw his destruction as a form of expression, some sort of aesthetic statement. The thought left Thatcher deeply shaken.

Outside in the corridor, Bolo Van Buren was still waiting when Gibbs and Thatcher left the courtroom.

"What's this?" Gibbs asked.

"Hello, Bolo," said Thatcher.

"You people ought to know," the artist said quietly, "that we aren't through. We have only begun. The revolution is coming to you too."

"Now what's that supposed to mean?" Thatcher snapped.

"When you get back to the Museum," Bolo replied, "you'll see what we mean, Mr. Thatcher."

Traffic on the East River Drive moved so slowly that Thatcher wished they could have taken a boat upstream—the tugs and barges to starboard were actually pacing them. He heard Gibbs's analysis of the decline in attendance since Thanksgiving (partly the lack of an exciting show, and partly the inevitable slump following a holiday), but his thoughts were on what they might find waiting for them.

At last they pulled up in front of the Museum.

"For Christ's sake," Gibbs said. "More of them."

They were all there—the same group they'd seen at the courtroom, augmented by half a dozen newcomers. This time two policemen were standing by, as well as Dolan and one of his guards.

Bolo Van Buren was waiting beside the entrance to the Museum. Thatcher stopped when they reached him. "Bolo—"

"Relax, man."

"We don't want any trouble."

"Look—we're not keeping anyone from going in or out. We're *peaceful*. Just here to spread the word, that's all."

He handed them a mimeographed sheet of paper.

"Read," Van Buren said. "Don't think 'cause it's not pretty it's not important—and don't put it down. We may not have a printing press like you do, but it's a certainty we have the *troops*."

Thatcher flinched at his choice of word, then nodded and went into the Museum, tucking the piece of paper under his arm.

10

PULL DOWN thy vanity, I say pull down."

WE DEMAND

1. That the Museum be open free to the public at all times.

2. That at least three of the fifteen elected members of the Museum's board of trustees be artists, both known and unknown, and that "pseudo-artists" and society painters be excluded from consideration.

3. That a "Black Wing" be established at the Museum for the display of the work of black, Puerto Rican, and American Indian artists.

4. That the Museum lend its prestige and resources to the struggle against discrimination, poverty, social injustice, the pollution of our environment, and war.

5. That the Museum sell a large number of works in its collection at least thirty years old and use the proceeds from this sale to buy the works of living, vital, unknown young artists.

6. That a plan be evolved by the Museum to give the artist a fair share of the resale price of his work.

7. That the artist retain undisputed copyright in his own work, regardless of who owns it, including the right to determine when and where it will be displayed or reproduced. He should also be able to see it freely whenever he requires.

8. That the Museum devote a section of its space to the permanent exhibition of works by artists without galleries.

9. That the Museum maintain rooms for the·mounting of art environments, and that there be at least one such environment continually on view.

10. That the Museum encourage the creation of tech-art pieces which can be manufactured in large quantities for the masses, and the Museum also undertake to dissipate the bourgeois commercial mystique surrounding original works of art.

Signed for the Artists' Round Table:

Abraham Zachary
Howard Van Buren (Bolo)
Athos Philippides
Dennis Scal
Russell Willoughby
Elizabeth Oppenheimer
John Thompson
. . . Backed by 150 other art workers!

A BILL OF RIGHTS FOR THE ARTIST!

End Repression in the Arts!

"To have gathered from the air a live tradition or from a fine old eye the unconquered flame. This is not vanity."

11

THE STAFF MEETING Thatcher called two weeks after Zachary's trial and shortly before the Christmas holidays began in an atmosphere of relative calm.

They were grouped around the low, round marble table in Thatcher's office, still drinking coffee: Alex Gibbs, who'd been the first to arrive; George Trueblood, looking as though he had one of his ghastly champagne hangovers; Homer Karp, head of the Film and Photography Department; Ted Porter from Painting and Sculpture; and the only woman who had any authority at the Museum, Patricia Sidney, the director of the Drawings and Prints Library.

Alex Gibbs had the floor.

"I don't see why wielding a paintbrush gives a man any special privileges," he said. "Or any special claim on the Museum."

"Who has a better right to make such a claim?" Thatcher asked. "Without them, what reason would we have for existing?"

"Turning your question around, Lloyd," George Trueblood said, "don't they need us far more than we need them? I mean—think of how many artists there are just begging for recognition. The chance to have their work hanging on museum walls—*that's* what they want."

"I don't think any of us really knows what artists want," Thatcher persisted. "At any rate, we should listen to them."

"But these demands!" Gibbs said. He held up the mimeographed sheet, much creased from having been folded and refolded and sent from office to office through the Museum. "Of course we'd like to have the Museum open free to the public—but we simply don't have the funds to make that feasible right now. As for some of these other points—"

"Perhaps they're making impossible demands," Thatcher said, "so we'll be forced to consider what *is* possible. Opening the Museum free to the public one day a week, for example."

"Suppose we do acknowledge and then perhaps yield to some of these demands," Gibbs said. "What next? Why shouldn't the artists insist on running the place themselves? They can't manage their own lives—yet they probably think they know how to manage a multi-million-dollar institution."

"You wouldn't put a haberdasher in charge of the U.S. Government, would you?" Thatcher asked. "I for one think that haberdasher turned out to be the best President we've had this side of World War Two. Anyway, Alex, they're not asking to run the place, they only want a few seats on our board."

"Only! Do they realize what being on the board means?"

"If it's money you're thinking of," Thatcher said, "you know yourself we have a board member or two who make no financial contribution at all."

"I'm speaking of prestige, too," Gibbs said. "To be effective, our board has to be composed of distinguished men and women. Unlike our professional staff, which has its talented *arrivistes*, its—"

"Birds of paradise?" Trueblood suggested.

"And its workhorses," Gibbs concluded. "A category in which I include myself—and Harry Truman."

"Maybe one or two artists would perk up our board," Thatcher said. "Keep Dexter Llewellyn company."

"I would oppose that idea," Gibbs said.

"You went to Yale, didn't you, Alex?" Thatcher asked.

Gibbs nodded.

"So did Bolo Van Buren."

"It takes more than a Yale degree to qualify for the board," Gibbs said. "But maybe we can put Van Buren in charge of your new black wing, Lloyd."

"You mean the third demand? Somehow I don't think we'll ever have a Jim Crow gallery in this museum, not as long as I'm director."

" 'Young Lochinvar is come out of the West,' " Gibbs muttered.

The temperature in the room was rising swiftly. George Trueblood elected himself peacemaker.

"I think we all know you both to have the Museum's best interests at heart," he said.

Just then Mal Crawford walked in. Though it was now almost noon, he neither excused nor explained his tardiness.

"We're talking about the militant artists," Gibbs announced to Mal.

"I can give you a bulletin from the front lines," Mal said. "I've been with Bolo Van Buren and Abe Zachary."

"Where?" Thatcher asked.

"At Bolo's studio down on lower Broadway. I suggested the meeting myself. It was unofficial, of course."

"I hope they understood that," Thatcher said.

"I'm sure they did. In fact I think they'd prefer it that way. . . . They told me they weren't willing to buy your suggestion of a blue-ribbon committee to study the problems of the artist, Lloyd."

"The problems of the arts—not just the artist," Thatcher said.

"They won't have any part of it. We all know such a committee could be extremely useful if it were properly set up. But think how long it would take to get it going—and who's going to be your chairman? The guy would have to be a saint, at least. Where would you find a thick-skinned sensitive man who could satisfy both Ira Garvey and Abe Zachary?"

"We'd find someone."

"They aren't gonna wait that long," Mal said.

"All right, what's coming next?" Gibbs asked him.

"It's hard to say. Another demonstration, I suppose. I don't know what form it'll take," Mal said. "But I know this—it's a situation all primed to blow."

Gibbs winced. "I wish you wouldn't use expressions like that," he said. "And please don't take it on yourself to conduct any more pourparlers."

"He's right, Mal," Thatcher said. "We should coordinate what we do and say."

"Sorry," said Mal. "Anyway, I told them we would respond to them—soon. That I would try to persuade you, and all the other powers-that-be, to sit down in the same room and talk straight to them."

Gibbs lifted the artists' proclamation like a pennant.

"How many of these people are really artists anyway?" he said. "Athos Philippides and this fellow Willoughby, to name two, can't claim a shred of artistic ability. Unless you regard a pile of metal plates and a backlot full of wet sand as art."

"Philippides," Thatcher mused. "George, isn't he—"

"You're right," Trueblood said. "We just added one of his sculptures to the permanent collection."

He grinned. So did Thatcher. Even Patricia Sidney flashed a wide smile, and Homer Karp chuckled in a remote, self-absorbed way. So far he'd remained silent. The oldest man on the staff, now nearing sixty, he had a mild but degenerative liver ailment which caused him to doze off occasionally. And he hated meetings—how he hated them! He glanced down at his watch and shuddered.

"*Could* we press on?" he asked in his deep, resonant voice. "I have an important appointment coming up."

Thatcher looked annoyed.

"With the new head of the Ford Foundation," Karp added.

"All right," Thatcher said. "Unless one of you has something else to say about the artists' demands, I'd like to take up the fund-raising program."

George Trueblood pressed his eyelids lightly with the tips of his fingers and groaned softly. "Must we?" he murmered.

"What we're going to do today," Thatcher said after they had helped themselves from a sandwich tray, "is start on two lists Marcus Hammer's people have prepared. Needless to say, these lists are highly confidential."

He passed out two sheets with xeroxed names.

"The first," he said, "is the so-called Gold List. It has on it the names of all the individuals and foundations we think are capable of giving the Museum one hundred thousand dollars or more. . . . Clearly, it would be to our advantage in raising sixty million dollars to have sixty people give us a million dollars each. So we begin at the apex of the pyramid, approaching the largest contributors first and then working our way downward and outward until we reach those who will donate fifty dollars or less."

"The betas," said George Trueblood.

Thatcher ignored him. "Hopefully, we can mail to these small contributors. As for this second list, the Silver List, these are the names of people who may be expected to give less than one hundred thousand dollars."

"Or nothing at all," Homer Karp interjected. "You've got Henry Field Masters IV on this list. He wouldn't give five dollars if we renamed the Museum for him."

"That's exactly what we want to find out," Thatcher said. "We'll start at the beginning and go through as many names today as we can."

Thatcher crossed to the door and opened it.

"Lise," he said, "would you call in the girls down the hall? We'll need you to sit in, too."

Before Thatcher could step back into his office, George Trueblood slipped out and waylaid him.

"Can't it wait, George?"

Apparently it could not. "While I respect the Museum's budget," Trueblood said, his expression revealing that he did no such thing, "I must say that I consider the opening night party for my Goodman Hart show to be of *critical* importance. . . . Here we are, less than a month away—why, Mal Crawford needs more time than that just to prepare the invitations, and I'm told we don't have money in the entertainment budget for a decent party. I mean—not even a little cocktail party with those dreary potato chips and peanuts instead of *canapés*? Are we so poor now that we can't afford to do things in the proper way?"

"I've already given your problem some thought, George."

"And?"

"This might be an opportunity to bring potential donors into the Museum."

"Mmm."

"I can ask Marcus Hammer if he'll release some of the fund-raising budget for a party, VIPs only. . . . Can you get some of Goodman Hart's famous friends to come?"

"Nothing simpler," Trueblood said. "I can promise you a *radiant* assembly."

"All right. We'll get the party for you."

George seemed prepared, literally, to jump for joy. "I'm so glad that's settled," he said happily. "It would be a disgrace to open a show this important without a party."

98

"Oh, I don't know," Thatcher said. "Don't you sometimes think we may carry this compulsive gaiety too far?"

Trueblood looked shocked. "What an odd idea, Lloyd."

The two miniskirted girls who entered the office with Lise a few minutes later brightened the room considerably, one carrying the records of donations to the last Museum capital drive, the other a steno pad.

"The first name on the list is Charles P. Appleton," said Thatcher. "Anyone know him?"

"I do," said Trueblood. "He's donated works valued, let me see, maybe in the high four figures."

"He gave five thousand dollars once before," Lise volunteered.

"On the Silver List then," Thatcher said. "Next—Amory Bernstein."

"Which Bernstein is that?" someone asked.

"Is there more than one?"

"Well, this one lives at 1407 Avenue of the Stars."

"Avenue of the *Stars?*"

"It's in Central City. You know, some damned Hollywood movie lot-turned suburb."

"Never heard of it. Or him."

Thatcher again: "The Cardman Foundation."

"Who's running it?"

"Victor I. Cardman and Grace G. Cardman."

"Both good friends of Ira Garvey," Homer suggested. "He'd be the best one to make the pitch."

"You get that down?" Thatcher asked the stenographer.

"Yes, sir."

To Thatcher it was an amazing list. There were sixty-eight names under Gold, and seventy-six under Silver. It was like crossing the Social Register with Dun and Bradstreet's and the Almanach de Gotha. The Museum's own Domesday Book. Financiers, movie producers, the city's leading banking and investment firms, foundations of every size and kind, including one whose only known beneficiary was the estate of its founder. There was a maharajah, a member of the peerage, and a knight of the realm—all celebrated for their art collections. The important names were all there: the Boardmans, the

Frankses, the Zimmerman family, Mrs. J. J. Lake who gave only to institutions in Washington—the Blocks, whose money was so new the ink was hardly dry on it, coming from a trucking chain into the galleries and studios of the most fashionable artists in town.

"Saul Berger gave a hundred thousand to Lincoln Center last year, but only two thousand when we had our last drive. Who'll tackle him?" . . .

And: "Who runs the Brownell Foundation?"

"The Ives family. She's a Mrs. Vanderhanks."

Suppose all these people were gathered into one room at one time, and wined and dined, and then solicited? *Ladies and gentlemen,* Ira Garvey might announce, *the waiters will now pass among you with bushel baskets to receive your contributions. Stocks and bonds will be acceptable, along with personal checks and IOUs. . . .*

Within the office the discussion was swirling from one corner of the room to the other, the voices becoming more raucous and more numerous, the trips to the liquor cabinet more frequent.

"Leslie J. Kannon? How about Leslie J. Kannon?"

"Does anyone know him?"

"He's a shit," George Trueblood called out. "A number-one."

"Let's put him on *that* list then," said Homer Karp.

Thatcher called a short break.

Now it was Mal Crawford's turn. He pursued Thatcher inexorably down the hall and into the men's room. They stood next to each other at the urinals. Thatcher sighed. His forehead had begun to throb.

"What do you take for tension, Mal?"

He was not to be diverted. "Permatil. Look, Lloyd, I need you on two talk shows and a radio interview. 'Night Owl'—"

"No. I told you to lay off booking me, and now here we go again. Can't you understand I have to settle down to the work of running this Museum, which is what I was hired to do? At first I figured the elevators would go up and down all right without my help, the cleaners would keep cleaning, and the guards would go on guarding. Now I'm not so sure. There isn't time—"

"Jesus, Lloyd, all right, I won't book you. But it's just a couple of little shows, and you *know* you're good in front of a camera. . . ."

"Cut the flattery, Mal. What you mean is, I like showing off."

"I don't know—do you?"

"Probably," Thatcher said, already regretting his show of temper. Vain himself, Mal suspected everyone else of great vanity—in the same way he no doubt assumed Thatcher to be a latent homosexual. "Anyway," Thatcher went on, "that's no reason to go *on* showing off."

"Even if it helps the Museum?"

"I can't believe these babble shows do. But if you line up a program that really adds to the Museum's prestige or helps us in fund-raising, of course I'll cooperate."

"We can't always get what we want."

"Go ahead and try. If anybody can manage it, you can."

"Now who's using flattery?"

At two o'clock, while they were giving the Gold List a rest and just as Homer Karp rose to bolt for his appointment, Ted Porter, the youngest man in the room, seized the floor in a sudden flank attack.

"I don't know how many of you know this," Porter said, "but some of us newer curators have been meeting lately."

"I've known," said George Trueblood.

"On our own time," Porter added. "We believe that we ought to have more voice in the operation of the Museum."

Thatcher sighed. It was the first he had heard of it, but somehow he was not at all surprised. "How many of you are there?" he asked.

"About thirty," Porter said. "We have a representative from every curatorial department—and from Administration, too."

"Who?" Gibbs demanded.

"Curt Bingham, your assistant."

"Curt certainly didn't mention it," Gibbs said to Thatcher.

"We agreed that I would be the one to open the discussions," Porter said. "And present our demands."

Thatcher motioned for Gibbs to hold his tongue as Porter took a small scrap of paper from his pocket. "There aren't many. We couldn't think of ten." He smiled and unfolded the paper, then cleared his throat. "First of all, we want to say that we don't wish to join a conventional union, although we have been approached by an organizer from the UAW."

"The *Automobile* Workers?" Thatcher said.

"Ah, yes. We would rather form our own organization. And we have—the Museum Workers Coalition. We're asking for the right to review the Museum's exhibition schedule before the exhibitions are . . . scheduled . . . and for the right to make recommendations to the board of trustees. Ditto for the publication program. Next—we want across-the-board cost-of-living salary increases, large enough to make a real difference. We want a sabbatical system, the same as in a college or university. And we want compensatory time for the hours we work late. That's about all—"

"Surely you can think of other possibilities," said Gibbs. "A two-month vacation?"

"We think six weeks would be reasonable."

Gibbs abandoned sarcasm. "Of course, these are all matters for the board of trustees to consider."

"When?" Porter asked.

"The agenda is already full for December, you can skip January —vacations, you know—I'd say this could all be brought up in February, or maybe March."

Porter looked at Thatcher and then back at Gibbs. "Is that all I can tell the others?"

"You can tell them that of course we'd *like* to give substantial salary increases. On the other hand—"

"We ought to be able to do better than that," said Thatcher. "George?"

"May I give it more thought?"

"Pat?"

"I agree with Alex. We should wait—let the board decide."

Thatcher turned back to Ted Porter. "Will you put your requests in writing?" he asked. The young curator nodded.

"Since I've just learned about your coalition, I can't give you a reply now—and you wouldn't want me to answer from the hip. But you will get an answer, you'll get it fast, and you have my personal word that when I take your case to the board, I'll plead it as though it were my own. Will that do, Ted?"

"Thank you," said Porter. "That's just fine."

"I think we'd better adjourn this meeting," Thatcher said, rising. "Alex, would you stick around?"

"Of course."

The office was quickly emptied; Gibbs started in before Lise had finished clearing away the sandwich trays and empty glasses.

"My God, Lloyd, those salary increases alone would sink us in red ink."

"Alex," Thatcher said, "Ted Porter's salary is eighty-five hundred dollars a year."

"We have several assistant curators in that range," said Gibbs, "and one, Bonnie Macrae, at an even lower figure."

"But Porter is no kid just out of college," Thatcher said. "He's thirty years old, with a wife and baby. And a master's degree and forty-some hours toward a doctorate. Not to mention three years' experience with this museum."

"He'll get some sort of increase, of course," Gibbs said. "But we can't afford to raise everyone's salary to the top of the field, you know that as well as I do."

"I hope you don't feel, Alex, that Ted Porter's salary is contributing to our inflationary spiral. He could earn more money teaching. Or as a bank clerk."

"This is the work he chose," Gibbs said. "Please try to understand my position, Lloyd. I too have listened to the Sermon on the Mount, but I've also been charged to keep this museum running smoothly, first under Robert Saint-Simon and now under you—and that assignment can't be done with good intentions. Charity does not begin here at the Museum—in my view, it *ends* here.

"And at the risk of giving unsolicited good advice, let me remind you respectfully that you are not an ordinary staff member here—be as sympathetic as you choose, but there *is* a tangible field of authority and privilege separating you from staff members like Ted Porter. You just can't have it both ways."

"I appreciate your position and your advice," Thatcher said stiffly. "But please get me the figures on what these new benefits would cost. . . . How about a week from today?"

"I can have it in three days."

"Even better," Thatcher said.

He accompanied his deputy director to the foyer, one hand lightly touching his elbow, steering him past Lise's desk.

"By the way," Gibbs said, lingering in the doorway, "I've been asked by Garvey to file a supplementary report on the Zachary affair."

What a thick dossier Abe is going to have compiled on him,

Thatcher thought. And how he'd laugh at the notion of being a case study in Ira Garvey's file cabinet.

"Fine by me, Alex."

"I just wanted to be sure you knew. . . ."

And what about the dossier on me, Thatcher wondered. How thick is that getting to be?

12

THATCHER SAT ALONE in the Patrons Room, a chamber that might have served equally well as an auditorium, a ballroom, or a basketball court. A single spotlight shone down on him and on the folders and printed sheets spread out on a huge, T-shaped rosewood table. The only sound in the vast room was the scratching of his pencil on the pages before him.

He had arrived a half-hour early for the tribal conclave—the monthly sitting of the board of trustees. Since he still had his own report to the board to go over, he welcomed the chance to sit by himself in the one room in the Museum where he might work undisturbed. For nearly twenty minutes he studied the figures and comparisons of Museum receipts and expenditures. When he had finished, he read through the agenda, checking off the items on which his comments would be expected. This was Garvey's show, not his. The staff was there to supply information, to be put through their paces and receive the Word. Only Thatcher himself played a dual role: trustee as well as staff director.

He felt light-headed, and his eyes stung. The figures and names on the page in his hand seemed to move slightly.

He wished he could somehow get more rest. Too many dinner parties, too many late meetings and early risings, too much work toted home in his briefcase—he was beginning to pay the price in lost sleep and racking dreams, in chafed nerves and, far too often, a tight ball of pain somewhere between his stomach and chest.

Trustee meetings were as stylized as Noh dramas. The staff usually gathered at five minutes to the hour. Precisely at four o'clock Ira Garvey would arrive, accompanied by his personal assistant for Museum affairs, Frank Henley. Almost immediately the room would fill with trustees, and, within a few minutes, all those who were going to be there would have drifted in, either separately or in flocks. Four-ten: Garvey would call the meeting to order. At four-twenty-five Austin Vanderhanks would rush in, looking as though he had just stepped off a jet, or was about to board one—apologetic, out of breath by just enough to make his apologies convincing—and smilingly, intelligently attentive. Nothing that went on at these meetings seemed too monotonous for him, nothing escaped his notice.

It was five of four. Alex Gibbs walked in, bearing a large sheaf of documents. With him came several members of the comptroller's staff.

And then, promptly at four, Frank Henley arrived. Without Ira Garvey. Thatcher looked up at him in surprise.

"Dr. Garvey is right behind me," he said. "He just stopped to wash his hands."

An improbable picture forced its way into Thatcher's mind: Garvey stepping into the men's room and extending his hands, while an assistant brought up a metal tray bearing distilled water and PhisoHex. . . .

"Good afternoon, Lloyd," Garvey said affably, and nodded to the others.

He stacked his row of papers together, blocked them neatly, and glanced around the room.

"Undoubtedly Mr. Vanderhanks will be along shortly. We'd better begin. . . . May I have your attention please, ladies and gentlemen?"

At the very least, half of the twenty-two trustees could be counted on to show up for the monthly session; this afternoon there were fifteen, including all those who had been at Garvey's dinner party except Serena Lord, unaccountably missing.

Martin Stanley, a frequent truant, was there—founder, owner, manager, and spokesman of a chain of conservative daily newspapers. Next to Stanley slumped Gray Butler, Sr., and his first cousin, old Thomas Seabury, who had wedded wealth and aged gracefully in Newport. Beyond him at the long table the faces got older and grayer. There were two women, Grace Stearnes and Mary Lawless—and two withered playboys, Harry Carstairs and Robert Browerman.

106

At the foot of the table sat Barney Specker, a man whose capital enhanced itself by about a thousand dollars every half-hour he spent at the Museum Patrons Room, or anywhere else. Completely bald and perhaps sixty pounds overweight, dressed in the most beautifully tailored British suits Thatcher had ever seen, Specker almost never spoke at these meetings. He just sat there—there seemed to be some mysterious quality about the Museum that drew him there and held him in his seat: a feeling of his own about the place not far from a kind of love.

Thatcher crossed his legs and forced himself, by kneading his forehead and cheekbones with his fingertips, to listen to Ira Garvey's parched voice.

". . . The Nominating Committee will not report today owing to the absence of its chairman, Mrs. Ashbrook Lord."

Where *was* Serena? Thatcher had not talked to her since the Garvey party.

At this point Austin Vanderhanks hurried in, head forward, hands efficiently hooked to the patch pockets of his navy-blue blazer, cheeks flushed from the cold outside. Where could he be coming from in such a costume, Thatcher wondered. Or where could he be going, this man who almost always wore banker's brown or broker's gray? Spring, and the yachting season, must have come early to Wall Street. Vanderhanks smiled apologetically and sat down alongside Ira Garvey, who nodded and continued talking.

"I'm happy to report that the state Board of Regents has looked favorably on our petition to enlarge our board by twelve additional members. This means we can broaden the base of our board without— and this is important—without sacrificing the experience and maturity of those board members who have served us for such a long time."

"I assume," said Marcus Hammer after his raised hand had been recognized by the chair, "that we'll take advantage of these new openings in our fund-raising campaign."

"Well now, that can't be our only consideration," said Garvey. "However, it's a point."

"I just want to remind us all," Hammer said, in a tone that grated on Thatcher's ears, "that there are several extremely generous patrons of this Museum who would welcome the opportunity to serve on the board of trustees."

Austin Vanderhanks looked up at Garvey and smiled with satisfaction.

"In any case," Garvey said, "I have instructed Mrs. Lord to assemble her committee and to consider possible candidates for these seats."

Thatcher was a habitual doodler. At about the time the melancholy strains of the treasurer's report sounded in the room, his pencil began to move across the mimeographed agenda as though it had a life of its own. His drawings were always elaborate and detailed, ranging from surrealistic nudes and fabulous animals to baroque sketches of castles and knights in armor; sometimes he drew Art Nouveau furniture and bizarre architectural structures. Today he sketched a monkey wearing corduroy trousers, a leather belt, and a butterfly tie. The monkey was staring down at a fish in a pond. From the mouth of the fish a thin stream of water spurted out, heading straight for the monkey's bulging eye.

As he drew, Thatcher listened attentively to the report. In the absence of the treasurer, Harry Mountjoy, executive vice-president of one of the city's largest investment firms, Alex Gibbs was reading now from last year's operating statement. ". . . You can see from page two that although total income and contributions have increased to approximately seven point three million dollars, expenses have grown at an even greater rate—to seven point eight three million dollars, resulting in an operating deficit of approximately five hundred thirty thousand dollars for the year. . . ."

As Gibbs spoke, Thatcher's eyes raced rapidly over the columns of figures. They were neat, they were convincing, and they were disquieting. Particularly alarming was the way the deficits had been increasing —by fifty or one hundred thousand dollars every year, and more rapidly the past two years than before.

Professor Wood's hand rose into the air, signaling urgently. Garvey must have seen, Thatcher realized, but he paid no attention.

Gibbs had passed on to more pleasant figures. ". . . Collection now valued at approximately ninety-one million dollars, an increase over the last appraisal six years ago of forty-seven million dollars; buildings and equipment estimated at twenty-one point five million dollars; endowment funds now worth more than thirty-two million dollars. . . . Other assets—"

108

Thatcher remembered a conversation with Robert Saint-Simon not long before his death.

"It's one hell of a place to administer," he'd said. "Maybe impossible. What you must try to do is cut out the part of the whole role you know you can perform, do that to perfection, and hope that somehow your concept of that role is large enough, grand enough in scale, to give the Museum the splendor it should have. As for me, I was always weak in details, particularly where money was involved. There I always depended on the astuteness of the professionals."

And shouldn't I, Thatcher wondered. Increasingly, it was becoming apparent that his role could not effectively encompass all the important aspects of the Museum's operation.

At last Garvey recognized Oscar Wood.

"I hope we're not going to pass over these figures without comment," Wood said. "These somewhat shocking figures, I ought to say."

"Do you wish to speak on the subject of the budget, Professor Wood?"

"I certainly do. At our present rate of spending and borrowing, it will not be long before our annual deficit equals our total expenditures ten years ago."

"You are as familiar as any of us with the state of the economy, Professor Wood. The times—"

"Are we out to emulate the federal government in our financial affairs?"

"I don't think that statement requires a serious answer. I suggest—"

"I suggest we are courting bankruptcy."

"That's rather a strong term," said Garvey. "Our problems are not hopelessly insoluble. . . ."

"I repeat—bankruptcy."

"Will the secretary please see that Professor Wood's last remark is *not* entered in the minutes?"

And so it went, on and on, until Thatcher's now-blunt pencil had covered several pages with doodles. Grace Stearnes had reported on the Museum's overseas program and provided them with an inappropriately gushing description of a spring meeting to be held in London; Thatcher himself had bored them all thoroughly with reports on attendance, sales, and the Museum's circulatory system, watching Manley Stringfellow's fingers make one cat's cradle after another as he spoke.

The motion to adjourn was seconded by three voices at once.

"Are we in danger of bankruptcy, Alex?"

"Not by my lights." Gibbs smiled stiffly. "You heard the figures, Lloyd."

"Yes, I heard them."

"Now wait a minute. If I'm not handling the budget to your satisfaction—"

"Alex, please. Why so defensive?"

"I'm not defensive. Look, you and I and Harry Mountjoy will get together as soon as he's back from the Islands. . . ."

"I must say, Lloyd, I'm pleased with this month's Bookstore sales. But what can we do to improve the Restaurant receipts?"

"Ira, they're bound to pick up as soon as our liquor license goes through. Lunch receipts are excellent. It's in the evenings that—"

"Undoubtedly. And, of course, these matters are unimportant compared to our first priority. . . ."

"Beg pardon?"

"I mean the fund-raising campaign, of course."

"Yes, well, it's progressing."

"Speed, Lloyd, make all possible speed. My financial advisers are forecasting a bear market. Now is the time. . . ."

"Yes, Ira."

"Lloyd," said George Trueblood, "could you come down to my office for a few minutes? There's someone here I'd like you to meet."

Thatcher tried first to beg off. "I've got to ride herd on the Junior Friends of the Museum. They're planning a folk-art cruise to Puerto Rico."

"Please? I won't keep you long."

"All right, George."

Where Thatcher's office was spare, almost monastic in its tidiness, Trueblood's was prodigiously cluttered: books in high piles, mounds and drifts of correspondence, and almost all the available wall space used for prints, drawings, posters, and proofs. Any day now, Thatcher expected to walk into this fantastic cave of paper and canvas and find objects and broadsides hanging down like stalactites from the ceiling.

In the midst of the disorder were George and a Buddha-like black man he introduced as Hannibal Hamilton.

"Lloyd, I know you haven't much time, so I'll stick to essentials. Hannibal is director of the Toussaint L'Ouverture Museum of Art on St. Nicholas Avenue and 112th Street—" Hamilton inclined his large oval head with a fleeting smile. "—which he took over in January, isn't that right?"

"That is correct. We used to be the Harlem Fine Arts Center, Mr. Thatcher."

"Inactive for the most part," George put in.

"We just scratched along on hardpan these past few years, Mr. Thatcher—no endowment, no permanent collection, and almost no visitors. Now our brothers have raised enough money to take over a whole building—we used to have only two floors—and we're expanding."

"I'm glad to hear that, Mr. Hamilton."

"We'd like you to help us stage an inaugural exhibition. Mr. Trueblood said I should just ask you straight out."

"What do you want most?"

"Original prints, lithographs, and etchings. We have sculpture and drawings, and a sampling of oils, but we'd like to show the community a variety of media—dealing, at least in part, with themes of interest to blacks. Not much still-life, you understand, and no abstract-expressionist paintings. Our people want their art to sing and dance too, Mr. Thatcher."

Trueblood took over. "Here's the list I've prepared, Lloyd." He handed it to Thatcher. "I'd like to take Hannibal to the print library and show him this selection. Then, if you approve the loan, I'll take care of everything else."

"I see no objections," said Thatcher, rising. "Nice to meet you, Mr. Hamilton. . . ."

Back in his own office, Thatcher checked over the list of lithographs George had given him. It was a fine historical perspective of printmaking—a Goya *Bulls of Bordeaux*, several outstanding Daumiers, Manet's *The Execution of the Emperor Maximilian*, works by Fantin-Latour, Odilon Redon, and three masterworks by Toulouse-Lautrec. The Norwegian expressionist Edvard Munch was on the list, along with such Americans as William Gropper, George Bellows, Stuart

Davis, and Thomas Hart Benton. George had even included two Riveras and a rare Siqueiros. A good show, indeed.

"Isn't Hannibal a jolly black giant, though?" George said later. "He couldn't get over how easy it was to borrow."

"He'll learn."

13

From Martha Crane's column, The Entertaining Arts, December 12:

. . . At the end of our recent interview, I asked the articulate young director of the Museum if he had any specific plans to carry out his idealistic concepts of what the Museum should be in the Space Age.

"This winter," he replied, "we intend to mount a showing of environments at the Museum. We expect to give over the entire ground floor of the building, more space than has ever been allotted to a single exhibition, to a group of artists who will be encouraged to create their own forms of expression from the inside out, *in situ.* They will have their choice of materials, and will enjoy complete freedom, within the Museum's physical limitations, to explore the changing dimensions of technology."

Pressed further, Mr. Thatcher conceded that this kind of exhibition is neither altogether new nor unique, having been done in a similar fashion in other cities, notably Paris and Stockholm. Deriving from so-called earthworks, these artistic experiments are a stimulating part of today's aesthetic climate.

Was the decision to do this show a reaction to recent protests by militant artists at the Museum?

Mr. Thatcher denied that these demonstrations were the primary reason for staging the show, but agreed that the artists had raised some valid criticisms of Museum policy, "which must be dealt with honestly and promptly." He also expressed the hope that the dissident Artists' Round Table would welcome the new environmental show.

When questioned as to whether the Painting and Sculpture Department or the Department of Architecture would be supervising the show,

Mr. Thatcher said that he himself would direct the exhibition, working with the artists involved.

And would Abraham Zachary be one of the participants?

"That will be decided at the appropriate time," Mr. Thatcher commented. "Abe Zachary's work doesn't exactly make him the ideal choice for this exhibition, but I see no other reason why he couldn't be included."

Among some of the other possible changes Thatcher visualizes for the Museum: dispersing the Museum's collection among a number of branch museums around less advantaged sections of the city, creating a special children's wing within the Museum, starting a television film and tape archive, publishing an avant-garde journal of design, and a series of instant, disposable art books. His long-range aim is to see a revolution in the teaching of art appreciation.

Quite a versatile young man, Lloyd Thatcher, and apparently a true friend of the artist, though his critics, more cynical perhaps, might ask if this *wunderkind* from the west is not trying to be, in the words of the Apostle Paul, all things to all men. . . .

Two days after the Martha Crane interview appeared, Thatcher was summoned to meet Ira Garvey in the doctor's office at the East River Clinic: purpose unspecified, agenda unknown.

Just before noon a cab deposited him at the entrance to a towering white beehive that resembled a Saarinen building torn from the drawing board before the architect had finished it. Built of poured concrete in cold flowing lines, its windows drawn back from the street line like small cells, the East River Clinic seemed to promise technological marvels like artificial hearts and man-made chromosomes.

Along one wall of the lobby stretched a Chryssa neon construction in cast acrylic and glass—deep blue and glowing. Nearby hung an Andrew Wyeth landscape. If the definition of originality is to go against the grain of one's own time, Thatcher thought, to follow one's own bent regardless of hostile criticism, no artist today is more original than Andrew Wyeth.

An elevator featuring Montavani playing Gershwin bore Thatcher swiftly up to the twenty-ninth floor.

Directly outside the entrance to Ira Garvey's private office hung a work by Pierre Soulages called *L'Espoir*. Behind a dense network of monolithic slabs and disruptive slashes of thick black oil could be seen faint glimmers of pure white and yellow light, challenging the darkness of the canvas.

This painting, which sent a shock of excitement along his spinal column, reminded Thatcher of one of Garvey's more widely circulated remarks: "I just wish there weren't so much emphasis put on the investment values of art," he had said. "When men no longer wish to own works of art, it will be because they are living like machines on a plastic earth. . . . Anyway, a person who buys a good painting, one he loves, can't *lose*."

After the Soulages, Thatcher was unprepared for what he found inside Garvey's office.

The room was just this side of monumental, and furnished entirely in a mixture of English and New England period pieces. The paintings here were portraits in subdued grays and browns, several Renaissance pieces, one Caravaggio and a Rembrandt miniature, and several limpid, sunny American primitives. The only distinctly modern painting Thatcher could see was a Charles Burchfield landscape.

What fascinated Thatcher most were the antiques: a Massachusetts bombé chest of drawers, a long teak refectory table, and a fantastically ornate desk with two hinged side sections spread out like wings, with brass and ivory drawers and filing compartments.

"If you're admiring that desk," said Garvey, "it came from the old Wells Fargo office in Jefferson City, Missouri. My grandfather once used it. See that nick on the side? Bullet scar from a holdup—never repaired. . . . How are you Lloyd?"

"Fine, thank you, Ira."

Garvey led the way to a conversational grouping of a wing chair, a Gebrüder Thonet rocker, and a Chippendale love seat in one corner. Choosing the love seat for himself, he switched on the hurricane lamp on a nearby end table.

"Now we can talk comfortably."

And Garvey did look supremely comfortable. This was clearly an atmosphere that suited him—this detailed and carefully composed tableau of solid furniture and elegant artifacts. Meant, Thatcher was sure, to impress the healthy visitor as well as the sick. *Nothing can go seriously wrong within these walls,* the room seemed to say.

"There are two things that trouble me," said Garvey.

"Yes?" Thatcher had chosen the rocker, and found himself accelerating the chair's gentle motion.

"Our acquisitions program, for one."

The Museum, unlike many institutions of its kind, had no general funds set aside to acquire art. It had to either draw on capital funds or find someone willing to buy a coveted work of art and donate it. Occasionally, an artist gave his work directly to the Museum, and collectors often made gifts of art for the tax deduction or for prestige. The problem here was to decide whether the Museum actually wanted the gift or not. This was scrounging of a high order indeed, for beggars had to be choosers in every sense of the phrase.

Garvey had lifted a sheet of paper from the drawer of the end table.

"I am concerned—about some of the acquisitions at the last meeting of your committee," he said. "I've just seen the minutes."

The monthly meeting of the Acquisitions Committee was an elaborate dance at which curators wooed patrons, patrons danced court around curators, and both joined to circle seductively about artists. Thatcher served as staff chairman of this committee. Garvey sometimes, but not always, attended; he was not a formal member of the committee.

He began to read aloud in his high, flat voice.

" 'Mr. Porter then showed a large oil painting by Achille Moreau, a gift of Mr. and Mrs. William Geller. The painting was achieved, Mr. Porter said, by having the artist's nude model coat herself first with red and then with purple paint and having her do exercises on the canvas.' "

"The painting is called *Exhalations II*," said Thatcher.

"Exercises, Lloyd?"

"Yes. Well, you see—Moreau has a theory about the human body in art, and he plans to work on various systems of the body. The cardiovascular system, the respiratory system—"

"I trust he won't overlook the reproductive system."

"The theory may seem cockeyed to us, but what matters is how the work is done, not why. Moreau's theory is probably no better or no worse than any other. Did Jackson Pollock's intentions matter? Only his actual accomplishment."

"I forbear to ask the Philistine's favorite question, Lloyd, but. . . ."

"Well, Ted Porter thinks it's art, and I'm inclined to back Ted. It may not seem a masterpiece in twenty years, but in our terms, it's definitely a work of museum quality."

"I hope you're both right," Garvey said, in a tone which indicated he didn't really think so. He turned a page and continued reading:

" 'Mr. Trueblood showed photographs of two conceptual works, from an exhibition recently held at a downtown gallery, called *Visionary Landscapes*. Mr. Trueblood pointed out that the objects in the photographs no longer existed or, rather, existed only at the moment they were being photographed. He said that the effects in one of the works, *Repainted Desert*, were accomplished by running a highway asphalt spreader containing dry pigments over a section of the Mojave Desert, and then agitating the surface of the sand with a wind machine.' "

Thatcher smiled and then shrugged. "What can I say? Serious artists are choosing to do a hundred things that have nothing to do with art as it has been practiced for centuries. They're experimenting with new materials, new methods, new ways of working. Flirting with computers and microelectronics, smuggling tiny aesthetic messages in decal form aboard space capsules headed for other planets. Ordinary objects are being turned inside out and upside down. Artists are enraptured with novelty, yet they're summoning art to perform all its old miracles of illusion and insight. . . ."

Garvey was listening—attentively, not just politely. Thatcher could feel the intensity of his desire to understand, and was grateful for it. Why, then, in speaking to Garvey did he feel like the misfit of the tribe trying to explain to an elder why the tribe's resident artist had decided to execute a flower on the cave wall instead of a wild boar?

"And if we don't attract the young, we won't have much of a future," he finished quietly. "It's a crazy, revolutionary world outside."

Garvey sighed. "I would rather we created a world inside our walls which offered harmony and beauty . . . 'a still point in the turning world.' "

Now it was Thatcher who strained not to understand but to agree.

"Some of us, Lloyd—some of us think your curators have already gone far enough afield. Of course I can appreciate that art may be found in the most commonplace objects—but blowing paint across the desert? How far will all this go?"

"Fifty years ago," Thatcher said, "the problem was to persuade people to accept any modern art. Now it's hard to convince them to let go of it, and accept anything new."

"Granted. But I'd like an answer to my question. How far?"

"Well, I've never yet found a satisfactory definition for the word 'art,' " Thatcher said. "Maybe it can't be defined."

Garvey stared straight at Thatcher for a long moment. "Why then, man," he said finally, "what *is* it you think you're doing as director of this art museum?"

Thatcher felt himself flush, and resented it—as he would have resented Garvey's suddenly ordering him to strip to the waist for a physical examination.

"And what do you mean," Garvey pressed on, "by giving newspaper interviews like this one?" He threw the clipping of Martha Crane's column down on the table between them. "Did you say what you're quoted as saying?"

"It's pretty close."

"So I may take it that this represents your philosophy of museums?"

"I wouldn't be pretentious enough to call it that, Ira."

" 'What I mean by art,' " Garvey read from the clipping, " 'is the vast population of individual works of art, just as the world itself is the three billion or so human beings who live on it. The so-called art world—artists, museum directors, critics, gallery owners, private collectors—is no more the *world* of art than the hierarchy of the Catholic Church—the bishops and cardinals and priests and nuns—is the Holy Ghost. . . .' I'm not misquoting you?"

"No."

"As a member of the so-called art world," Garvey said, "let me call some fundamental facts to your attention. After you have the work of art it must be housed in a building with four walls and a floor. This structure needs curators, guards, custodians—it needs trustees who will give the money to build and maintain it. Since the paintings can't all be hung at once, it needs space for storage. All this physical plant exists just to shelter the work. Well, let me ask you this. If the Holy Ghost is not to be found in the house of God—if the spirit of art is not to be found in a museum—where *do* you expect to find it?"

"I was trying to suggest that the institution as we know it is not the only answer."

"Wrong," said Garvey. "The institution is the skeleton of which society is the body. Destroy it and the body dies. Destroy the Museum and art dies."

"I can't accept that—without qualification."

"As for your suggestion to disperse the Museum's collection through the city—it's plain dangerous. Are you suggesting that we destroy the Museum piecemeal?"

118

"And just what do you want *done?*" Thatcher asked. "I won't go back on anything in that interview."

"I hardly expect you to discredit your own remarks. But you can abandon your plan to stage this whatever-you-call-it environments show."

"Are you speaking for all the trustees?"

"I speak for myself. No doubt many of the trustees will agree."

After a moment, and in a much gentler tone, Garvey said, "I understand how you feel, Lloyd. The show *is* your idea, after all. But you'll have other opportunities—"

"This is too serious a matter to be settled in one brief conversation," Thatcher said. "There are other things at stake besides my feelings."

"You're right, of course," Garvey said. He leaned forward in his seat and touched Thatcher's arm, startling him. "Much of the world is sick, you know that, Lloyd," he said softly. "We must keep that sickness out of the Museum. The militants, the crazy crowds, the demonstrators and vandals—they *must* be kept out. That is your most important charge."

He took his hand off Thatcher's arm and stood up. "I'm going downtown for an appointment. May I offer you a lift to the Museum?"

"All right," Thatcher said. He would rather have been alone just then, but it wasn't worth a lie to excuse himself. Still, it would be hard to be polite and attentive to Garvey, imprisoned in his car.

He needn't have worried. Most of the ride in Garvey's chauffeured limousine was accomplished in an air-conditioned, hermetic silence. Garvey consulted his *Wall Street Journal,* and then certain slim blue folders. Thatcher opened his own briefcase and shuffled meaninglessly through the papers on top.

Almost as an afterthought, Thatcher told Garvey of the loan he and George had arranged for the Toussaint L'Ouverture Museum. To his surprise, Garvey frowned when he saw the list.

"I thought you'd be pleased," Thatcher said. "We're bound to build goodwill with this loan—and good public relations."

"I daresay. You've checked carefully into who's behind this museum?"

"It looked fine to me." In truth, Thatcher had recognized only a few names among the museum's sponsors—a famous concert musician, a film actress, and a Pulitzer Prize-winning novelist. The rest had meant nothing special to him. Nothing alarming, either.

"I've heard reports that the Panthers are involved, Lloyd."

"Is that certain?"

"It ought to have been investigated thoroughly, in any case."

"But Ira, even if it were true, I shouldn't think it would reflect credit on the Panthers. What could be healthier than setting up a museum?"

"Who knows what those people have in mind?"

"Anyway," Thatcher said, "we're transporting the prints ourselves, and the borrowers will assume the insurance charges."

"They'll be high, with a collection this valuable. . . ."

"Only a few thousand dollars, Ira. They can afford *that*."

He shook his head. "I don't like it. I'd far rather have the collection intact than collect insurance on it."

"Isn't it *more* important to have the collection seen by people who've never been exposed to it before?"

"They might have come to the Museum to see these prints."

"But they won't—they just *won't*, dammit! Any more than we'd make the trip up to Harlem to see their pitiful collection."

Garvey locked his arms across his chest. He let Thatcher sit there for a moment or two before speaking again.

"Well," he said finally, "it seems to me a lot of risk to take just to earn favorable publicity."

"It's *not* just for favorable publicity."

"Please be calm, Lloyd. I'm not impugning your motives, I'm sure they couldn't be worthier. No doubt it would be embarrassing for you to back out now—"

"We'd all look foolish."

Garvey let out a theatrical sigh. "If you feel that strongly about it, then go ahead."

Thatcher was relieved to have Garvey capitulate, though why the man couldn't understand—well, the hell with it!

He thanked Garvey with one curt, ungracious syllable.

When they drew up in front of the Museum, Garvey seemed reluctant to let Thatcher get out of the car.

"Lloyd," he said, more urgently than he had said anything during their long visit, "Give up that environment show. Cancel it now, I implore you. I know I'm right about this."

"Thank you for the ride, Ira," Thatcher said. He stepped to the curb, and shut the door, careful not to slam it.

14

IT WAS STILL snowing when Thatcher left the Museum that evening: a fine, sharp snow that came down in slanting gusts. Most of it melted as fast as it struck the steaming pavements, but the wind was rising from the north, and the temperature falling; soon it would begin to stick.

It wasn't the snow he disliked, it was the filthy slush it became the instant it touched a Manhattan street. Only in the air itself, in the fresh wet flakes beating against his cheeks and forehead, was there any fleeting purity.

There were, of course, no empty taxis. Thatcher walked past shop windows dressed in rich Christmas colors and in streams and clouds of gold and silver—displays glorious with lights, some flashing rhythmically, some shining like fixed stars on the walls of buildings and in windows. Passing a charity Santa Claus with his strident handbell, he dropped some change into the papier-mâché chimney and then, out of silver, put a dollar bill into the collection box of a Salvation Army squad playing "Good King Wenceslaus" on a trumpet, a trombone, and a concertina. (At least he *thought* they were playing "Wenceslaus"; the wind tore away most of the sounds they made, sending fragments of discordant music off into the darkness before they could reach him.)

It seemed to Thatcher that his nervous system was less in cadence with Christmas every year, that he had to wait longer and longer for

122

the sense of irrational delight, the ability to feel the miraculous in the ordinary, which the holidays were meant to bring to those who remained faithful to them. He didn't particularly mind the commercial aspects of the season. The buying and selling, the compulsive spending, piles of gorgeous wrappings and foolish gifts at the foot of the Christmas tree—these seemed childish but warmly human. Religious symbols like carols and candles and mangers were childlike too—and human, not divine. What he waited for each year, and now had to wait so long for, was some strong, happy emotion rising inside him, shamelessly close to the surface.

For the most part, that warmth and delight had come over the years through Susie. But now she was almost an adult herself, and searching, just as he was, for her own private epiphanies.

As usual, Thatcher was behind on his shopping. Lorraine did most of it for the family, but he couldn't count on her for everything. In addition to Lorraine's own present, there would be one large, extravagant gift for his daughter, and something fluffy and cheerful for his mother.

For Lise Deering he might buy a basket of wines, a selection of cheeses, or an exotic flowering plant—some ephemeral gift that would bring her pleasure without embarrassment. They had a precarious balance to maintain between the impulse to touch and the intense pressures of their work together. So far, they'd handled the situation skillfully, keeping the undeniable attraction at a comfortable level.

He paused in front of a Bonwit Teller window, dazzling yet austere in blues and silvers, framing a lavishly trimmed thin silk robe. Was this what was missing—a completely gratuitous, even frivolous gift for a beautiful woman on whom he had no claims, to whom he owed no obligations?

He thought of Serena Lord. She'd called him that afternoon and invited him to dinner. Black tie, he had asked. No, dress any way you like, come directly from the Museum if you want—I'd like to discuss the last trustees' meeting with you, the one I missed. And we missed you, Thatcher told her. She'd been in Washington, she'd tell him all about it when she saw him that night.

When he hung up the phone, Thatcher's lips felt dry, and there was a fluttering sensation in the pit of his stomach. His curiosity was aroused. In all her encounters with Thatcher, Serena had been open, candid, dignified, and apparently admiring. He liked her—more today than yesterday or last week. Moreover, he was eager to see her again, to give her something that would please her.

What did he want her to have?

She liked games of all kinds, and was good at them: golf, tennis, chess, backgammon, Russian bank, bridge, even poker, he'd heard—she played them all hard, and to win.

He turned away from Bonwit's window with a small sigh. Maybe, he thought, I'll give her the game of skittles in the window of Abercrombie and Fitch—and a case of Danish beer.

And one day soon he'd have to decide whether or not he was falling in love with her.

Thatcher stopped by the apartment to change into a white silk turtleneck and a maroon blazer.

"You have to go out tonight?"

It wasn't like Lorraine to nag. At least half Thatcher's resentment was guilt, of course, because the dinner sending him back into the snowstorm was more than just another appearance at court.

"Susie wants you to help with her homework, Lloyd."

"Well, now—" Thatcher began.

"I think she really just wants to spend some time with you. You haven't given her much lately."

As he walked down the hall with Lorraine, he nearly tripped over a painter's drop cloth.

"I wish they'd get this muck out of here."

"The contractor said they'd definitely be done this week."

"Well, they've got to clear out before Christmas. George Trueblood and I picked out some paintings and prints from the Museum collection to hang as soon as the walls are ready. I'd like to give a staff party early in January."

He found his daughter curled up in a wing chair in the living room.

"*Bon soir, papa.*"

"So it's French tonight," Thatcher said. "Thank God—I was afraid you might need some help in math."

"If I did, Daddy, I wouldn't ask you. Not after last time."

"*Alors,*" he said crisply. "*Commençons?*"

124

"If you'd rather," Susie said, "we can wait until after dinner."

"I'll be going out for dinner, baby."

Her smile faded quickly. "Okay, Daddy. So it's now or never. Would you like me to fix you a drink first?"

"No, thanks. I'm much more French without gin."

She gave her exercise book to Thatcher to hold while she repeated her lessons.

"*Au téléphone,*" she said. "*Allô, Passy 22-15?*"

"That's Passy," Thatcher amended. "The accent is on the second syllable in a two-syllable word, always. Remember?"

"*. . . Oui, qui est à l'appareil? . . . Ah, bonjour, madame. Ici Pierre. . . . Bernard est là?*"

"Bernar' without pronouncing the 'd.' *"Bernar' est là?* Make it sound like a question, Susie."

They went on. She was shaky in grammar and somewhat uncertain about speech rhythms, but she had a fine ear for the music of the language; her vowels were clear and sweet, and she rolled her r's lightly. A month or two in France and she'd speak the language like a European.

"Not bad at all," he said, waiting for her to say what was really on her mind. He'd long been used to her roundabout way of communicating. She got to sex by way of athletics, to schedule problems after talking about, say, the weather. Thatcher had learned to wait. This time it was the school itself that was troubling her, and she reached it through French, her French teacher, and at last the headmaster.

"I hate it," she said finally.

Thatcher sighed. He'd managed, thanks to some discreet pressure from Ira Garvey and another trustee, to enter Susan in the Rowayton School on West 73rd Street. It was expensive, selective, and firmly endorsed by those who couldn't get their children into Brearley or Spence or Dalton.

"Am I stuck there, Daddy?"

"Not if it's all wrong, Susie." His reply was not precisely true. It would be hard to get her out of Rowayton and into some other school before the end of the school year—if it could be done at all—without sacrificing the fees for the first term.

"The place is so snobbish, Daddy," she said. "And I don't have any friends—after almost three months."

"No friends at all?" he said softly.

"Well, one girl. She's Jewish."

"So?"

"Daddy, it's *because* she's Jewish. The other girls don't pay any attention to Lora either."

Thatcher shook his head sadly and took her by both hands.

"Look, darling," he said. "Remember that story I read you a long time ago—*The Little Prince* by Saint-Exupéry?" She nodded. "Well, it won't be long before you'll be able to read the story yourself in French, and you'll enjoy it even more than you did then—at least, I hope you will. Anyhow, there's a place in the book where the Little Prince says: *'J'ai un ami. Tout le monde n'a pas un ami.'* Can you translate that for me?"

"I have a friend," she said. "Not everybody has a friend."

"Well, you might want to remember that if you have only one friend, a real one, you're still way ahead of the game. Also remember you hated Denver at first, too—you begged me to send you back to San Francisco to school."

"I'd forgotten. Look, I'll try, Daddy, honest—but don't be surprised if I turn into a nasty little WASP myself."

"Better not."

She sighed. "I wish there were some way we could get back to the Coast. For good."

"What do you mean?"

"You know, say to the people at the Museum—I'm sorry, folks, but it's been a big blooper, I really don't belong here at all. Back to God's country—you know?"

"Susie, what *is* this?"

"You're a great museum man, Daddy, everybody agrees on that, but maybe the city just isn't the place for us—*this* city, I mean. It isn't the place for *me*, that's for sure, but I know that isn't the important thing. What you want to do, where you want to be—that's important. But even you don't have the time to see what's happening to you."

"And *what's* happening to me that's so terrible?"

She bit her lips, and then rushed on.

"Well, you're smoking much more, for one thing, and drinking a lot more, too, and what's worse, I bet you don't even notice it because you're too busy to keep track. There's nothing in your life but the Museum and a few minutes now and then for us. You don't get much sleep, and you're sure not having any fun—how could you be? Why shouldn't you have a girl friend, and even get married again . . . while you're still young enough?"

"Listen, Susie," Thatcher said evenly. "You just let me worry about that part of my life. And don't count my drinks—or my cigarettes either."

"I didn't expect you to go for it. I'm sorry."

"All right," Thatcher said. "Let's forget it."

"Forget what?" said Lorraine, entering the room.

"Susie apparently hankers to play matchmaker," Thatcher said lightly. "Thinks I ought to get married and settle down."

"Oh?" said Lorraine. "Anyone I know?"

"No candidates," Thatcher said. "Are you sure you want a mother so badly, Susie?"

"I don't want a mother at all," she said softly. "I just think you should have a wife."

Thatcher did not answer.

"Dinner is ready, Susie," his sister announced.

"All right, Aunt Lorraine. Good night, Daddy."

"Good night."

As Thatcher's sister turned away with Susie in tow, Thatcher suddenly felt constricted. He needed space to move around in, the cold air and the evening sky. Neither Susie nor Lorraine understood how much the Museum meant to him right now, how important it was to give it all the time and energy he could. He was building something, and it couldn't be done all at once or easily. God knows he would rather enjoy himself more. And in time he would. They might even wind up out West again, who could tell? In ten years' time, especially if they were successful years for the Museum, he could choose what appealed to him most.

But this chance, and the guerdon it carried with it, were likely to come only once. How had Chaucer put it? "The lyf so short, the craft so long to lerne, Th' assay so hard, so sharp the conquering. . . ."

"Well, Lloyd," Serena said when she opened the door, "you're proof that one should never give up hope."

"Am I that late?"

"I didn't give you a set time, did I? Come along in, let me take your hat and coat. . . . I bet you're dying for a drink."

She led Thatcher into her formal living room. The room was certainly one side of Serena, Thatcher thought, the *pro bono publico* side. The only functions he could imagine taking place naturally in this room were meetings to plan charity balls and theater benefits. An early-nineteenth-century clock was reflected in a mirrored panel, framed by flowered draperies caught back and tied Victorian fashion. The couch too was Victorian, and hard as repentance. Perched uncomfortably on the edge of it, Thatcher shifted his weight back to find more room and found himself wedged in so tightly that his legs nearly knocked over the delicate coffee table. He looked around the walls at portraits of various Lords and Ashbrooks of the recent and distant past, and then back to Serena.

There were no overhead lights in the room. The lamp beside the sofa shone on the right half of Serena's face, leaving the other half in shadow. Her eyes were wide and alert, a brilliant blue. Her hair, a warm, burnished blond, was drawn tightly back from her forehead and caught in a swirling curve behind her ears, held in place on one side by a bright diamond clip.

A maid brought in a tray with a bottle of Pernod, a decanter of ice water, and two goblets.

"I have *ouzo* too if you'd prefer, Lloyd."

"The Pernod will be fine. It's just—well, I haven't had any for years."

"Absinthe is a memory drink, isn't it? Does it remind you of your student days in France?"

Thatcher poured the colorless liquid into the goblets and then added water, watching with pleasure as the liquid turned a cloudy yellowish-white.

"It reminds me of my first trip to Paris with Jeanne—my wife. We were very young, very unused to Pernod. After the second glass, I discovered that some weird kind of paralysis had struck me from the waist down. I just couldn't get out of my chair at the *café-terrace*."

"This probably isn't as strong."

"Nor am I as susceptible," Thatcher said.

They sipped their drinks in silence for a few minutes.

"Are we waiting for any other dinner guests?" he asked finally.

"I thought Aaron was going to come, but he begged off. He's dining with the Shah of Kuwait."

"Just like that?"

"Aaron loves breaking bread and making conversation with the celebrated. It's his frustrated ambition, I think, to be the host of a television interview program."

" 'This world is divided by temperament into hosts and guests'?"

"Maybe it's not that simple. I'm by nature a guest, but I've been trained from childhood as a hostess. Now I can't escape it."

They were tacking, Thatcher felt—and toward what destination he could not yet tell.

A phone rang in a nearby room, dozens of times, or so it seemed. Finally it stopped.

"Mr. Garvey calling, ma'am."

"Yes. Please excuse me, Lloyd."

Thatcher spent a moment or two examining the portraits in the room, without much satisfaction. They had been commissioned out of duty, apparently, or filial affection, and were not particularly good. It was hard to realize that Peale and Copley and West had been painting at the same time—why had such mediocre workmen been chosen instead?

He could find only two books in the room—a novel by Nathalie Sarraute and *Love Respelt*, a volume of Robert Graves's poems. Lifting the book of poems, he leafed through it. One poem, "Whole Love," had been checked and heavily underscored with a pencil:

> Every choice is always the wrong choice,
> Every vote cast is always cast away—
> How can truth hover between alternatives?
>
> Then love me more than dearly, love me wholly,
> Love me with no weighing of circumstance,
> As I am pledged in honour to love you. . . .

Serena returned to the living room with a preoccupied frown on her face.

"Ira's concerned—" she said, and then stopped. "He's anxious to have a slate of candidates for the new openings on the board as soon as possible."

"You're making progress?"

"That's why I went to Washington. I'm trying to get John Carew to fill one of those ten slots."

Thatcher smiled.

"You like the idea?"

"Yes," he said. "Very much." Among the congressmen Thatcher knew, Senator Carew stood out like Thomas Jefferson at a convention of Rotary International. He had more than one man's share of intelligence, money, eloquence—and a robust plurality from his native Connecticut. He was a collector, too, and not at the expense of the public treasury.

"He likes the idea that Aaron Redburn may also go on the board with him," Serena said.

"They're friends?"

"Not precisely. Admirers. Johnny agrees with us, Lloyd, that what we need on the board is young money."

"And what about Ira?"

"Oh, Ira *wants* younger blood in the picture, so long as it's blue, and so long as he's still in charge. Actually Ira does pretty much what Austin Vanderhanks tells him to do, don't you know?"

"Robert suggested as much."

"Yes. Well, Ira wasn't president when Robert was director. Austin was, and Robert got along beautifully with Austin, as he did with everyone else. He had the most exquisite manners of any human being I've ever known. . . . Anyhow, Aaron is the only one I've nominated so far. Have you lunched with him yet?"

"No."

"I hope you will soon."

"I will as soon as it can be set up. He's a terribly busy man."

"I have a date with him next week," Serena said. "I'll suggest he lunch with you instead."

"If you don't mind, I'll take care of it myself."

"Sorry—as you wish. But we shouldn't delay. If we can add nine younger people to the board, all more or less sympathetic to you—"

"I see."

"And if you can count on at least three other present trustees besides myself—and *if* Austin Vanderhanks at least stays neutral—you should be able to make the board do pretty much what you want."

"Serena," Thatcher said, "I know you believe we're both in agreement, and *I* feel that we are. But I'd like to be sure we know what we agree about."

She looked up at him in surprise. "All right, Lloyd."

"I want younger trustees on the board because I think they will be more sympathetic to my kind of program."

"Yes?"

"And I know some of my proposals are going to be called radical."

"I expect they will."

"Are you prepared for the kind of criticism I'll draw? You may attract some of it on the ricochet."

"Why don't you try me?" Serena asked. "Do you think you're the only one who realizes that the Museum is threatened? Who regrets the way we seem to play it so safe—in what we buy and what we show? I think I know as well as you do what's going on, and *not* going on."

"All right. This is where we can start," Thatcher said. "There's a show I want to do. I'm calling it 'Dimensions.' Ira Garvey's against it."

"I know."

"He told you?"

She nodded.

"Let me tell you about it."

Serena listened without interruptions, concentrating fiercely, as though trying by the pressure of her fingers against her forehead to *see* the exhibition. When he had finished, she sat back and looked straight into his eyes.

"You don't know quite what it will be . . . do you, Lloyd?"

"Neither will the artists, until they start to put it together. Although the idea isn't new, the show will be unplanned—improvisational."

"Is there any risk, do you think?"

"Only to my reputation, probably."

She sighed. "All right," she said. "I'll get on the phone first thing tomorrow. I'll organize a lobby for you."

"Thanks. I'll bet you're good at it."

"I am. . . . You see," she said, "we do want the same things after all. Don't we?"

The question seemed to hang in the air. Serena got up and moved toward the door.

131

"You must be starved, Lloyd—I'll see how dinner is coming."

She returned shortly and led him into a candlelit dining room gleaming with silver and crystal. The meal they were served, unlike the dinner at Garvey's, was simple and delicious, set off by good wine and by conversation that was never forced or awkward. Those who say that neither a friendship nor a love affair can properly begin until two people have broken bread together know what they're talking about, Thatcher thought as they returned to the living room couch after drinking their coffee.

"Serena . . . about Aaron."

He was speaking to her again as a trustee. But without waiting for his question, she answered him on the easy level of intimacy they'd achieved at the dinner table.

"Aaron is a kind of watchdog—I'd better explain that. He's primarily interested in keeping Aaron Redburn single, and he knows I'd never try to trap him into marriage—or anyone else, either."

"You'd never have to, Serena."

"What's the truth about a husband who makes a habit of philandering? That his marriage has been adulterated."

Thatcher made no comment, and she went on:

"I wouldn't *think* of marriage again unless there was a complete commitment on both sides. . . ."

"That isn't always possible."

"Don't I know!" Her laugh seemed, for once, metallic. "Anyway, Aaron keeps lesser—and less determined—men at bay. As for the single-minded, I can live without them. And I can live without the big drinkers, thank you very much, and without the masculinity hangups. . . . I'll tell you something I've never told anyone before, Lloyd—my husband Bill was stingy, too. God, was he tight! He didn't believe in making his money useful—in getting it to *do* something. But I took his divorce settlement and gave the whole thing to Alcoholics Anonymous. Anonymously."

Now the laughter was almost out of her control. When it subsided, she sat down next to Thatcher and shook her head, hard.

"I'm fine," she said, and blinked. "But it *does* get lonely sometimes. It does indeed."

Without a word, Thatcher put his arm around her shoulders and drew her close to him. She stiffened slightly, and then her body turned gratefully toward his. At first, the embrace held no desire. She trembled for a moment or two, then kept perfectly still. Thatcher's mouth felt hot and dry, and the arm of the couch jabbed painfully into his kidney. He shifted closer as she lifted her face.

The kiss, when it came, was long, warm, and sweet, but strangely complicated and inhibiting. On Serena's part, it seemed an attempt to probe the depth of his passion; for Thatcher, the pressure of her body against his unlocked a deep longing. But even as they broke apart, a helpless sense of loneliness, difficult to tell from despair, swept over him, and his eyes—inches away from Serena's sapphire brightness— went gray and remote. He was conscious of an attraction so powerful his loins ached; at the same time, his brain was cruelly aware of the choice he must make before his body made it for him.

The needle of the scale wavered. His tragically short, enchanting marriage. Susie. His career. Serena—her presence, her perfume, the percussion of her heart—all there for the taking. Mrs. Lord. Madam Trustee. The needle came to rest.

Serena knew the answer first. She drew back and smiled, blew a stray lock of hair away from her lips. Then she sat up straight.

"I can't play this both ways," Thatcher said. "It's got to be clearly one thing or another, and—"

She stopped his mouth with a graceful, impersonal touch of her hand.

Thatcher walked home that night through a driving blizzard outside, inside him a turmoil of self-reproach and martyrdom. He had only one consolation—he had been honest both with himself and with Serena. His own kind of damn fool, in short.

The next morning a letter on peach-colored stationery came hand-delivered to his office. Lise handed it to him unopened, without comment. When he was alone, Thatcher slit the envelope open.

Lloyd—

You're a gentleman.
You're also a gentle man.

I was almost ready to go down for the third time.
Thank you for being strong enough to bring me
back to shore.

S.

He had her respect, then. And his own—he had not chosen to sink under the glittering surface with her.

"Damn," he said softly, and dropped the letter and envelope into his wastebasket.

15

It was Monday, December 20. It *had* to be Monday—a day of lunar foolishness.

Arriving for work, Thatcher found the sidewalk in front of the Museum piled high with lights, cables, cameras, and dollies. At the curb stood two large vans with the legend "Virgo Films" and the sign of the maiden painted boldly on their flanks. The doors of the vans were wide open, while men and women in parkas and sweaters passed in and out, carrying scripts and chairs and containers of coffee. One van had been fitted out as a traveling office; the second resembled a commissary, with a galley oven, formica table, and chairs up front. From panels beneath the vans, cables spilled out like entrails onto the sidewalk and into the Museum.

Thatcher picked his way through this elaborate obstacle course, searching for someone in charge. Hearing a bearded man in a ski jacket give what sounded like an authentic command, Thatcher headed for him.

"This your crew?"

"Mind stepping out of the way? We're gonna light this strip of walk for our next scene."

"Kind of a mess, isn't it?" A polite understatement; actually it was Chaos and Old Night. "I thought you people were coming next week."

"We're ahead of our shooting schedule, so we cleared today with your publicity wallah. Who're you?"

135

"I'm the Museum director."

The film maker thrust out his hand.

"Well, pleased to meet you Mr.—Thatcher, isn't it? My name is Gordon Finn."

"Lloyd Thatcher. You the producer, Mr. Finn?"

"Second unit director. . . . *Cut that spot!*" he shouted to one of his lighting men. "*All right, people, get in place.*"

Thatcher watched, both annoyed and fascinated.

"Look, we're awful busy," Finn said. "You know how it is. Nice to meet you, Lloyd. Stick around and watch if you're curious, I'll introduce you to the kids in the cast during coffee break."

"I'm pretty busy myself, Mr. Finn. But I'd like to know—"

"We're filming the final boy-and-girl scene."

Boy and Girl stood silent and shivering in front of the vitrine. Girl looked vaguely familiar to Thatcher. Now Thatcher remembered— she'd been a "superstar" in one of Andy Warhol's subterranean films several months ago. Boy looked too much like so many other late-twentieth-century creatures—thin, hairy, round-shouldered, and slouching awkwardly to port—to be distinctive.

"Girl is on the verge of a breakdown, in deep identity crisis, and Boy is trying to keep her from blowing her stack," Finn continued. "Boy thinks coming to the Museum to look at the art will phase her down. The camera follows them into the Museum—we get a glimpse of some great art—and they go into the restaurant for a sandwich."

Thatcher wondered how in God's name anyone else was going to get into the Museum to look at great art so long as Boy and Girl and their spiderweb of equipment were blocking the front door.

"I like it the first way better!" Finn called out harshly. He had already forgotten Thatcher, who saw Mal Crawford standing at the edge of the set. Set? This madness was contagious. Thatcher made his way to Mal's side.

"Exciting, isn't it?" Mal said.

"It's too bad they had to come on the day of an opening," Thatcher said.

"Oh, they'll be out of there long before then."

"They'd better be. And what happens when they start taking all that machinery into the restaurant?"

"They'll cope, don't worry. They want pictures of the crowds. And they've given me their *absolute* promise they'll be gone by one o'clock."

"All right, but let me know if they don't clear away on time."

If the scene in front of the Museum was *cinéma vérité*, what Thatcher found back in the South Exhibition Galleries was pure Dada.

Huge metal gantries stood along the walls like Martian insects waiting to be fed, while the paintings that were their ultimate prey leaned against the walls or nested in pine crates. Several towering sculptures, hooded with canvas to protect them from plaster dust and paint, were poised in the center of the second room. Workmen pushed and strained at a massive crate. A rubber-wheeled truck, steered by one of the custodians, came sliding eerily toward Thatcher and then veered off into another gallery just before reaching him.

These galleries were designed for temporary exhibitions; only the exterior walls were load-bearing. The other walls were meant to be, and always were, torn down after an exhibition and rebuilt for the next one. As Thatcher entered the gallery he kicked at a rolled-up drop cloth and skirted a five-gallon can of calcimine.

It was just like home.

"Get that goddam thing over—to the left I said! Three inches to the left!"

George Trueblood was perched on a stepladder, glaring across a distance of some ten feet at workmen hoisting a giant canvas into position.

"That's it . . . hold it right there! Okay, Vinnie—fix it."

He nodded to Thatcher and descended the ladder, bearing a floor plan of the galleries. On a cardtable behind him, a paper model of the gallery had been set up for reference. The curator looked from the stamp-sized square pastel in the model to the painting itself with apparent satisfaction.

"A bastard to hang, right, Vinnie?" The workman, a fleshy young man with mottled skin, nodded and smiled, showing a good many gaps in his back teeth.

"It's right, now, though," said Thatcher.

He knew well enough how many hours went into the planning of an exhibition like this—months and even years sometimes—especially in the case of an unflaggingly prolific artist like Goodman Hart. As recently as this past week, George had gotten final approval for one work he had almost despaired of obtaining. And now, with the opening that night, he was still driving himself and his men to finish on time.

"Anything missing, George? I'll be glad to help any way I can."

"I wish you'd speak to that impossible Stanley Westerman. I can't talk to him myself—I want to kill him. He won't promise the catalogs for tonight."

"I'll look into it."

"Fine, you can kill him for me."

Thatcher changed the subject. "Where's Goodman?"

"Oh that son-of-a-bitch is around here somewhere, making life miserable for all of us. . . ."

Thatcher discovered Goodman Hart in the smallest exhibition room, seated in a wheelchair talking with one of the workmen, one foot lazily extended, his chin on his right hand.

The wheelchair was ordinarily used by the director of an exhibition to rest during the setup, or to convey him quickly from one crisis to another. As soon as he saw Thatcher, Hart slapped its wheels and propelled himself across the littered room.

"How can we *possibly* open tonight?"

"This is about what I expected to find, Goodman."

"God almighty, you're all mad around here."

"George will make it, he always does. Somehow we finish on time no matter how frantic it looks."

"Who's frantic? I'm not frantic! I just—"

"Good, we appreciate your concern, but George is under pretty high pressure—don't make it worse. This is hardly your first show here."

"Well, it will sure as hell be my last. I'm too goddam young for a retrospective, anyway. You don't want people to think I'm *dead*, do you?"

"George is worried about his catalogs," Thatcher told Stanley Westerman.

"Oh, George is always worried."

138

Thatcher fought back a growing irritation. Westerman was not ordinarily one of his prima donnas, though he had his own brand of arrogance. Stanley was short, obese, and distractingly ugly, and for all these reasons—for the further reason that it sometimes seemed to Thatcher that any useful publication in the museum field was all but impossibly difficult to produce—Thatcher made allowances.

"*Are* the books going to be late, Stanley?"

"Being bound now. They'll be delivered to the Bookstore tomorrow afternoon in time to go on public sale, and that's the best we can do."

"What about the party tonight?"

"I don't know what we can do about *that*."

So Westerman hadn't been invited to the party. The slip was George's, and Thatcher was sure it was deliberate.

"You might ask the bindery to send over five hundred copies by truck. Or we can send someone to pick up any number they'll give us."

"That'll cost us. They'll have to stop the machines."

"I know."

"All right, I'll do it, but we've already run up high costs. *Mostly* because George Trueblood has changed his mind so often. . . ."

Though it had appeared on the Daily Schedule of Events for several days running, Thatcher almost overlooked the announcement. This morning it leaped off the page.

12:00   Noon Film Showing   *Broadway Magic of 1935*

How many years had it been since he had seen that movie, or heard the title, or even thought about it. . . . Fifteen? Twenty?

"Lise," he said, "put a party invitation in the interoffice mail to Stanley Westerman. And if anyone calls—"

"Yes?"

"You'll find me down in the auditorium. Strolling down Memory Lane. But take a message if you can."

The auditorium was dark when he reached it; the showing had already begun. Thatcher took a seat near the back. As soon as he sank into the velvet cushions, he found himself crouching down, doubling up his knees, and pressing them against the back of the seat in the next row. Though the auditorium had only a scattered crowd today, he could hear the piping voices of kids packed into the front rows when he shut his eyes, and smell the mixed odors of popcorn and the cigarette smoke that had always drifted down in blue coils from the loges.

The picture on the screen was hopelessly bad and naïve—and yet so beautiful that Thatcher was fascinated. The actors seemed bathed in a creamy Renaissance light of intense clarity. Highlights gave the blondes a silver glimmer, the brunettes a dark radiance; faces and hands were like ivory brought to life. It seemed incredible that these stars with whom Thatcher and everyone else in America had grown up had ever looked so young. His mother, too, had looked young and china-doll pretty in 1935, but she was only two years younger than the century, after all, and she'd waited a long time for this chance.

There she was now, in a heartbreakingly brief scene. How could they ever have hoped for her to be discovered through it and transformed into a star? She couldn't have been on screen longer than a minute and a half! She was playing the established star of the Broadway musical theater who refuses to entrust her career to the hands of young Jerry or Larry or whatever Dick Powell's screen name was—the neophyte director taking over the big musical from his stricken mentor Warner Baxter—or was it Warren William? There they all were, clustered on the stage of the Times Square Theater; Vivian, the girl played by Thatcher's mother, was saying in a throaty warble: "You expect me to let some kid who ain't dry behind the ears direct *me*, Vivian Dawn? Listen, Morrie, either you get me an experienced director or you get yourself another star!"

And that was how Dick Powell happened to pluck Ginger Rogers out of the chorus line and offer her the chance to step into the starring role:

"Gee, you mean you want me to play the lead?"

"You can do it, Mickey, I know you can."

"But Jerry—I don't know what to say. It's what I've dreamed of, my big chance, but—"

"Bigger than you know, baby. . . ."

And in their rehearsal costumes, Mickey and the chorus linked willowy arms and sang:

> If it's maa-gic
> It's the Broadway kind,
> If it's tragic
> It's Broadway too . . .

While an outraged Vivian Dawn, played by Merilew Thomas, born Mary Jane Ermentinger, now Mrs. George L. Thatcher, stalked off the stage of the theater into oblivion. A cruel joke, altogether— casting a struggling bit player as an established star, while a famous star played an obscure chorus girl. And that had been the high point of his mother's career. She never got another speaking part: a few walk-ons, then she was an extra again. Nor had she given up the struggle gracefully; so long as anyone wanted her on a set, she was willing to work.

Had she ever had a chance, Thatcher wondered, or had it always been hopeless? And what was missing from her career that others had? Was it just luck? Had she failed because of her marriage and children? Because she'd fallen in love with an indolent Welsh bartender instead of an actor or producer? She'd had an agent once; Thatcher remembered her references to him. Or perhaps that too had been one of the dreams she sometimes confused with reality in those days. And even if there actually had been an agent—what was ten percent of nothing?

> There are teardrops
> In the bright lights
> Of Broadway.
> There is laughter
> And heartache too . . .

Thatcher didn't notice Lise slipping into the seat beside him, she came so quietly. She waited a moment, then touched him on the arm. He trembled and blinked down at her.

"I'm sorry," she said. "You're needed."

"Needed?"

She put her hand on his arm again. "Are you all right?"

"Of course." He got up. "It was a lousy movie anyway."

Lester Dolan was waiting upstairs. He stopped pacing as soon as he saw Thatcher and folded his arms.

141

"Those movie people . . ."

"What movie people?" Thatcher was still with the brothers Warner.

"The Virgo Films crew. They're in the restaurant now, it's the height of the lunch hour, and we're having traffic problems."

Thatcher consulted his watch.

"They're supposed to be gone by one. Let's go."

Downstairs, the usual line of people waiting to get into the restaurant was exceeded by an even longer line waiting to pay and get out.

"And look over there," Dolan said. "By the fountain."

Thatcher could not see the illuminated fountain in the center of the restaurant for the crowd that had formed around it. Even some of the waitresses were hovering near the ring of bystanders. Thatcher and Dolan pressed their way through the crowd, using their elbows and knees when they had to, and ignoring hostile stares and murmured complaints.

At the center of the throng they found themselves blocked by the bearded Mr. Finn and his camera crew, who had set up their lights and camera equipment right at the edge of the fountain. The scene was blindingly lit, and the fountain was at the heart of this artificial sun; a rainbow had formed in the white glare of its flashing spray.

"Jesus God," said Dolan.

Girl, soaking wet from the spray, had her back to Thatcher and Dolan; Boy was facing them, up to his knees in the pool, standing with his arms outstretched to her in pleading. As the cameras ground and Finn towered over the scene like some hulking, rufous satyr, Girl stripped away her glistening wet silk dress. She was now wearing only the shining fall of water from the fountain.

"Beautiful, beautiful," Finn murmured.

"Poontang!" Girl cried out. "Bang me!"

"Great day in the morning!" This from Dolan.

She turned restlessly in a kind of hopping pirouette, perhaps, Thatcher thought, because she found the water freezing cold. She seemed to be trying to execute a dance of sorts—some sacramental offering of herself to the elements—arms spread wide, head thrown back, her dark-brown hair plastered down by jets of gleaming spray.

Now she had turned toward Thatcher and Dolan. To Thatcher she was a pathetically unerotic sight—her legs and hips much too thin and bony, her breasts pendant, the nipples standing out under the chilling spray like figs.

"Now I've seen everything," Dolan muttered. Thatcher was startled to see that his security chief was deadly serious; his face was dark with anger.

The crowd seemed to be enjoying the spectacle. Laughter was a common reaction, some of it embarrassed, some frankly appreciative. The noise level from conversation was uncomfortably high, though Thatcher noticed that a few hardy souls paid no attention at all to the filming, but kept right on eating their chef's salad and lobster Newburg.

Another shrill ripple of laughter from the crowd pulled Thatcher's attention back to the fountain. Boy had now shucked off his shirt and trousers and was slouching purposefully through the water toward his co-star, his genitals dangling limply in the vapor. Thatcher reached out and tapped Finn on the shoulder.

"Break it off, will you?"

"Don't get excited."

"Hare Krishna," Girl cried out in a thin, breathy voice. "Om Om, Om! Plant me like a god!"

"Thatcher," Dolan murmured, "I do believe he's going to board that girl."

"Can't beat the old macaroni, can you?" Finn opened his mouth in a wide grin.

"Turn that thing off!" Thatcher said again.

"Yah, we got enough. Okay everybody, that'll do it."

"Thank God—I'm freezing my tail off in here," said the girl. They stepped out and accepted raincoats from a technician standing nearby.

Dolan and Thatcher moved closer, Dolan pressing quite near the film director, as though he meant to seize him by the lapels—if Finn had been wearing any.

"You people—" Dolan began.

"You have no right to come in here and disrupt things like this," Thatcher finished.

"Why so nervous, we got a permit."

"You'd never have gotten one if we'd known what you were planning to do."

"Whaddya mean, I showed a script! What's so unusual, a thing like this?" Finn waved his arms melodramatically. "You got nudity all over this place. Look over there." He pointed to a Maillol statue partially concealed by a stand of ferns on the other side of the fountain—a monumental bronze of a woman crouching on great sleek metal haunches, her breasts thrust out like cannon. A member of Finn's lighting crew was leaning against her hip.

"Tell him to get away from that bronze," said Thatcher.

Finn was agreeable. "Hey Sonny, bug off that statue, will you . . . ? Don't get excited now, we won't hurt anything. And like I say, Lloyd, with nudes everywhere why get so worked up over a girl with no clothes on?"

"Would you mind not calling me Lloyd? And I'm sure you know perfectly well there's a difference between a nude sculpture by a talented artist and a naked girl in a blue movie."

"Hey—watch that blue movie stuff, buddy. This film is *art* if it's anything at all. What's the matter, aren't the flicks good enough for you?"

"If you'd wanted to take a nude scene, it could have been done when the Museum was closed—*if* the scene was really necessary. But what choice did we have? You just came in here, set up your gear, and did what you pleased."

"Well, your people saw the script, what's the fuss about?"

Dolan, convinced nobody was getting anywhere, put in a plea. "Will you please leave now?"

"If you'll get out of our way, that's what we're trying to do."

Just then Mal Crawford arrived, out of breath and apologetic.

"I got here as soon as I heard," he said to Thatcher.

"Not soon enough, I'm afraid. Will you make sure these people are out of here as fast as possible?"

"Certainly."

"Then come see me, please—I'm going up now."

Electricians were rolling up the cables, and a kind of bucket brigade had been set up to move the other equipment back through the crowd to the lobby. A hundred people or so were still standing around watching.

Dolan could not resist one last assault on the enemy.

"Don't let us see you back here again," he said to Finn.

At first Finn went right on dismantling his equipment. Then he turned around and looked at Dolan. He was puffing on a cigar,

144

which Thatcher felt sure was at least part marijuana. The burnt-honey odor was unmistakable.

"Back again?" Finn said. "What would we want to come back to this place for? We make pictures, we don't look at them."

"Mal, do you mean to tell me you didn't *read* this script?"

"Of course I read it. I swear to you Lloyd, the nude sequence wasn't in the version I saw. They must have written it in later. Or improvised it."

"Couldn't you tell what kind of picture it was?"

"I don't know yet what the picture is going to be like. Do *you* know? I mean—it's hard to tell. I figured so long as Russ was connected with it, we wouldn't have to worry."

"Russ?"

"My friend Russ McAlmon is the PR man for Virgo Films, that was how it was all set up. Wait'll I get to him about *this* booboo."

"Never mind that," Thatcher said. "What I can't understand is why you weren't right there watching them. You know someone from the Press Department is supposed to oversee filming at all times."

"George Trueblood needed some material checked for his opening and—"

"Then why didn't you leave one of the girls in the department behind to watch?"

"It was, you know, lunch hour, Lloyd. They—"

"Oh for Christ's sake, can't you stagger lunches? You should know better than to be caught on a limb like this. The trustees are sure to hear about it."

Mal Crawford took a deep breath. For an instant his face went quite blank, and then one corner of his mouth rose in a familiar, mocking smile, belied by the restless, darting movements of his eyes.

"Look, Lloyd, I'm not going to beg for my job, no job means that much—believe me. But I want to stay here until I finish what I started. I'm sorry for what happened—"

"You said that."

"What else can I say, then? I just don't want to leave until the Press Department is in good shape. And, please, don't you think I've earned some consideration? Who do you know in the business who could have matched the coverage I've gotten for the Museum since last year?"

Thatcher was close to firing Crawford at that moment, closer than he had been before Mal had begun to talk, and he was angry enough at the beginning. It was bad enough for Mal to have been such a damn fool, but this scene was impossible. Before the silly creature broke down in tears, Thatcher should push him out of the office and be rid of him for good.

Just then, Crawford started to laugh, a hiccuping, near-hysterical laugh. He raised his hands in mock despair.

"It would be . . . would be just my luck," he stammered, "to be fired because of some goddam stupid fairy . . . like Russ McAlmon."

All this time Thatcher's pencil had been darting across the scratch pad on his desk. A canoe on fire; Mal Crawford dressed as an Algonquin brave, stoic in the thickening flames while overhead a *deus ex machina* hovered, in the form of a helicopter with butterfly wings.

"What are you going to tell Ira Garvey when he asks how this happened?"

"I'll tell him the truth—it was all Russ McAlmon's fault, his and that Finn person."

He stopped talking and sat motionless, waiting.

Outside the window, the air had turned dark gray, heavy with gathering snow. Along the adjacent street pedestrians bent their heads and hurried through the early twilight. Inside, the two men sat looking at each other with faint distaste, caught in the lee of a common embarrassment.

Thatcher sighed and rose from his chair. "How does tonight's opening look?"

"Quiet," was the answer. "For a change."

After Mal's departure, Thatcher rested his head in his arms for a moment, then got up and started to straighten out his desk. As he emptied his ashtray, he was relieved to see the last traces of Mal's visit—several badly chewed filter-tips—disappear into the wastebasket. Odious man. Was it just because Mal was such an obvious queen? He hoped not. Already he'd begun to regret his leniency.

As he stacked the morning's unopened mail on top of yesterday's, a torn slip of paper with a telephone number written on it fluttered out from somewhere: 823-1942. Whose number was it? Then he remembered—the opening at the Walker Gallery. Alexandra.

As he dialed, the muscles across his shoulder blades tightened in anticipation.

He sat for a moment listening to the steady ring at the other end of the wire, counting to six . . . seven . . . eight. Then, with a disappointment out of all proportion to his original impulse, an access of almost primal loneliness, he let the phone slip back to its cradle.

At five-fifteen Thatcher proceeded to the Estelle Vanderhanks Wing to see how George Trueblood and his artist had weathered the afternoon.

In one of the exhibition rooms, two workmen were playing a variation of bocce with several empty wine bottles and a ball improvised from terra-cotta. Seeing Thatcher, they broke off the game abruptly.

"Nothing to do?" he asked one of them.

"All finished here."

"Then punch out or go see your foreman."

They wandered sheepishly away.

Thatcher found Trueblood and Hart in the inner hall, seated cross-legged on the floor. The artist was bent over a metal bucket, stirring what appeared to be wet cement. His shirt was open to the waist and his chest glistened with sweat.

"Offissa Pup," said Trueblood.

Thatcher picked up his cue. "What is it, Krazy?"

"Ignatz Mouse here," Trueblood answered. "He don' wanna get dressed up for our pahty in Coconio County tonight."

Hart sighed. "Why should I dress?" he inquired of the cement bucket.

"I explained to him," Trueblood continued, "that I'm gonna dress up, you're gonna dress up, all God's chillun gonna dress up—why not him? It's his party."

"That's why I won't do it," Hart said. "It's as unlike me to wear a tuxedo as it would be for Ira Garvey to wear coveralls. Besides, what's more destructive of caste than evening clothes—everyone standing around in the same uniform? Perversion of the democratic process."

"It doesn't matter what you wear, Goody," Thatcher said. "If you want, you can come as you are."

"Wouldn't have time to change anyway. I've got to stay here and work for a while."

"It all looks fine to me," Thatcher said.

"The Barney Specker *Misericordia*," said George. "It's damaged. "And no wonder—Specker kept the figures in his dining room, until one of his maids threatened to quit if he didn't take those dirty statues out of her domain."

"You'd be surprised how rottenly people take care of things they don't understand," said Hart. He looked as though he would not trust Trueblood or Thatcher too far, either.

"This kind of show gets harder to do all the time," Thatcher said.

Trueblood rose awkwardly to his feet; he wasn't used to the lotus position. "I don't know what the answer is. I told Goody about your mad plans."

"And?"

"Not my style," said Hart. "Not that I disagree with your idea. The key to all great art is improvisation. The happy accident. But I don't want anything to do with any group or school. I go solo."

"I've *heard*," Trueblood said, "that three out of your four wives are coming tonight."

"And the fourth?" Hart said. "What's the matter with the fourth?"

From the galleries Thatcher hurried back to his office, where Lise was waiting with his dinner clothes on a hanger. He was already out of his coat and necktie and unbuttoning his shirt by the time he reached his desk.

"Studs?"

"In the box."

He tossed the shirt across the room; Lise stood looking at him in his T-shirt with amused appreciation. His arms and throat were pale but muscular.

"Pretty good for a sedentary type," she said.

"Secret of good health," said Thatcher. "Never put one unnecessary foot in front of another."

He rubbed his chin with a scowl. "Shaver?"

"Here it is."

"For propriety's sake, close the door behind you."

On the way out, splendid in his dress suit and ruffled shirt, he stopped at her desk to sign the outgoing mail.

"You haven't got much time to get ready yourself," he said.

"I don't have to stand in the receiving line, I'll make it."

He handed the correspondence back to her. "Don't imagine I'll see you at dinner, so I'd like, right now, to claim the first dance."

"It's yours."

She went into his office and picked up the littered clothing briskly and matter-of-factly, as a wife might. Then she sat down to put her desk in order. The room seemed suddenly, abnormally still. Did he, or didn't he, love that Lord woman? Was she, or wasn't she, in love with him?

And what else was new?

16

BY THE TIME Lise had taxied to her apartment, changed, and returned to the Museum, the party was in its full glory. The sound of it carried all the way to the main floor: all voices at first, a susurrant choir growing to a roar. The full-throated diapason of a cocktail party at organ pitch.

For Thatcher it was a rapid flow of images. The reception line with Thatcher and the Vanderhanks standing next to the Garveys. (Had Serena Lord got to Ira Garvey yet about his "Dimensions" show?) Vanderhanks murmuring happily to Thatcher: "Most beautiful show we've had in years." (As usual, he had gone down before the reception for a private viewing with George Trueblood.) George himself, at the other end of the line: gorgeous in a flaming red tuxedo, smiling broadly. (He had achieved the miracle—every painting in place, every piece of sculpture standing firm.)

The smoke from a hundred cigarettes eddied about the room into eyes dazzled by the sight of the painter Hugo Levy in a zebra-striped suit, or by Sandy Stafford in his hand-made aluminized paper suit (which he offered to sell on the spot to one enthusiastic collector), or by an oddly put-together woman in a red skirt and black scarf top from which her Renoiresque bosom kept emerging, to take a bow perhaps. Martha Crane drifted by in a red panne-velvet jump suit and a flowing military coat; Serena Lord in Mainbocher pink and gold brocade with sable cuffs. Three women had painted their faces silver.

Thatcher himself moved unobtrusively through the crowd, his feelings hidden behind a polite smile which he carried like a mirror from person to person until he found Lise.

Later on the party flowed into the galleries, where Goodman Hart brooded over a group of admirers waiting vainly for him to explain his work. He had kept his promise not to wear evening clothes, or a smile.

From there Thatcher and Lise moved with the swirling crowds toward the South Galleries, where the dance and light show were beginning.

"How did my speech go?"

"To the point and not an instant too long," Lise said.

"Did you enjoy your dinner table conversation?"

"Very much. I was with Marcus Hammer and Manley Stringfellow. . . ."

Hammer had a roving eye for Lise, as Gibbs surely knew, which was no doubt why she'd been seated next to him.

"You look beautiful," he said. And she did, in a black paneled gown with a high collar and bared shoulders. It was, Thatcher thought, the most becoming dress in what seemed more and more an exhibition of fashion than of art.

Long before they reached the galleries they met the pounding beat of rock music flowing into the hall. Thatcher could feel it in his teeth, feel it vibrating in the pit of his stomach. The galleries were bathed in a hard yellow sodium vapor that washed the color out of every face in the room. Thatcher's white shirtfront had turned a color as bilious as the wall. In one corner a long bar had been set up: champagne and steins of lager beer, with bottles of gin and scotch and bourbon at the ready for those creatures of habit who could not or would not change brands, not even for one night. Most people were swilling champagne. Was that the right word? Yes. Though some sipped the wine, most were drinking it as fast as it could be poured. Next to the bar a grill-cart dispensed frankfurters with piccalilli relish, catsup and mustard, and sauerkraut, great dripping frankfurters in bulbous yellow buns; spectators who weren't dancing sat on bleacher seats along the side of the room with their hot dogs and champagne or beer steins.

Thatcher drew Lise out to the dancing area and they tried to find their way into the beat as couples crouched and writhed and shook and lunged all around them. When a young man wearing jeans and a ruffled evening shirt squeezed in between them without an apology, they gave it up and headed for the bleachers. Thatcher, pulling rank, had grabbed a full bottle of champagne and two glasses; now, as they sipped, he surveyed the crowd. Across the gallery, Serena Lord waved at him. He lifted his right arm in greeting and then realized he had raised the champagne bottle and not the glass.

"You ought to mix," Lise shouted. Her eyes were shining in the relentless bath of yellow light.

"In a minute," he said.

The command post of the dance was a platform near the west wall of the room. There sat the master of the revels, a disc jockey surrounded by speakers, mixes, feedbacks, stacks of records, yards of wire, a buss console, and a squat black transformer. When the dancers slowed down or threatened to move off the floor, the disc jockey churned the air with his hands in abrupt, whiplike motions.

Was it Thatcher's imagination, or was the light actually changing to a quiet, lime-green shade? It *was* changing. The effect of the new light was eerie, submarine. Some of the strong colors in the room now came out in high contrast; the dancers resembled tropical fish swimming through an emerald-tinted grotto.

Thatcher could recognize the young of a half-dozen celebrated tribes: the Ives boy, the Boardman girl, a Franks, and a Zimmerman. Young Jason Cardman and Marcus Hammer's son Gregory. It was the kind of party that encouraged name-dropping on an orgiastic scale. Martha Crane's column tomorrow would be full of the droppings.

Lester Dolan asked Lise to dance; Thatcher felt the impact of her departure almost at once. Suddenly the room seemed insufferably hot and oppressive. He felt caught inside the music like a beast in a trap; suffocated, battered, paralyzed by it. He kept his eyes fixed on Lise as she danced by, glad to see that the dance required her to stay at least a yard away from Dolan. At one point Dolan vanished from sight in a crowd of other dancers; he reappeared just as swiftly, peering around for Lise while his hips and elbows still pumped rhythmically on. How gracefully Lise moved! If he had never seen her before, Thatcher would have chosen her instantly as the girl on the floor he most wanted to meet. . . .

George Trueblood came along and climbed up to the bleacher

seat next to Thatcher. He was cradling a bottle of champagne; Thatcher's was now empty, and he lifted his glass.

"A success, isn't it, George?"

"Too subdued a word. It's an orgasm."

"The show looks immaculate."

"An immaculate orgasm."

"Are you drunk?"

"Not so much as. High. Stoned."

"You look it."

"Don't make faces. In time it'll be common as chewing gum." He reached into his pocket.

"Like one, Lloyd?"

"No. No thank you."

Mal Crawford appeared in the doorway, saw Thatcher and Trueblood, and leaned toward them as though he would join them if they gave him a sign.

"Stay away, you bastard," George muttered. "Just look at him," he said to Thatcher. "Pretends to be your best friend and all the time he's feeding confidential information to Ira Garvey."

"What?"

"How d'you suppose Garvey finds out what's happening here? As distinguished from the official news *you* give the old man?"

"Now look, George—"

"Ever since Mal came. . . . He was always Garvey's man and not even Robert knew, shrewd as he was."

"You're full of surprises tonight, George," Thatcher said lightly.

"Just want you to know I'm—grateful, friend. . . . Here comes Mal. I'm going to leave. Can't stand him. Not right now, anyway."

Then Mal was standing alongside Thatcher, brandishing a champagne glass.

"Why's old George rushing off?" he said. "Do you suppose . . . ?" he hiccuped. "Never mind. . . ."

Thatcher had never seen Mal really drunk before; now he recognized the signs: the mannered sweetness in his voice, an elaborate, almost courtly politeness—and a sad, sad smile.

"Just want you to know," Mal said, "how much I appreciate your understanding and support today. Made all the difference in the world. . . ." As he talked, he looked Thatcher squarely in the eyes and caressed the lapel of his jacket. "I'm gonna do anything I can to help you. . . ."

Thatcher took Mal's hand off his coat.

"Mal," he said, "don't overdo it."

"But I *mean* it."

"You're exaggerating."

"No, no, Lloyd, I *do* mean it. You'll see, believe me."

Thatcher got up and put his glass carefully down next to the empty champagne bottle. He took Mal gently by the arm, intending to lead him to some place where he could sit down, or collapse quietly.

"Shall we dance?" Mal murmured. He draped one arm over Thatcher's shoulder, raising his lips so close to Thatcher's face that the flecks of saliva at the corners of his mouth were clearly visible. His breath was enough to kill flies.

"Dance with me instead, Mal," said Lise, appearing suddenly beside them. Her face was damp, and one lock of hair, a brilliant green now in the changing light, hung over her forehead. Mal permitted himself to be led away meekly to the dance floor. As she left, Lise threw back her head with an expression of mingled bravado and determination.

The jockey was playing acid rock:

> Get it all together,
> Open up your head;
> If you won't see
> We may be
> Walking with the dead.

Now the light was changing again from green to cobalt-blue, the music coming more powerfully than ever from the battery of speakers. To Thatcher it was a scene from Doré's illustrations of Dante: the death's-head glare of light on the dancers' faces, no shadows or contours—just flat, blue glaze over everything.

> With the dead,
> With the dead,
> With the dead,
> The dead.

After the blue came magenta, freshening and softening the faces —and then white light, which gave the dancers back their normal colors. As the tempo of the party quickened, the lights spun faster from one color to another: sodium:green:cobalt:magenta:white:sodium:green:cobalt:magenta:white. The thrust of the music ranged up and down, too—the boom boom BOOM boom, boom boom BOOM boom of the beat hammering away at them all, the occasional tinkle of broken glass in some far corner of the galleries, loud raucous laughter, and speech rising in pitch until it became pure scream, shrill and torrential.

Now Lise was dancing with Thatcher again. Were it another kind of dance, those he'd grown up with, the orchestra would be playing "Stardust." Instead the music was The Four of Pentacles playing a desolate wail of "Woodstock Rock."

"Sixteen hours ago . . ." said Thatcher.

He was walking with Lise Deering through the doors of the Museum.

"Sixteen hours ago I stepped into this place, still a relatively young man."

"Want to walk for a while?"

"All right. This air feels good."

And then he began to tell her about the party he'd been thinking of for his "Dimensions" show.

"If the weather is mild enough," he said, "I'd like to get the city to close this street off at both ends—after hours, of course—and have one big gaudy block party, with Japanese lanterns and pushcarts with food and big tuns of wine and beer . . . and let the party go on the livelong night, until the last musician and the last dancer fall exhausted on the pavement."

"Oh yes! Like the Feast of San Gennaro."

"Only a feast for the artists and art lovers."

"To the patron saint of art," murmured Thatcher.

"St. Catharine of Bologna."

Lise's apartment building was twelve blocks north and several blocks west of the Museum. Cab after cab passed them by; not one showed a roof light.

"You don't have to take me any closer," she said. "I can walk on alone from here."

He said nothing, and they walked on.

At the entrance to her building, she stopped and looked up at him. "I have a feeling you think something special's expected of you, Lloyd," she said. "Or that you're trying to figure out what *is* expected. For me, it's been a funny, lovely, crazy evening—and to top it off, I smuggled a bottle of that champagne out of the Museum." She opened her wrap and showed it to him.

He held her gently by the arms: "Will you keep it on ice?" Slowly she drew her wrap closed again.

"For now," she replied. "But not indefinitely." Then she added: "Let me know when you're ready to celebrate something," and turned away.

Thatcher waited, smoking a cigarette, thinking soft colors and bright sounds, long enough for Lise to take the elevator up to her floor, open the door of her apartment and enter it. . . . Then he was walking homeward in a bitterly cold, gray night—gray overhead where zinc-colored clouds swirled about a sliver of moon; gray underfoot where yesterday's snowstorm was hardening into dark marbled ice.

He was, he suddenly realized, deeply displeased with himself.

17

The Toussaint L'Ouverture Museum of Art was to the Museum what a storefront church is to the Cathedral of St. John the Divine—yet on the night of its formal opening, the rooms glowed with a baroque luster, some of it borrowed from the works of art that had been crowded into its bare rooms, most of it the glamour of Cinderella dressed up for the ball.

What calcimine could do to cover years of neglect had been done to the plaster walls; the floors which had been swept and washed ferociously clean, dipped and creaked, and the new tile on the steps had already started buckling; steam hissed and clanked in the pipes of mottled radiators. For all that, it seemed to Thatcher that the place sparkled like a Christmas tree.

Harlem was out in force, at least its patrons of the arts. One contingent came in a beautiful variety of fur hats and metal dresses, boots and dashikis, gaudy shirts and beads and silver belts—a dazzling array of fabrics and textures, hair styles and body-art worn, carried, and trailed into the exhibition.

The second contingent moved through the exhibition rooms with stately precision—the Ira Garveys and Marcus Hammers and Barney Speckers of Central Park West and Riverside Drive and the Grand Concourse—the men in business suits and ornate evening clothes, their women in high-fashion cocktail dresses and evening gowns, chatting and smiling and nodding politely to each other. They might, Thatcher observed, have been the subjects of those rotogravure society sections in the Sunday papers—with everybody turned out in various shades of sepia.

Hannibal Hamilton, dressed in a bottle-green corduroy jump suit with a lemon-silk stock held in place by a silver bullet made into a tie pin, swung from one contingent to the next, his face looming over the crowd like an ebony moon.

"Having fun?" he bellowed. The noise in the small rooms was deafening. "Have a drink, Lloyd." He pressed a paper cup into Thatcher's hand. In the cup sloshed a dark liquid which turned out to be a dubious bourbon. Thatcher sipped it, then gritted his teeth in a mask of cordiality. Neither he nor George Trueblood ever really stopped smiling for a minute.

"Must be four hundred people here!" Hamilton announced.

A quartet of small boys dressed like diminutive Edwardian dandies muscled through the crowd, bearing cokes and singing loud snatches of street song, violent and profane.

"Doing the ethnic bit, Mr. Director?"

Thatcher turned to face Bolo Van Buren, whose hands were cocked on his hips. Thatcher took Bolo in swiftly: Mao jacket, tie-dyed dungarees, Navajo moccasins, and the baleful glare of a hanging judge. Next to Bolo stood three men in Moslem costumes and dark-violet motorcycle glasses, their faces almost identically pitted and stubbled. To Thatcher they resembled nothing so much as *fellahin* crossed with Tontons Macoute: they created, he noticed, a zone of silence around themselves.

"Hello, Bolo. I consider myself lucky to have an invitation."

"That's more'n I got," Bolo replied. "What *shit*, man—this place ought to be called the Simon Legree Museum of Art. Right, brothers?" The three men made sounds somewhere between laughter and groans; one of them muttered something in an accent incomprehensible to Thatcher.

"Mosta these cats don't know what they're seein'—uppity niggers, all of them." With this remark Bolo drifted off, followed by his corporal's guard.

"Where's Hannibal?" Trueblood asked.

"Wandered off somewhere, I guess."

"I wish he'd stay nearby. Some of these people are a shade menacing. Makes me nervous."

"If it's any consolation, so am I."

158

George brightened suddenly. "Look over there!" He pointed to an obvious black homosexual strutting by. "The African Queen!"

Thatcher laughed, and refrained from saying he'd seen *The Boys in the Band* too. George probably was convinced by now that the line was his own, anyway.

By now Thatcher and Trueblood were not quite so ethnically isolated; a number of white and Puerto Rican city officials had shown up, and a handful of other whites Thatcher recognized as either collectors or conspicuous Afrophiles.

The crowd had thinned out enough so that they could pay more attention to the exhibition. In the room where the Museum's lithographs were hung, a knot of visitors had formed in front of *Zamboula Polka*, the major Lautrec print in the show—"a hand-colored first-state proof before text," according to its label. Watercolored, in fact, by Lautrec himself in 1901.

"There's a pet nigger for you," somebody remarked.

"Yeah, and dig those Mickey Mouse gloves. . . ."

Thatcher had always prized the delicacy and humor of *Zamboula Polka*. Like all Lautrec's later drawings, it achieved its effects with elegant simplicity and assurance, through an absolute economy of line. Now he saw the drawing as it might appear to a certain kind of black. The lady seated at the piano remained much the same— prim, rather plump around the throat, her pouter-pigeon bosom nicely complemented by mutton-chop sleeves and a skirt that billowed about the piano stool—eyes half-closed, rabbity teeth showing in a grin of immense self-satisfaction, the right hand daintily raised to attack the keyboard. A Prussian blue hair ribbon completed Lautrec's portrait of a monumentally demure *vieille fille*. But to see her companion through a Panther's eyes was to find a cartoon, affectionate perhaps but essentially caricature: the solidly planted bowlegs encased in striped pants; rococo watch chain swinging from his vest pockets; tiny jacket set off by an enormous butterfly necktie; and, the cruelest part of the lampoon, a pineal head, sharp, pointed teeth, bulging strabismic eyes, and grotesquely exaggerated ears with gold rings dangling from them. Like *Chocolat*, the dancer was one of Lautrec's randy, stylish aborigines, a stereotype of this period incarnate.

Listening to the comments around him, Thatcher was dismayed. He hated to see art whose only purpose had been to give pleasure turned into evidence in the Case Against the Caucasian Race. Yet the malcontents were right—Henri de Toulouse-Lautrec had looked at a black man and seen a darky.

The meeting of the Museum representatives with the Artists' Round Table had been arranged over a three-week period of negotiations hardly less complex than the disputes in Paris a few years ago over the shape of the table for the Vietnamese peace conference.

For one thing, the spokesman for the artists kept changing. First it was Athos Philippides, whose parliamentary gifts proved inadequate to the occasion. Since the talks could hardly be conducted in demotic Greek, he yielded to Bolo Van Buren—Howard Van Buren as he was called on ceremonial occasions. But then, as a black artist, Van Buren was apparently considered too fiercely committed to a single one of the artists' demands—a wing at the Museum for black and Puerto Rican artists. Bolo was followed by Elizabeth Oppenheimer, who introduced an eleventh demand into the list of ten—a separate wing for women artists, promptly nicknamed the GYN wing by some of the curators.

Abe Zachary had dropped out of sight for the moment; it was rumored that he found the political maneuvering within the organization uncongenial. Abe held fast to his concept of an Independent Organization of Unorganized Independents—no bylaws, no statutes, no constitution, no dues, and no membership requirements.

So, by the time the meetings were to begin, it was not possible to say *who* would speak for the artists. Thatcher, of course, was to speak for the Museum.

The agenda, too, was a problem. The artists wanted to follow their original ten points, their "bill of rights." Thatcher asked for an ad hoc agenda, one that would deal with specific points on which both the artists and the Museum staff felt concern, for which there existed some genuine hope of agreement.

And who would attend the meeting? All of the artists in the association? (It wasn't clear whether there were forty, sixty, or more members.) Thatcher insisted this would mean a meeting too large to be effective. He proposed that the Museum send ten representatives and that the artists also send ten. The artists pointed out that they were a democracy, not a republic, and that they could not leave out of the meeting any of their members who wished to attend.

Finally some things were decided. The artists would call for a voluntary, representative turnout of their membership; the Museum would send as many delegates as it thought proper, and as many staff members to sit by and observe the session as it could spare from their duties. An ad hoc chairman would be appointed at the meeting; presumably Thatcher. The press would be admitted, but only if they asked to come; the proceedings would be taped and transcribed.

Then the date of the meeting was discussed. . . . Like the flipping calendar pages in an old movie, days passed—in futile disagreement and fallow postponement—until a concordat was finally reached and Thatcher returned from the far country of Negotiation to make his report to his president.

Garvey listened to Thatcher's account rocking steadily back and forth in his chair. When the plans had all been laid before him he leaned back, holding his chair poised at its apogee, and said with a smile: "And was all this necessary?"

"*Necessary?* Ira, we're in a battle, like it or not. We can't just sit around and wait for the next attack. Furthermore, this was a damned hard meeting to set up. I'd hate to think you didn't approve of it."

Garvey rocked forward in a near lunge.

"Approve? I deplore this meeting, Lloyd."

"A strong word."

"I feel strongly."

"We need to speak to the artists—face to face. We can't hide any longer behind letters and news releases."

"On the contrary, it's much too soon to meet with them. If we wait a few months, this whole organization may evaporate."

"I don't think we'll be given the time."

"Artists have enjoyed a peculiar position in society for centuries," Garvey said, rocking slowly again. "The Renaissance turned them from ordinary craftsmen—artists and workmen—into demiurges. Michelangelo, da Vinci—the godlike creators. The Industrial Revolution made them into entertainers of the middle class—gifted servants of the rich, if you will. Now we treat them like children—spoiled sometimes, scolded when they need to be. Occasionally they become outcasts, criminal types, as that fellow Zachary seems to be. I'm aware that artists play an ambiguous role, and I'm sympathetic to their ambitions. But—negotiate with them? They have no grounds on which to negotiate."

"Ira, you speak of them as if they *were* children!"

"Perhaps I do—and with some reason, if you consider recent events. My point stands all the same. Artists are privileged creatures. They ought to recognize that fact, not go marching into the galleries of a fine museum, desecrating them with angry talk and dirty vandalism."

Thatcher sighed heavily. "Ira, I'd like a member of the board of trustees to be present at this meeting." The rocker went back and hung precariously on its points. "Will you nominate somebody?"

"I have a board meeting here at the hospital myself. Nor would I come if I could."

"I wasn't asking you to come."

"Lloyd—you do understand the art of collective bargaining?"

"I like to think so."

"Then you should know how imprudent it is to send your most powerful person into the first stages of negotiation—that leaves you with no place left to appeal. It would be much better if you sent a junior person to this meeting."

"I feel I should be there myself."

"So be it. But there will be no trustee present." He smiled. Thatcher stubbed out his cigarette in a nearby ashtray, grinding it to shreds. "I consider myself a reasonable man," Garvey continued. "If any one of your artists wants to come here and talk to me, and tell me what his organization wishes us to do about poverty on the Lower East Side, or the war in Southeast Asia, or even the high price of art—well then, I'll talk to him. I will tell him what I think can be done, and what can't. But I will not take part in any of these carnivals."

He tapped his knee with the index finger of his right hand. "And I'd appreciate it if you would not plan any more of them yourself."

"If you're talking about my environments show—"

"I am indeed."

Thatcher and Lise were sharing a box lunch from *La Brasserie* in his office—*pâté de foie gras*, cheese, chicken, salad, and fruit, with a bottle of wine which Thatcher had ordered as a tranquilizer.

"That stubborn old man," he said, "is trying to undermine everything I want to do here."

She waited for him to come to rest.

"I feel like chucking it all up."

162

"No, you don't, Lloyd—you feel like slugging somebody."

"What really gets me is that I let him sit there and belittle the meeting without telling him what I thought of his attitude. I just *argued*, politely, and—"

"Maybe that was wise."

"Jesus—what was running through my mind. . . ."

"What are you going to do now?"

"Talk to Garvey again—right after lunch."

She reminded him of all the disputatious *ira*'s in the dictionary: *iracund, irascible, irate, Irish*. She reminded him of his long-range plans for the Museum, his personal ambitions, his blood pressure. No use—he was determined to go back to Garvey's office.

"You'll be careful, Lloyd?"

"I hope not."

"Come in, Lloyd, come in—you're always welcome." When he removed his glasses, Ira Garvey's face seemed softer. He beckoned to Thatcher with one wiry hand. "I wasn't expecting you so soon, but now that you're here. . . . Sit down, Lloyd."

Thatcher took a seat, and a deep breath.

"I talked to some of the trustees about your environments show," Garvey said, drawing the sentence out with painstaking deliberation.

"Yes, Ira?"

"And they think, or so they tell me, that perhaps I'm being too hasty. . . ."

Thatcher remained silent, politely attentive, wary.

"I certainly don't want anyone thinking I'm out of step with the times," Garvey continued. "Though I don't see why I should struggle to be in the mode either." This last was delivered with a self-deprecating chuckle. "But I get the impression from some of my colleagues on the board—one of them argued with particular zeal—that I'm being rather. . .stuffy."

Thatcher smiled uncomfortably.

"Now, I must say I don't for a moment *think* I am. On the contrary, I believe that the rash young people who cry Anything Goes are the ones who are being unstylishly backward. Nevertheless. . . ."

Thatcher waited. What on earth was there for *him* to say?

"You can keep the show—'Dimensions,' you call it—manageable?"

"I'm sure I can."

"All right, Lloyd, I withdraw my objections. Still. . . ." He sighed and stopped talking. Obviously, his reservations about the show had not been laid to rest at all; just as obviously, he was trying to be fair. He smiled at Thatcher and they traded amusing comments about last night's party. Thatcher began to share some of his feelings about his own show, and what it might mean to the artists; he was sorry when the conversation drew to a close.

"If there's nothing else, Lloyd—"

"No, not really, and I've got to get back myself."

"I have a patient coming in," Garvey said with an odd note in his voice. He led Thatcher to the door. "The first patient I ever had, actually, when I was a young sawbones just starting practice. I still see him for good luck, the way some men keep the first dollar bill they ever earned."

Thatcher found himself speculating what Garvey might have been like as a younger man—and conceded that he probably wouldn't have gotten along with him much better then.

"The man is dying, of course," Garvey said. "Old age, really. I got him through everything else, but this. . . . Thank you for coming, Lloyd. Take care."

Take care. Be good. Don't rock the boat.

Out in the hallway, awaiting the elevator wired for beautiful sound, Thatcher found his anger with Garvey and with himself returning. He had no appointment back at the Museum, he had in fact counted on being at the hospital much longer. He had to have more time with Garvey—he *must* get through to the man. And Garvey was patronizing him, of course—with great finesse, it was true, but patronizing him all the same.

The elevator door opened. As Thatcher stepped forward, a bent, ghastly-pale old man hobbled out, supporting himself on two canes, metal braces clamped to his frail arms. As the two men passed each other, Garvey's patient looked up at Thatcher, his face etched with deep lines of pain and determination.

He might have reached out and touched the man, and said, *I'm one of Garvey's patients, too, you know.*

164

18

*From the official transcript of the meeting of the Artists' Round
Table with Museum representatives, held Tuesday, December 21, at
4:22 p.m. Present: 52 members or sympathizers of ART; 15 Museum
staff members:*

THATCHER: Ladies and gentlemen, welcome to the Museum. Contrary to some opinions, we are not inhospitable to the arts, or the
artist.

(*Laughter*)

VOICE: You'll be sorry.

THATCHER: We are glad to see so many of you here this afternoon. . . .

(*Noise and confusion*)

THATCHER: Without posters and handbills.

(*Laughter mixed with boos*)

THATCHER: May we have order, please? Our first item of business
is to nominate and elect an ad hoc chairman for this meeting. The
floor is open to nominations.

TRUEBLOOD: I would like to nominate Lloyd Thatcher as chairman.

VOICES: Seconded.

VOICE: Are we open for further nominations, or does the Museum
intend to run this meeting by itself?

THATCHER: Of course we're open.

165

VOICE: My name is Howard Van Buren, and I nominate Mr. John Thompson as Chairman.

(*Applause*)

VOICE: Second.

VAN BUREN: I now move that the nominations be closed.

VOICE: Second.

THATCHER: Any additional nominations?

VAN BUREN: Vote, put it to a vote.

THATCHER: . . . That's thirteen votes for Lloyd Thatcher and 54 votes for John Thompson. I yield the chair to Mr. Thompson.

THOMPSON: Thank you, Mr. Thatcher. Let us proceed to our agenda. As you know, we are following the demands originally presented to the Museum, with some modifications which have since been introduced.

THATCHER: Yes, we have the agenda here.

VOICE: Mr. Chairman, sir. Mr. Chairman.

THOMPSON: The chair recognizes Athos Philippides.

PHILIPPIDES: I question the good faith of the Museum in taking part in this meeting.

THATCHER: In what way?

THOMPSON: Please, Mr. Thatcher, Mr. Philippides has the floor. Would you continue, Mr. Philippides?

PHILIPPIDES: As I look around I see artists by the score, here in solidarity to help each other make their voices heard. A real breakthrough this is. Never before have artists joined in working toward a common goal. Is possible to imagine how the Founding Fathers felt in Convention Hall in Philadelphia when—

THOMPSON: Would you mind skipping Philadelphia, Mr. Philippides, and coming to the point?

PHILIPPIDES: I come to the point, don't worry.

THOMPSON: Would you please come to the point more rapidly, then?

PHILIPPIDES: Not even in my native Greece, cradle of arts—

THOMPSON: *Please*, Mr. Philippides.

PHILIPPIDES: I was saying—I look around this room and see artists by the score, yes. I see a museum director, Mr. Lloyd Thatcher, yes. I see Mr. Trueblood, the chief curator of the Museum. Hello, George. I also see one . . . two . . . five other members of the staff, yes, such as—

166

THOMPSON: We all see them, Mr. Philippides.

PHILIPPIDES: But—I do not see any trustees present here, not one.

THOMPSON: Mr. Thatcher, would you care to comment on the absence of trustee representation?

THATCHER: Certainly. We felt—the staff felt—that this meeting would be better served if the artists and the staff could join in an informal discussion of these demands, and that any conclusions we come to then be submitted to the trustees as recommendations for action.

THOMPSON: I see. You have come here then without any real authority to grant any of the demands?

THATCHER: I have my authority as director of the Museum. No single trustee can act for the full board in any case.

THOMPSON: Yet you realize that the first demand is that the trustees appoint artists as members of your board. Are you prepared to recommend this action?

THATCHER: No, I am not.

THOMPSON: Why not?

THATCHER: Because the board will never accept it, and I cannot recommend a proposal I know has no chance of being considered—even if I should favor it myself. Can't we talk about the things we *can* accomplish together?

THOMPSON: How else are the artists to have any real power to influence the decisions of the Museum?

THATCHER: As artists, I should think.

THOMPSON: I don't understand. . . .

THATCHER: Let me explain. Our power as staff members is considerable. But a staff member serving also as a trustee might find himself forced to vote against his own interests, instead of defending those interests to the board. Rather like a defense attorney—or a prosecutor —also trying to serve as judge and jury. The same thing is true of the artist. He maintains his integrity better by remaining an artist, not by becoming a trustee.

VOICE: That's all rhetoric.

THATCHER: Well, I believe it. In any case, there is one artist on the board of trustees—Dexter Llewellyn.

(Loud laughter)

THOMPSON: Order. Order.

(Continued laughter and some catcalls)

THOMPSON: Order. I think the feelings in the room about Mr. Llewellyn have been made only too clear, Mr. Thatcher.

THATCHER: You may be as emphatic as you please, he still remains an artist. And a trustee.

THOMPSON: Point two on our agenda is that the Museum establish a wing for black and Puerto Rican artists. How do you feel about that?

THATCHER: I'm opposed to it, on the grounds that art has nothing to do with that kind of distinction. The Museum should recognize and encourage talent wherever it can be found. A separate wing for black artists would be practicing discrimination in reverse.

THOMPSON: A highly reactionary point of view. I'm speaking now as an individual member of ART, not as chairman pro tem of this meeting. The black artist is discriminated against already, in every possible way. Why not discriminate in his favor for a change? Anyway, isn't discrimination the very heart and soul of a Museum curator's function?

THATCHER: I don't consider myself a reactionary. I brought the work of black artists into both major museums with which I was previously associated. I will fight against *racial* discrimination in this museum if I find it here. I will search out talented black artists wherever they are working. But I don't think—

(Loud noise and commotion in rear of room)

VAN BUREN: Well, here we are, big man. Lots of us right in this room, you don't have to look far.

THOMPSON: You're out of order, Mr. Van Buren.

VAN BUREN: Put me in order then, will you, Johnny?

THOMPSON: The chair recognizes Howard Van Buren.

VAN BUREN: I been listening to all this stuff Mr. Chuck Dude Thatcher here has been saying, but now I'm fresh out of patience. Man, are you trying to tell us that all the art in this Museum is great?

THATCHER: I wouldn't make such a claim.

VAN BUREN: You think all the art in this Museum is even *good*?

THATCHER: We thought it was good when we acquired it, but tastes change, and time makes its own judgments. Sometimes those judgments correct our mistakes.

VAN BUREN: What you mean is, you don't make final judgments.

THATCHER: No, we don't.

VAN BUREN: Well then, another question. Why, with all the bad

168

white art in this museum, bad by your own admission, isn't there an equal quantity of bad black art? Since you don't make final judgments about art, how can you say the black artists don't meet the same high or low standard? You know what I conclude from this? I conclude the Museum is racist.

THATCHER: The Museum recognizes no color barrier—

VAN BUREN: Well, I got news for the Museum then. There *is* a color barrier. And black art is different from white art, just like black food is different from white food, and black music from white music. If you don't put us in for what we are—black—you leave us out altogether.

THATCHER: I repeat, we don't care what an artist's color is. Or his sex or birthplace or his peculiarities.

VAN BUREN: Now that *is* generous. You let the kinky ones in too, long as the kinks are in their sex lives. My, my, you people surely are big-hearted. . . . Mr. Chairman, this is impossible.

THATCHER: Not if we show goodwill.

VAN BUREN: *(Obscenity)* When Bolo Van Buren don't like a thing, he don't sit for it.

THOMPSON: Order here. Order.

(Commotion in back of room)

THOMPSON: Sit down, you people. Order. . . . We can't have people milling around and still conduct a meeting, Bolo. What is this?

VAN BUREN: There's no room in this Museum for the black artist, so why should I stay?

VOICE: Stop pushing.

VAN BUREN: Who's with me?

THATCHER: This is getting out of hand. Mr. Chairman, may I suggest we—

THOMSON: The chair can't allow—

VAN BUREN: *(Obscenity)* the chair.

(H. Van Buren and 16 supporters leave the meeting.)

THOMSON: Order. The chair recognizes Mr. Walter Williams.

WILLIAMS: Thank you. As a sculptor for over fifteen years, I've been wondering about all this concern with the Museum, since it seems to get increasingly dull each year. Why do people want to get involved in such a dull place? Then I started thinking about it. Well, I just wanted to say, I don't see that the establishment of a black wing is going to make it a more interesting museum than to establish a wing for bearded artists, or women artists, or blond artists. What's the point?

THOMPSON: We are all wondering.

THATCHER: May I suggest that we move along, Mr. Thompson?

THOMPSON: I couldn't agree more. The chair recognizes Elizabeth Oppenheimer.

OPPENHEIMER: Mr. Chairman, I'd like to ask Mr. Thatcher a question.

THOMPSON: Go ahead, Bess.

OPPENHEIMER: Mr. Chairman, why do you call me by my first name, and not even my full first name but by my nickname, and the others by Mister and their last names?

THOMPSON: Force of habit, I suppose.

OPPENHEIMER: Just because we're married, Mr. Chairman, that doesn't mean we shouldn't be formal when formality is called for.

THOMPSON: Miss Oppenheimer, please continue.

OPPENHEIMER: Ms. Elizabeth Oppenheimer.

THOMPSON: If I'd known how to pronounce Ms., I'd have used it.

OPPENHEIMER: Mr. Thatcher, may I ask what is your attitude toward our demand for a wing devoted to the work of women artists?

THATCHER: The same as my attitude toward a black wing. I'm against it.

THOMPSON: That demand comes later in our agenda. It's out of order here.

OPPENHEIMER: I don't see why we can't discuss it now, while we're on the subject. Women are even more discriminated against than black men, sometimes. Everybody knows that.

(Applause)

THATCHER: Forgive me for stating the obvious, but the Museum does own work by women artists, and hangs it regularly.

OPPENHEIMER: Mr. Thatcher, I'd like to ask George Trueblood some questions.

THOMPSON: Go ahead, Ms. Oppenheimer.

OPPENHEIMER: I submit that this Museum is aware of only a few kinds of art, the most conventional and popular—the commodities. Where does the Museum stand regarding Acid Art? Why have you had no display of Erotic Art? Why have you completely overlooked

170

the work of such groups as The Motherfuckers? And how about Earth Art? Tech Art?

TRUEBLOOD: You're not asking questions, Miss—Ms. Oppenheimer, you're making a speech.

OPPENHEIMER: No, I'm drawing up an indictment. J'accuse, sweetheart. J'accuse.

(Commotion in back of room)

THOMPSON: Order. Order. Order.

TRUEBLOOD: This meeting is becoming an exercise in hysteria.

THOMPSON: Mr. Thatcher?

THATCHER: The answer to Bess Oppenheimer's demand for a women's wing will always be no. For the same reasons I've just given against opening a black wing.

THOMPSON: The word "always" has a terrible ring of finality, Mr. Thatcher.

OPPENHEIMER: In any case, I see no reason for me to take further part in this meeting.

(Elizabeth Oppenheimer and 20 of her followers walk out, accompanied by reporters for Time and Newsweek, and the CBS cameramen.)

THOMPSON: May we have a head count, please?

(Count shows 14 members of ART remaining, and 15 Museum staff members.)

THOMPSON: I guess we still have a quorum. At any rate, maybe now we can get down to business.

Afterward, Martha Crane stayed to talk to Thatcher.

"Sorry, Lloyd. No story."

"We aren't exactly looking for publicity just now, Martha. But I think we're making progress. We're going to do a show with the artists —that's all we've agreed on so far, but at least it's a start."

"What if they decide to pick Abe Zachary to direct the environment show?"

"He wouldn't be acceptable," Thatcher said. "It will be hard enough to get this show done in any case. With Abe it would be impossible. The trustees would fight us every step of the way."

"And does Bolo Van Buren get a place in this show?"

"If he's picked, yes."

"Oh, my dear," Martha Crane said, smiling happily. "You do like to sail close to the wind, don't you?"

Together, Thatcher and Trueblood reread the *Times* story silently.

Officials of the Toussaint L'Ouverture Museum at 97 St. Nicholas Avenue yesterday reported extensive damage to one of the galleries as the result of water damage. Apparently, pipes froze during Wednesday's sub-zero cold and then burst, flooding almost one entire floor of the Museum and damaging a number of works on exhibition. The destruction was particularly severe in the room devoted to prints and drawings.

"Have you found out which prints were damaged, George?"
"The Davis and the Kuniyoshi were water-soaked. *Zamboula Polka* was hopelessly stained—a total loss."
"Will the insurance cover it?"
"We should get about seven thousand dollars. Of course, the print should bring more in an open auction."
"Garvey'll have a fit. . . ."
"Wait till he reads the last line:"

Although Hannibal Hamilton, the director of the museum, has attributed the damage to an accidental failure of the antiquated heating system, police in the precinct have not ruled out the possibility of sabotage, and are continuing their investigation.

When Thatcher got home that evening, Lorraine met him in the hallway, helped him off with his overcoat, then inclined her head toward the living room.
"What is it, Lorr?"
"He's waiting for you in there—that artist. I told him you'd be late, but he insisted on waiting."
"Who?"
"Abe Zachary."
"Did you offer him a drink?"
"He wanted beer and we don't have any."
"See if you can order some up, will you?"
The living room was ninety percent finished and perhaps ten percent furnished: a Danish chair, a shag-covered studio couch, a wastebasket. Paintings leaned against every wall waiting to be hung. Dark

and bearlike, Abe Zachary prowled softly along the far wall, peering at them intently.

"Hello, Zach."

"All this stuff belong to you, Lloyd?"

"Or the Museum."

"How about this one?" Zachary held up a study of a girl standing beside a palomino horse, one hand holding the bridle, the other resting on the horse's left flank. Behind them lay a line of swirling gray and burnt-umber escarpments, shaped by a palette knife, fading into the sky. "This isn't the Museum's."

"Ah, no."

"Of course." Zachary nodded with satisfaction. "Why not say it's yours? Embarrassed by it?"

"I'm not embarrassed."

"It's pretty good." Zachary smiled for the first time since Thatcher had greeted him. "It's almost quite good."

"Thanks. That's almost a compliment, Zach."

"Well, what do you expect? I'm talking to you as I would to an artist, not to some old lady painting by numbers and thinking she's Grandma Moses."

"I'm glad of that."

"So you didn't quit altogether. . . ."

"Haven't done much since Jeanne died."

"That her with the horse?"

Thatcher nodded.

"I remember her now. She was a beautiful girl, like a Marie Laurençin."

There was an embarrassed silence, and then Thatcher said hastily, "How about sitting down? There ought to be some beer here soon."

"Don't bother on my account."

"I like it too," Thatcher said. But he hadn't drunk beer in—was it fifteen years? Somehow it seemed to belong to California and the years with Abe: pitchers of foaming beer on the tables of back-street taverns; six-packs on the beach when they all chipped in their small change and, if they had to, shared the cans.

"You don't mind if I sit down then?" Thatcher sank down on the couch. "Sorry it's not better organized around here. Work in progress."

"Hell, I don't care," Zachary said. "I even maybe prefer it this way

—looks almost like a studio now, with that unobstructed north light. When it's finished, I'd hesitate to come into a room like this for fear of busting a teacup or farting in some big shot's face."

"Zach," Thatcher said, "I missed you this afternoon."

"Yeah?"

"Don't you think . . . well, Jesus, Zach, you *started* this whole thing—bulling into the Museum and smashing up your painting."

"Yep."

"And then you don't even show up for the talks. Is that kosher?"

"Now Lloyd, you know me too well to talk to me about doing what's expected. There are only two rules I follow. One—get the work done. Two—keep your pipes clean and unclogged."

"Nice and pat," Thatcher said. "And safe for you. But what about your friends—the ones who have to do the fighting?"

"That's all political," Abe said. "And I don't want anything to do with aesthetic politics. This ART thing isn't going to give the artist stature or freedom—pride in himself and his work. It's going to give him dues and red tape—officers, for Christ's sake. Who needs another *union?*"

"You're a flaming anarchist!"

Abe bowed. "And proud of it. But when you talk about friends—"

"I mean it, you're letting them all down. Lord knows they need intelligent leadership."

"Maybe I'm more concerned about my friends than you think," Abe said. "Could be that's why I'm here. To warn you."

"You're a great one for issuing warnings, Zach."

"Look, you're angry because I let *you* down, not the artists. They'll manage all right by themselves, but now you've taken their problems on your shoulders—and mine too, or so you think."

"That's a crock."

"I'm not so sure your museum isn't already obsolete, beyond help anyway. And that show of yours—which you think is such a great idea—"

"What about it?"

"Lloyd, could you try not to be so touchy, so *personal* about this? This show is like all the Museum's other shows, a musical comedy put on to build attendance. It's got nothing to do with the new art, it's just a coat of rouge and lipstick slapped on a corpse. Give it up, that show."

174

"No."

"Postpone it, then. Think about it more carefully."

"No. I mean—why should I?"

To Thatcher the conversation seemed to have taken a wholly bizarre tack. It was as though Ira Garvey's high voice were issuing from Abe Zachary's massive head. "Why?" he asked again.

"Because I think maybe somebody or something's going to get hurt if you give that show. Listen to me, we've got some mean people on our side—not really artists, but guys who think art is some form of welfare. They could try to ruin the show because they don't want to see it succeed—or they might wreck it just for the hell of it. Any show would do, but yours is the one they'd pick because it *is* yours."

Thatcher shook his head. "That's hard to believe."

"So believe it."

Thatcher looked at Abe Zachary intently for a moment, wondering how far he could take the old artist into his confidence.

"The trouble is," Zachary said, "that you're thinking like an artist, and I sound like some crazy museum director."

"You didn't mention any names, Zach."

"I could. But I don't know them all yet, just the faces and mentalities."

Lorraine carried in a tray with a half-gallon bottle of beer and two glasses. "I'm sorry this is so late," she said.

"Thanks," Thatcher said. "Just put it down."

"Where?" she said, looking around her.

"All right, I'll take it." Thatcher put the tray on the floor. The two men waited until the sound of Lorraine's footsteps had receded down the hall.

"Thirsty, Zach?"

"I could use some."

"Here."

"I take it you'll be going ahead with the show."

"I'm going ahead with it."

Zachary took a long swallow of beer, and then sighed. "I came here to warn you about my . . . associates. Which makes me to them some kind of fink. Now I have to go back and try to get them to call off the war. And what does that make me?"

"That's a rhetorical question, isn't it?"

"Don't split hairs, I'm still a fink. So—I might as well go all the way, and volunteer my services. You want my help in the show—and I don't see why you should—I'll be glad to give it to you."

"I'd have to be honest with you, Zach. I'm not so sure of my judgment right now."

Nor am I sure of so many other things, Thatcher thought. Who my friends are, and who my enemies. And whether I have the right to be so stubborn if the Museum's security is at stake.

Zachary grinned. "Well, now, if you're thinking of crying, we got the right stuff here for it." He hoisted his glass. "Happy days."

"I'm glad you came, Zach."

"Pay me a visit downtown. If you think *you've* got north light, you should see my north light."

"MEET ME AT THE Numbers," Aaron Redburn said to Thatcher on the phone the following morning. "Make it twelve-thirty."

When Thatcher announced that he was Aaron Redburn's guest, the smiles at the door of the 21 Club brightened. Thatcher was hardly surprised; Redburn's name had performed its magic recently at the Brussels, where Thatcher, Serena, and Redburn had met for a get-acquainted lunch.

The headwaiter, after greeting Thatcher warmly, told him Mr. Redburn had phoned: he'd be fifteen minutes late.

"Would you like to take the table, Mr. Thatcher?"

Thatcher nodded and headed for the stairs.

He had done his homework on his host before their first meeting. Redburn was reported to be a billionaire—most of it earned from a data-processing service firm in Tulsa, with branches throughout the Southwest. He had just begun to buy art; the Redburn collection at this point was heavily weighted in favor of a few artists in the Minimal and Hard-Edge schools.

Now Aaron Redburn, collector, wanted to become Aaron Redburn, trustee. During lunch at the Brussels, he had pumped Thatcher and Serena relentlessly for information about the Museum:

How many trustees were there?

How were they selected?

What were their names—how often did they meet?

And, finally, speculatively: "When are they elected?"

"Not until the annual meeting in May," Thatcher said.

"So long a wait?" Redburn asked.

"Those are the bylaws."

"So I wait," he said, with a smile that accepted the absurdity of waiting for something one wanted. "It doesn't seem like much of a sacrifice."

"Hello, Lloyd."

It was Dexter Llewellyn, crossing the room toward Thatcher's banquette. Trailing in his wake was Winthrop Briggs, slim and light-footed.

"What brings you to Twenty-One?" Llewellyn asked. "Lunching all by your lonesome?"

"With Aaron Redburn."

"Oh. How *lucky* for you. . . . I thought you might like to join us, but obviously you can't."

"Thanks all the same."

"May we sit for a moment?" Llewellyn did not wait for an answer. "Aaron Redburn," he mused. "All that *new* money. A possible donor?"

"Trustee, maybe."

"You *don't* say! Serena Lord's idea, I suppose. . . . Well, isn't that interesting! Tell me, Lloyd, I meant to call you—would you be good enough to meet Marcus Hammer and me for tea at the Museum this evening?"

"I'm sure it can be arranged."

"We'd like to talk to you about the fund-raising program."

Thatcher thought rapidly. Today was the day of the Museum's Christmas party. It would be tight, but if he cut short his appearance at the party. . . .

"Shall we say four-thirty?"

"I'll be there."

"You know, I'm fascinated by the idea of Aaron Redburn as a trustee," Llewellyn said. "Aren't you, Winnie?"

"Oh, absolutely. The man on horseback."

"I could tell you a story or two about Aaron Redburn that would curl your hair," Llewellyn continued. "Including one famously wild party that took place right here, in a private dining room. A gathering of executives—sales managers and plant managers, that kind of thing. Anyhow, Redburn put one of those men through a hazing about his college—University of Florida or one of those glorified high schools—that ended with the poor man down on his hands and knees, baying like a basset hound. Imagine that, Lloyd."

He could; all too easily. He hoped the story was not true.

"Just one of the boys," Briggs suggested.

"No more than Caligula," Llewellyn corrected him. "But perhaps we shouldn't be too choosy. He has a lot of money, our Mr. Redburn, and we need a lot."

"Dexter, I wouldn't recommend anyone for the board I didn't think qualified. And certainly Serena wouldn't."

"I should hope not, Lloyd. There are some things we must not eat, no matter how hungry we are, isn't that right, Winnie?" Briggs, who was chewing on a bread stick, nodded his assent to this sentiment.

"So," Thatcher said, "we must judge Redburn on his merits."

"I'm sure he'd agree. . . . Wouldn't you, Mr. Redburn?"

"Wouldn't I agree to what?" asked Aaron Redburn, his hand outstretched to Thatcher.

"We're discussing the Museum's urgent need for new blood," said Llewellyn. "But excuse me, I'm—"

"Aaron, this is Dexter Llewellyn," said Thatcher.

"Yes, we've met."

"And Winthrop Briggs."

Redburn nodded—barely.

"We're just *en passage* to our own table, Mr. Redburn," Llewellyn said. "So nice to see you. Come along, Win."

Redburn sat down and shook his head as though to clear it of unwanted noise.

"I don't care for the man," he said. "And not just because he's effeminate."

"Why then?"

"Because he's the kind who sums you up and puts you down in twenty-five words or less. I flatter myself I'm not that simple. Sorry to be late, Lloyd."

"I've been enjoying your hospitality in your absence," Thatcher said, lifting his martini glass.

"Let's have another drink. Carl?" A waiter had materialized at Redburn's elbow with a martini. Redburn drank his first one rapidly, and called for another. Thatcher would have preferred limiting himself to one drink, but his host would have none of it. When the third martini appeared, Thatcher let it stand for ten minutes and then barely sipped it.

"I leave the food to Carl," Redburn said. "You don't mind?"

"Certainly not."

"It saves so much time, and it really doesn't matter as long as the food is perfect."

It was. Thatcher could not remember a lighter filet of sole, or a more luminous white wine. And while they ate, they talked of nothing of any consequence—mostly sports. Redburn had just bought a hockey team and wanted to discuss first the Rangers and then the prospects of his own team, now so low in the standings that the sports writers could scarcely conceal their boredom in covering its games. Did Thatcher ever want to use Redburn's box at the Garden? It was his for the asking.

A haze of cigarette smoke, sweet with the fumes of wine and espresso, enveloped them like a protective mantle.

Suddenly Redburn said: "You need help with your trustees, don't you, Lloyd?"

"What?" Thatcher's eyes had been fixed on Redburn, but his mind had been wandering everywhere else.

"I mean—I know Serena can be counted on, but I get the impression you aren't so sure of some of the others."

"No administrator can ever take his board for granted, Aaron. As you no doubt realize."

"I know that no board wants to consider itself a rubber stamp. You have to throw them something they can safely veto now and again—boards of directors and boards of trustees can't be too different, after all. But if you had your druthers, wouldn't you want a favorable board?"

"I hope I have one already."

"Well, if Dexter Llewellyn is any example, you don't. I don't know him well, Lloyd, but if I'm any judge of buggers, he's just waiting for you to trip and fall on your face."

Thatcher disagreed good-naturedly. "I think they all want to give me every chance to do my job well—but the world has changed, and the Museum, so far, hasn't changed much."

"Maybe I can help you," Redburn said. "Once I'm on the board, and when Serena has nominated some of the other candidates we've talked about—"

180

"I really shouldn't be listening to this, you know."

"Well, why *not*—it concerns you, doesn't it? As I was saying, once we get this thing lined up—and mind you, I won't say I don't have influence on a few present members of the board—you can go full speed ahead with your programs."

"I plan to anyhow."

"How about an after-dinner drink? Brandy? Cointreau? Drambuie?"

"Just more coffee, please."

Redburn turned to the waiter hovering nearby and gave his order softly. For an instant he remained in profile, his eyes on a lovely young woman who sat across the room from them, breathing idly on her fingernails. So completely absorbed was Redburn in his calm inspection of her that to Thatcher he seemed, ever so briefly, like a life-sized, lithographed cardboard figure—the billboard cutout for a fancy new cigarette, or a Southern California political campaign.

He turned back to Thatcher, unaware, obviously, that he had ever been gone.

"You want to do exciting exhibitions, don't you, Lloyd?"

"I want it to be the most exciting museum in all the world. It almost is now—and it *could* be." Thatcher felt he was babbling, but he was borne along now by the force of his own enthusiasm.

"Exhibitions of the new young painters, not just the old hacks?"

"There are young hacks as well as old ones, Aaron. It isn't just familiarity that breeds contempt—novelty can, too."

"Painters who should be seen more often, maybe. Like Tom Fischer."

So that was it. First the bait and then the hook. Now Thatcher remembered. Idiosyncratic as Redburn's collection was, and out of all proportion to any balanced representation of contemporary painting, it was particularly strong in the work of Tom Fischer. It was entirely possible that he owned as many Fischers as Fischer himself.

Thatcher's eyes smarted from the smoke, and he could taste his apprehension. "Fischer?"

"You know his work?" Redburn asked.

"Yes, I've seen it."

"What do you think?"

"He's talented."

"Is that all you can say?"

"We own a few Fischers at the Museum. . . ."

"That could be easily rectified. I'd be glad to give you a number of his best paintings myself."

"That would be generous of you, Aaron, but I'd have to know the conditions."

"What do you mean—conditions? I'm suggesting you might want to have a Tom Fischer exhibition, that's all."

"A major one?"

"That's up to you. Look—you make it sound as though I'm offering you a deal of some kind. . . . I just happen to like Tom Fischer's work."

And you just happen to own a lot of it, thought Thatcher. Work whose value will increase overnight if the Museum has a show of Tom Fischer paintings. What price a friendly board of trustees? A Fischer retrospective.

"Well, *aren't* you offering a deal?" Thatcher asked. He risked a smile.

Redburn, whose body had stiffened, sank back on his banquette. He too smiled—quite affably, Thatcher thought. "It's up to you," he said.

To Aaron Redburn, Thatcher thought, everything is a deal, some you lose and some you win. And it's logical enough that if you have an art collection you want it to be as valuable as possible.

"Aaron, I'm afraid Tom Fischer may not be ready for that kind of a show just yet."

"I'm sorry to hear you say that. I was hoping you'd agree with me on Fischer's merits."

"I wish I did—Tom's a likable fellow."

"I hate to be wrong about things like that."

"Think of it this way, Aaron—you're still one of the first collectors to appreciate Fischer's talent. The others may have to follow your lead some day."

Redburn had begun to look around the room as though he were expecting somebody or trying to find a clock.

"I was thinking of inviting you down to the wine cellar," he said. "There's a nineteen-thirty-seven Madeira down there you really ought to taste. But. . . ."

"Another time, perhaps."

"Perhaps. Well . . . I'm sorry, Thatcher, I have to run."

He rose and departed; so good a customer, Thatcher observed, that he wasn't even presented with a check. Thatcher was sorry to see him go—not because he would miss going down into the *cave* with its hoard of cobwebbed vintages, but because he had begun to like Aaron Redburn.

And he might have made a good trustee. But not now, not anymore. It wouldn't do.

And although they didn't seem to agree about much these days, this was one point on which he felt certain that Ira Garvey would share his conviction.

20

WHAT DOES A one-martini man do after a three-martini lunch?

Thatcher waited at the restaurant until he was reasonably certain that Aaron Redburn was gone, and then set out on foot—no particular destination, he just wanted to breathe a few gallons of air, cold if not altogether fresh.

He sauntered west on 52nd Street, glad to be momentarily free of appointments, tycoons, curators, artists, and trustees, possible or actual. Nobody knew where he was, or, if he was lucky, even cared.

Heading south, he found himself in the neighborhood of the Di-Cassino warehouse. He knew Austin Vanderhanks was receiving a new shipment of paintings this afternoon from his agent in Paris, on their way to one or another Vanderhanks residence. He had not specifically asked Thatcher to come and look at the shipment with him, but a number of the paintings would ultimately hang in the Museum, and Thatcher was sure Vanderhanks would want him to inspect them.

On impulse, and because opening these particular packages would be rather like having Christmas fall a few days early, Thatcher turned west again.

DiCassino's vast, smoke-stained hulk lay in the shadow of the West Side Highway, within sight of the Hudson River docks, battered all day long by the roar of trucks and cars and buses, pneumatic drills, cement mixers, giant cranes.

But Thatcher knew that at any given moment perhaps a third of the fine art in New York City was inside this building, either in storage or in transit. Leaving here, the great private collections moved from city to city and to every continent, while the stored works of art remaining within its walls made the warehouse one of the world's finest unvisited museums.

Thatcher banged sharply on the glass door of the receiving room. Vanderhanks must be upstairs in the loading bay.

"Coming!" said a harsh, distant voice. A man in gray coveralls appeared in the doorway.

"Hello, Mario," said Thatcher.

"Oh, hello, Mr. Thatcher—I wasn't expecting you. How ya been?"

"Fine thanks, and yourself?"

"Still on antacids. You need something?"

"I'm hunting for Austin Vanderhanks."

"Ya, he's on the fourth floor. Looking at that new bunch of stuff. Come on, I'll take you up."

They ascended slowly in a wheezing freight elevator. On a stool in the corner lay a half-eaten sausage sandwich, a crumpled buttermilk container, and a copy of the *Daily News*—a still life of sorts.

At the fourth floor Mario opened the elevator door and turned to Thatcher: "I see you're having some trouble at the Museum. With the artists."

"Oh, I think that's under control."

"It's the dope," Mario said solemnly. "They're all on the needle. They oughta calm down and go to work. After all—who needs 'em? There's enough art by the dead ones around, right?"

"Which way, Mario?"

"Bay D. See ya later, Mr. Thatcher."

Thatcher was quite unprepared, when he reached Bay D, to find that Vanderhanks was not alone.

"Hello, Lloyd," said Manley Stringfellow softly.

"Lloyd," Austin Vanderhanks said in a high, preoccupied voice. "Is it Thatcher?"

The two older men were standing in front of a row of magnificent canvases—Matisses and Picassos, most of them, though Thatcher also recognized two Mondrians, a Rousseau, and a Cezanne. A bright overhead light glared down on the paintings. Manley Stringfellow, holding a portable work light in one hand, was bent over on one knee before a Friesz landscape.

"How are you, Lloyd?" Stringfellow said. "You've come to see these?"

The way to the paintings from the doorway was almost completely blocked by empty cases, broken planks, and baling strips. Approaching the two men, Thatcher nearly tripped and fell.

"My new shipment," Vanderhanks said.

"I know."

"A superb group, isn't it?"

There was in Vanderhanks' eyes an intensity Thatcher had never seen before, a harshness and ferocity in his voice. The single-minded engagement of the collector caught up in his passion. . . .

"Lloyd," he said. "It wasn't necessary."

"What's that?"

"You needn't have gone to the trouble to come down."

"No trouble," Thatcher said, his mouth dry. "I thought you'd want someone from the Museum to examine them."

"Yes, well, Manley is here. By all means, stay if you like, of course. We'd be glad to have you look at them—"

"No, I should get back to the Museum. Manley's verification is more than sufficient."

Stringfellow had risen to his feet. The work light in his hand threw ghastly shadows on his thin, ancient face, and highlighted his bald skull.

"First-rate," he declared. "Absolutely."

They're used to each other, Thatcher thought. Like two old lovers. . . . The collectors.

Knowing the acquisitive instinct as well as he did, why should he feel resentful that Vanderhanks preferred to share his treasures first with Stringfellow? And why was this damned room so hot and oppressive?

As Thatcher left, he heard Vanderhanks saying, with unguarded joy, "Isn't this Bonnard nude exquisite, Manley? The light touches the body like gauze. . . ."

Thatcher walked into the Museum like a man breaking in new shoes. Finding his foyer empty, he remembered with a shock of annoyance that most of the staff were probably down in the furnace room at the Christmas party hosted each year by the Museum's maintenance staff. He closed the door of his office behind him and sat for some time in his chair, arms folded, staring out into the darkening room.

He knew it was childish to mind so much what was only an injury to his self-esteem, and yet he did mind. He did not want to move, or work, or go anywhere. Still, he was expected at the party, he would have to make an appearance. What else was there to do but carry his distress downstairs with him and try to lose it somewhere along the way?

When Thatcher reached the furnace room, the party had been under way for two hours, but showed no signs of winding down. A long table set up at the side of the room for drinks and hors d'oeuvres was now in prodigal disarray, with empty bottles crowding full and half-empty ones, and *canapés* and cheeses, breads and cookies piled every which way on the Christmas stripes of the tablecloth. A drummer, a guitarist, and a trumpet player pounded out rockabilly alongside the main furnace; half-a-dozen couples were dancing. Loud bursts of laughter and conversation echoed harshly in the room's structural steel walls, among the climbing webs of pipes and conduits.

Thatcher went to the bar and helped himself to a large scotch and water.

"Hello there, Mr. Thatcher."

"How are you, Jack? Hello, Marty, nice to see you. . . . Sorry I'm so late."

"We'd've kept the party going until you got here, Mr. Thatcher."

The warmth of his reception by the workmen, coupled with the burning effect of the scotch, which he had swallowed almost in one long draught, brought stinging tears to Thatcher's eyes. He turned his head away and, setting down his empty glass, blew his nose surreptitiously on a paper napkin.

"Try some of the gouda, Mr. Thatcher. There's plenty left, and it's the best one."

"No thanks, Ernest. I believe I'll have another scotch instead."

The foreman of the maintenance crew asked Thatcher what he thought of the music. "It's home-cooked, you know. A few of the boys."

"All the better, Harry."

"I'm glad you could come, Mr. Thatcher. Mr. Saint-Simon always used to say this was his favorite party of the year. Once even Mr. Vanderhanks stopped by for a couple of minutes."

At the sound of Vanderhanks' name, Thatcher found himself back at the edge of gloom. Knowing it would only depress him further, he refilled his glass. The hell with Vanderhanks and his aging Mazarin—this was a party.

He edged away from the table and began to move from group to group, trying to talk to as many people as he could in as short a time as possible. In the distance, he saw Lise dancing with Lester Dolan—close together, for the combo had switched to dance music of the forties and fifties; "Brazil" and "Perfidia" and "The Green Leaves of Summer." Thatcher waved at Lise, and Dolan nodded. Then, slowly, they glided over to Thatcher.

"I wondered if you were going to get here," Lise said. "I hope you don't mind my leaving the office for such a long time, but I have somebody next door covering the phones."

"It's all right," Thatcher said. "You deserve a rest."

"And a dance maybe?"

"Do you mind, Les?"

Thatcher took Lise into his arms and stepped out slowly with her. At first he danced awkwardly, for he was still preoccupied, but gradually the oppressiveness faded and he found the rhythms of the music and of Lise's body.

"Is everything all right?" she asked him.

"Why do you ask?"

"When you came in, you looked sort of . . . remote."

"I'm enjoying myself right now."

"Sir, I consider that answer evasive."

"Tell you later, Lise. Not now."

"It didn't go well at lunch then. . . ."

Thatcher said nothing, and they danced on.

"Knowing what Christmas office parties are generally like . . ." he began.

"Yes?"

"I wasn't exactly looking forward to this. I was wrong—it was worth coming."

"I'm glad you changed your mind."

"When I got here I felt completely cold," he explained. "Now I feel warm. It's not just the liquor, or the heat of the room, or the music and dancing. There's genuine affection here in this room—I can feel it, and I wish I could stay and enjoy it longer."

"May I cut back in?" It was Dolan, tapping Thatcher lightly on the shoulder. He held a drink in one hand, which he extended to Thatcher. "I brought this over for you, Lloyd."

"No thanks, I have a meeting up in one of the committee rooms."

Dolan gathered Lise up and moved away, staring down at her in a frankly sexual examination which seemed, at the same time, to sift its opportunities and weigh its chances of rejection.

Thatcher remained only a moment longer in the room, battered by insistent voices and by the music. Then he left, taking his loneliness with him.

"You're late, Lloyd," said Dexter Llewellyn. "By more than fifteen minutes," he added, as though it were essential to establish the precise measure of Thatcher's tardiness.

"I'm sorry about that. I've been in the furnace room at the staff party, and I guess I overstayed myself."

"The director of this museum is rather like a mayor," Llewellyn said. "Or so I've often thought. He has to rush from a ribbon-cutting ceremony to a six-alarm fire, to a gangland slaughter. No wonder the poor man is often late." He smiled slyly. "And harassed."

Marcus Hammer rose a few inches from his chair and reached out to shake Thatcher's hand—a quick, ceremonious greeting.

"Please excuse me, Marcus. I hope you and Dexter haven't been waiting long."

"We're having tea, thank you. Will you join us?"

The two men were sitting at a round table in the trustees' private dining room. Between their cups and the silver service stood the model of the Museum Tower Ira Garvey had unveiled at his dinner party.

"I'll fix myself a scotch instead, if you don't mind," Thatcher said. He took his time mixing the drink, conscious all the time that the two men were staring at his back—with, he imagined, disapproval. "I've gone over the plans," he said to them.

"What do you think?"

Thatcher went over to the model on the table. Beside it lay a roll of blueprints. He spread them out on the table.

"As it's designed now, we'll be building right over the glassed-in garden."

"That's right."

"And the first setback will come at the tenth floor. Won't that spoil the garden?"

"All it will block out," Hammer said, "is those soot-covered skylights."

"I'm sure that with the combination of natural and artificial light we have now, and its controlled temperature, we can preserve the garden," Llewellyn said.

"But it will change."

"Of course. How can the tower be built without changing the profile of this building?"

"And what about the profile of the block?"

"What do you mean?" Marcus Hammer was beginning to look impatient.

"We must consider what it will mean to bring another high-rise office building into an already overcrowded neighborhood."

"The city itself doesn't seem too concerned," Hammer said. "My friends downtown are confident we'll get the necessary building code variances."

"What we're asking," Thatcher said, "is that they allow us to build an office building over this Museum which will provide approximately two hundred thousand square feet of office space."

"For which we can expect income for the Museum of between two and three million dollars a year." Hammer reached across the table for the plans. "You do realize, Lloyd, how much endowment capital would be needed to produce that income every year."

"Over forty million dollars."

"Just so," said Llewellyn. "Lloyd—this plan could be our salvation. I deeply believe that."

"I'm not questioning the benefits of the Tower, Dexter. I'm only raising the kind of questions we should ask—before somebody else raises them. The press, for one."

Llewellyn chuckled and patted Thatcher on the arm.

"My dear Lloyd, we will certainly show the proper concern for public reaction. I myself have a public relations counsel on retainer— I wouldn't suggest anything less for the Museum."

"All the same," Thatcher said, "I think we may have a fight on

190

our hands to get this Tower through if our only concern is revenue. Now, there are things we could offer to make the Tower more acceptable."

"Such as?"

"Artist's studios. And apartments. Nobody's building any living quarters for the artists these days, or studios either. And most of the available space they can use is being destroyed. I suggest that we devote the first five or six floors of the Tower to studios and living quarters for artists, charging them a rent they can afford to pay—the way Carnegie Hall used to do for musicians."

Hammer said nothing.

"Lloyd, my dear man, that's marvelous!" Llewellyn exclaimed. "It does you credit as a man of spirit and a friend of the artist." He turned to Hammer. "Marcus, suppose you answer our resident idealist."

"First, there's the loss of revenue," Hammer said. "Business space brings fifteen to twenty dollars a square foot a year—studios would be lucky to bring five. Outside of that, there are a couple of other objections that come to mind. For one, artists are not reliable tenants. For another, the Museum might well not want to be in a position where it is landlord to its own suppliers, in a manner of speaking."

"But is the Museum interested in art and the makers of art, or in becoming landlords to commerce and industry? And what becomes of the Museum's purpose—when we're harnessed to some huge and complicated profit machine?"

Neither Llewellyn nor Hammer answered him for a moment. Finally Hammer spoke. "I think it's a damn-fool idea myself."

"Why?" Thatcher persisted.

"It is, practically speaking, eleemosynary," Llewellyn said.

"What did you say?" Hammer snapped.

"It's one of my favorite words. It means charitable. And that's what this Museum is *not*."

In the silence that followed, Thatcher fixed himself another drink. As he sipped, he realized that Marcus Hammer was speaking to him.

"I do want to be fair, Thatcher. But I'm beginning to think your people are dragging their feet on this fund-raising program."

"I don't think so."

"Alex Gibbs tells me you've barely gotten through the Gold List and haven't even started on the Silver List."

"That's about right."

"We need the fastest possible action if we're ever—"

"Gentlemen," Thatcher said, rising, his drink in his hand. "May I say something please?" He gripped his glass hard with both hands. "When I first took this job, I had a long talk with Robert Saint-Simon. During the course of this talk we discussed fund-raising very frankly. I told Robert that I expected to help with the money drives, boring as they might be, because they're necessary." He seated himself with elaborate care, and then went on.

"As I've said, I'll do what I must to insure that the Museum survives. But I also told Robert that I would not let fund-raising interfere with the real business of the Museum, which is showing art, not raising money. Do I make myself clear?"

Quite deliberately Dexter Llewellyn took the plans from Marcus Hammer's hands and rolled them up.

"Look here," he said to Thatcher, "you can't leave us high and dry like this. Goddam it, fund-raising may well be the most important thing you have to do in this place. Now, we know nothing of any agreement you may have had with Robert prior to joining the Museum —though I think it highly unfair of you to call on a dead man, a man who can't answer for himself, to support your position on this. You may be sure of one thing, though—you'll take your instructions from the board of trustees."

"Why Dexter!" Thatcher said. "You're getting angry."

"Aren't I just, though? And let me tell you—you'd better be damn careful I don't *stay* angry."

"I don't think we're getting anywhere." Marcus Hammer stood up and looked around for his hat and overcoat. "It never pays," he grumbled, "to talk about anything useful just before Christmas. But I must say—" he turned to Thatcher. "—I hope you'll look at this Tower business less emotionally the next time we meet."

That evening Dexter Llewellyn called Ira Garvey at home. Christmas Eve or no Christmas Eve, he wanted it known that the meeting had been an utter failure, that their fund-raising plans had been set back weeks as a consequence. That Marcus Hammer was most upset about it all, and, lastly, that Lloyd Thatcher had been drunk and quarrelsome.

"You're sure?" Garvey said.

"Of course I'm sure. He almost dropped his glass on the table."

"Yes, but—"

"He was drunk. He talked nonsense. And offended both of us." Then he added, gratuitously: "He tried to put Robert Saint-Simon in a bad light as well."

"Not like Thatcher," Garvey said. "Do you know of any particular difficulties he's having that might account for it? Personal problems, or—"

"Ira, I'm not a psychiatrist—how can I answer a question like that?"

"Very well, then. Thank you for calling, Dexter."

"You understand it was a painful duty."

"I'm sure."

"But I'm worried about our young Mr. Thatcher."

"So am I," said Ira Garvey.

21

"MERRY CHRISTMAS!" Thatcher was the first to say it on Christmas morning. "Merry Christmas, Susie. Merry Christmas, Lorraine. Isn't it a beautiful day?"

The invading hordes were gone—the painters, decorators, electricians, and plumbers—out by Christmas after all. A good deal of furniture still needed to be moved into place and the paintings were still lined up along the walls, but there would be plenty of time to put them up, and great pleasure for Thatcher in doing it; there were few things he enjoyed more than hanging and rehanging pictures.

At ten o'clock the Thatchers opened their presents: clothes and books and records for Susie; shirts and neckties in striped and checked abundance for Thatcher, along with a fantastically detailed and beautiful icon Lorraine had found in a Third Avenue antique shop. From his staff at the Museum came a recording of Dvorak Quintets, and from several gallery owners, bottles of scotch and cognac, and one large basket containing a magnum of champagne.

"Into the Museum liquor closet with it."

"But Lloyd, it's a gift."

"A business gift," Thatcher said. "Into the Museum closet." They kept two different liquor cabinets—one to hold their own supply, mostly wine for meals, and a second, much larger cabinet for the liquor Thatcher would use to entertain the staff and guests of the Museum.

Lorraine, who was happily trying on a suede wrap coat over her robe, did not argue the point.

After opening their gifts, they sat and admired the fifteen-foot balsam Thatcher had dragged home the night before from a parking lot several blocks north on Madison Avenue. They'd put it in the two-story stairwell area of the apartment, where it would tower over visitors as they entered the foyer. Then he and Lorraine and Susie had stayed up until all hours decorating its branches with homemade rings and angels, stars and bright paper mobiles.

"Can't stand any tree but a live one," Thatcher said.

"You're right," said Lorraine.

"Absolutely right," Susie said. "None of those gun-metal trees for us."

"The smell of the forests, the virgin pine. . . ."

Thatcher was happy.

At noon on Christmas Day the phone rang. Lorraine made a face.

"If it's the Museum calling—"

"Can't be," Thatcher said.

"But you know it can."

"Well, why don't you answer it and tell whoever it is that I'm busy playing canasta."

Thatcher and Susan had almost forgotten the telephone call by the time Lorraine returned, pale and shaken.

"What is it?"

"Bad news from Mercy Hospital."

"Mother?"

"Yes." She stood terribly still and straight. "They think. . . . She's sinking, Lloyd. It's her kidney failure. Oh Lloyd. . . ." Her voice crumpled, along with her unnaturally erect posture. Both Thatcher and Susie got up from the floor and went to her. Holding his sister close, his chin touching her hair, Thatcher could see through the living-room window to the terrace outside, streaked with long dark scabs of frozen snow. Inside the room, Christmas quietly died away.

"Both kidneys?"

"Yes."

"Damn," Thatcher said, with no particular force.

"I'll be all right. I promise, Lloyd."

195

"Silly. If you feel like crying, go ahead."

"There's no time now. We've got to make arrangements to get to Baltimore."

"Mmm. Will day after tomorrow be all right?"

"Day after tomorrow?"

"There's an important meeting about the curators' demands coming up. I'll cancel everything I can, though, and—"

"Meetings? Momma's *dying*, Lloyd, didn't you *hear* me?"

"Yes. Don't worry, I'll call Lise as soon as I can and we'll go down tomorrow."

"But the Museum always comes first, doesn't it?" she said. "Before everything."

"Now Lorraine, you're just upset. Let's not—"

"She's also right, Daddy!"

Thatcher turned to face his daughter.

"So she's right!" he snapped. "It's that kind of job, we knew it from the beginning."

"And we haven't *gone* anywhere, we haven't done anything in months that hasn't been connected with the Museum. Every party has been a Museum party, every—"

"That's not so. I mean—it *can't* be, Susie."

"Do you know how many nights you've been out to dinner, Daddy, or late?"

"No, and I told you to stop keeping score on me."

"You put on your dinner clothes three or four evenings a week, don't you *know* that?"

"Please, honey. I know it's been hard on you both. It'll ease up in time."

"You said that last summer. Well, when is it ever going to ease up? Next summer, Daddy? Maybe the summer of nineteen ninety-six?"

"You don't understand how hard it is. I don't know, I'll do my best—"

"Oh, I'm certain you will, Daddy." Her voice faltered under the strain of holding a pitch of irony. "But you love it, I know that whether you do or not. Getting all dressed up in your After Six and going to parties, your name in the papers, people who don't know you recognizing you—it means a lot, doesn't it?"

"It comes with the territory."

"I just hope you're having lots of fun—because we're not!"

"Enough!" Thatcher shouted. "Please—that's *enough.*"

Something in his face made her believe him.

"All right, Daddy."

They fell silent, but the aftermath of the quarrel lay around them like the crumpled gift wrappings scattered on the floor.

"Merry Christmas, Lise. And I wish I had nothing more important to say than that."

"Bad news?"

Thatcher told her.

"How can I help?"

"Somehow we have to move our Monday meeting to Tuesday or Wednesday. I don't know how we'll get ready for it if I'm in Baltimore. . . ."

"Could I possibly come along with you?"

"You think it's wise? I . . . hate to spoil your holiday."

"You won't."

Thatcher would have flown to Baltimore if he'd been alone—he detested eastern-seaboard driving—but Lorraine was one of the dwindling band who cannot or will not fly. They drove instead, in a rented Mercedes, leaving Susie behind with friends. Lorraine had accepted Thatcher's announcement that Lise was coming with apparent calm. "If you must," she'd said, and turned away.

As the trip began, Thatcher's thoughts were still of his sister and daughter, with the Museum as the intruder, breaking into his thoughts without warning as it broke into his family life. Ira Garvey wasn't going to like having the meeting postponed, and according to Lise Ted Porter had received the news with resignation, as though he expected no less from a self-absorbed, arbitrary administration. The other side of the coin, Thatcher thought. Lorraine and Susie resented his neglect of his personal life, while the Museum staff didn't seriously believe he had one. As for Thatcher himself, he was beginning to feel the weight of all his obligations like solid rock pressing down on him.

By the time they were well onto the New Jersey Turnpike, Lise was reading memoranda aloud to him as he drove. She'd begun with one from Homer Karp: " 'Much as I hate to admit it, Museum salaries among the junior members of the department are too low. It seems to me we are encouraging a form of wretchedly paid apprenticeship, by which we train our younger people to perform their most valuable service for other institutions. May I suggest. . . .'" Lise's voice droned on, flat and unemotional.

Thatcher found himself pressing the accelerator harder and harder as they drove through miles of New Jersey's smoking wastes—crowding and then surpassing the speed limit on the Turnpike.

"You'd better slow down," said Lorraine.

Thatcher's foot slackened on the gas pedal.

"Sorry, I was thinking. I mean I wasn't thinking."

"Horrible, isn't it?"

"Can you imagine breaking down here?" Thatcher asked. "You could be asphyxiated in the time it takes to change a tire."

"And yet human beings live here. Work here, anyway."

"They do? I haven't seen any. Just factories and oil towers and car dumps."

"You're being morbid," Lorraine said, as though that explained everything.

By the time they reached Baltimore Thatcher's eyes were smarting; he rolled down the window of the car to let cold air stream in. Lorraine drew her coat collar up around her face.

"Isn't this where we turn?"

"Not until we get to Saint Charles Street."

"I think it's sooner than that."

"Don't drive for me—please."

It had occurred to him more than once lately that he and Lorraine were coming to resemble a middle-aged married couple, without any of the comfort and joy of marriage. With all his esteem for her, she often got on his nerves in trivial ways, as he was sure he did hers. And for the first time, he was beginning to realize that they might be together for the rest of their lives, that neither of them might ever remarry—Lorraine because her marriages had all been failures, or so she said, and he because his marriage had been so successful he couldn't settle for less. Or so *he* said. Maybe there was another reason, the one hidden in his quarrel with Susie yesterday morning: too much Museum and too much Career, too little Thatcher left over for the imaginative effort it took to make even a marriage of convenience work, still less a love match.

How desirable that kind of love seemed to him, and how remote, as he drove through the fading winter afternoon.

"The motel is on the way to the hospital, isn't it?" Lise asked.

"Yes. Two blocks this side."

"Why don't you drop me off there first? I can check us all in while you two go on to the hospital."

"Sounds fine," Thatcher said.

"I can also start organizing some of these notes."

"All right, Lloyd," Lorraine put in. "But let's hurry."

Hurry? Thatcher felt almost certain that his mother would wait until they reached her before worsening.

The room was almost dark when they entered; the last traces of afternoon light were ebbing from the grime-covered windows, and a single lamp had been lit near the massive white bed. Mary Jane Thatcher looked frail and tiny under the taut sheets. Now that she no longer dyed her hair, it had gone a patchy gray, shot through with faded henna tufts caught up in a spidery net. How old she looked— so pale, almost the color of Gauguin's *Yellow Christ*.

They approached the bed, which had been cranked up so that she might look at an ancient television set across the room. The volume had been turned down, and images flickered soundlessly on the screen —like a ghastly Muzak for the eyes only, playing to the bare walls.

As Thatcher and Lorraine leaned over her, she opened her red-rimmed eyes.

"Hello, Mother."

She turned her head slowly to the left and stared first at Thatcher, then Lorraine.

"Both my darlings," she said in a hoarse whisper.

"It's good to see you, Mother," Thatcher said.

"Not as good—" Thatcher leaned over the bed and put his head close to hers to catch the rest of the sentence. "—as it is to see you." The faint odor of camphor and some kind of bitter acid rose from her skin. Quickly, he stood upright again.

"Will you stay?" she asked them.

"Yes, we'll be here for a while," Lorraine said, and took her hand.

She was breathing with difficulty now; her nostrils trembled with the force of the air drawn sharply into them. Her nose, Thatcher saw, was still fine, shapely—the last of her features to lose delicacy and definition.

Thatcher and Lorraine drew up two straight chairs and sat down on either side of the bed.

Their mother hummed. What was the song? Thatcher leaned over again, close to her lips, trying to identify the melody. There was none; just notes, random notes of music.

Watching her, Thatcher felt an impulse to lift her in his arms and rock her back and forth until she slept. Despite her worn, creased skin and cracked lips, she was a child. Had she ever really become an adult? Thatcher couldn't remember a time when she hadn't needed to be comforted, or encouraged, or prodded in one direction or another.

He took her hand in his; the thin, dry fingers tightened against his palm.

"Mother."

"Yes, Lloydy?"

"God, you were pretty."

The old lips parted in a trembling, ecstatic smile; almost immediately, she dropped off to sleep.

Thatcher looked across the bed at his sister: "I *have* tried to love her, God knows I have."

Their mother's doctor had only a few minutes to spend with them. "She's suffering from a progressive degeneration of the kidneys," he said. "Her uric acid level is running a count high enough to prove fatal in most cases. Putting it plainly, she's being slowly poisoned."

"How horrible!" said Lorraine.

"It isn't painful for her," the doctor said. "What usually happens is that the patient slips into a coma and then just sinks away. It could be any day now—or it could be weeks away."

"Do you think we should stay?" Thatcher asked.

"Suit yourself on that. We'll keep you notified of her condition if you go home, and if you stay—well, you'll find that sometimes her mind will wander."

"It has before, too."

The doctor nodded.

"Senility is a peculiar disease. We have no idea how it will strike, or when. I've known of cases among forty-year-olds. How old is your mother—seventy?"

"Sixty-eight."

"You see—it struck her early. Well . . . nice to meet you both, good-bye." He headed off down the hall, his white jacket swinging open. About ten paces from them he stopped suddenly and turned back.

"Oh, Mr. Thatcher."

"Yes, Doctor?"

"My wife recently inherited her family's old Victorian house up in Hamilton, New York," he said. "Place is full of antiques, you know, and quite a few oil paintings. Fancy gilt frames, too. I was wondering how we would go about finding out how valuable they are. Would your museum—"

"We don't evaluate works of art," Thatcher said. "Though we'll authenticate them if you believe they're the work of established artists. A good color photograph is often enough for that purpose."

"Oh?"

"Your best bet is to take them to a gallery, or a reliable antique dealer."

"I see," the doctor said. He nodded, but sounded disappointed and somewhat skeptical. "I thought your museum might buy that kind of thing, if it was old enough."

"Age isn't necessarily a gauge of quality," Thatcher said. "As a gerontologist, I'm sure you know that."

"Yeah?" The doctor grinned suddenly. "I get it," he said. "You know—you're right."

When they returned to the Motor Lodge, a scribbled note in Lise's handwriting was waiting in Thatcher's box.

"I. Garvey called. Asks you return call ASAP. RE 3-2183."

Garvey was unavailable when Thatcher placed a call to him from his room; he left a message with Mrs. Garvey. Then he lay down on his bed, just to shut his eyes for a few moments—and was asleep before he got around to taking off his shoes.

They dined that night in the restaurant of the Motor Lodge, primarily because Thatcher was still too tired to set out exploring the city for food. Not even the desire for Maryland crab cakes and terrapin could overcome his lassitude. Through the first part of the meal, they spoke little. Lorraine toyed with her food, while Thatcher gentled a second martini along into his dinner. He was midway through his London broil when the waiter summoned him to the telephone. It was Ira Garvey.

"Lloyd . . . at last. How's your mother?"

"Failing. But comfortable."

"Yes—that's important. She's in good hands?"

"So far as I know. But we're never told much about doctors, are we? We laymen, I mean. Doctors don't carry ratings, like hotels and restaurants."

Garvey chuckled in remote appreciation of Thatcher's joke, then inquired politely who the doctor was.

"Boyle? Don't know him. No reason I should, however. I'll tell you why I called."

"Yes, Ira."

"We need you back here early tomorrow morning for a conference at City Hall with the head of the zoning commission. . . . Marcus Hammer, yourself, myself. To discuss those variances for the Tower."

"I've wanted to talk to you about that, Ira."

"So I understand from Dexter Llewellyn."

"Can't we slow this thing down a bit? Hold off going to City Hall until we've had a chance to give the whole matter more thought?"

"I'm sorry, but I don't think it's possible, Lloyd. The climate downtown is favorable to us right now—a month from now it might not be. And Marcus has gone to considerable trouble to get this appointment set up."

"I see."

"You will be there? Ten o'clock sharp, Mr. Cole's office."

"I don't see how, Ira. I drove down with my sister and my assistant, Miss Deering. I don't see how we can possibly get back by then."

"I don't want to be unreasonable, Lloyd, but perhaps you could fly back early while the two ladies drive your car back."

It occurred to Thatcher that Garvey might think his unwillingness to keep the appointment at City Hall was not because of his doubts about the Tower but because it was going to be inconvenient for him to get back from Baltimore.

"Alex Gibbs couldn't do it for me?"

A pause. "He could."

"Perhaps I will fly," Thatcher said quickly. "I'll see what I can work out."

"Good. . . . Thatcher, I have the adjuster's decision on *Zamboula Polka* in hand. . . ."

"I saw it too, Ira, and I'm disappointed in the settlement."

"Shall we appeal it?"

"I intend to, though I don't think it will do much good."

"Thatcher, I—well, I know we're all sorry about this regrettable incident. It's always tragic when a masterpiece is destroyed."

"There are still four other hand-colored copies of the print in existence—"

"None of which belongs to us."

After another apology for disturbing him, Garvey hung up. Dr. Garvey regrets, thought Thatcher, disturbing me on Sunday, on a holiday weekend, at the dinner table. While my mother is passing on.

He returned to the restaurant too annoyed to care that the news he brought was bound to spoil whatever remained of dinner.

When they retired for the night, they left it that Lorraine, who did not drive, would either stay on in Baltimore or ride back to New York with Lise while Thatcher took the shuttle.

Along about midnight, Lorraine knocked on Thatcher's door and asked if she might come in and talk. He snapped the light on, and she curled up on the couch while Thatcher sat on the edge of his bed.

"I can't get the sight of her out of my mind, Lloyd."

"Do you want a drink?"

"No thanks."

"How about a sleeping tablet?"

"It wouldn't do any good—I see her too clearly."

"I see her," he said, "as she was, too. Even now, with almost nothing left that you could describe as beautiful."

"What's so important about being beautiful anyway? Some people never are at all beautiful—and what *difference* does it make?"

"It was what mattered most to her."

"Lloyd, that's a horrible thing to say. What about Dad? What about you and me?"

"We were always her audience. And sometimes we were lucky. When she decided to play the part of Mother."

"She *was* a mother."

"You may be right. I'm not feeling in a forgiving mood tonight, that's all."

"I'm sorry, Lloyd. I just can't stay here and watch her die. I want to go home with Lise tomorrow."

"All right, you don't have to stay."

She was beginning to cry now.

"Listen," he said. "She never was particularly successful, or spectacular—she didn't get her name up in lights, which is what she wanted most of all. But she had a long run. There's no reason to feel sorry for her now. A good run, and at least she had the guts to try."

"That's not important *either*," said Lorraine, and left.

Thatcher's room seemed oppressively silent, and moonlight streaming in through the fibreglass curtains gave every object in the room an unnatural distinctness.

Now I lay me down to sleep. . . . What comes next?

A bag of peanuts at my feet. . . .

Odd snatches of other songs: *No momma, no poppa, no food to eat.* . . . *Cuddle up a little closer, baby mine.* . . . *All alone, by the telephone.* . . . *Don't cry, Lloydy, don't cry.* . . .

He had only to pick up the phone and call Lise's room. Wasn't that what he wanted—the drowsy heat of a woman's breath on his face, the plain-spoken endearments and sweet vulgarities whispered in the darkness—all that Jeanne was, and that no one else had really been to him since—wasn't it the accumulation of body memories, the flesh as necessary as bread, and the marriage of flesh and imagination?

Thatcher groped in the dark until his hand touched the cool plastic of the telephone on the night table.

But was it Lise he wanted? Lise, who would not be satisfied with a desperately lonely phone call, or with pleasant nights when he could find the time? Was it just somebody he wanted, *any*body? Any body. . . ?

His hand slid off the phone and fell back on the bedcovers.

Someday, perhaps, he would riddle it all out. What has three legs, four eyes, and white hair? A lecherous old man wearing glasses. What is this face, less clear and clearer, coming to him out of the darkness behind his eyelids? The face of a beautiful woman smiling. No time for that now, not yet. Mustn't touch. For God's sake, let me sleep but *don't* make me dream. . . .

22

Thatcher spent only five weeks organizing "Dimensions," the Museum's show of environments—by far the shortest time ever spent in the preparation of a major exhibition. The whole point of the show, he insisted to anyone who questioned the speed with which they were working, was improvisation, immediacy, a quality of intense pressure and driving haste. They were all winging it.

Thatcher and his eight artists—seven men and a woman—worked literally day and night on the environments: begging, promoting, scrounging materials wherever they could get them, making do with whatever they could find. Each of the artists conceived and planned his own domain; it was Thatcher's role to clear the way for them, get the equipment needed, or the budget to buy it, any way he could. It turned out that manufacturers of plastics and electronics supplies were only too happy to offer materials, so long as their names were listed in the show's catalog.

The concept seemed ridiculously simple. Just take a room or an area and make it your own, Thatcher instructed the artists. Create an environment. It may be aesthetically familiar, or wholly inventive, whatever you please—so long as the idea is practical. (Athos Philippides was not. He began by wanting to construct a gigantic tank in his room, filled with underwater vegetation and hordes of angelfish and gouramis. Thatcher said no when his engineers despaired of sealing a room off that would be watertight and able to resist so many pounds of pressure.)

Finally the rooms were planned, one by one.

The first was entirely filled with sand, sand in heaps and slopes and miniature dunes. To keep this portable desert from flowing out into the corridor of the Museum, a special half-entry, like a Dutch door, with ascending and descending stairs, had to be built. To convey the feeling of desert wastes, the thermostat was set at eighty-five degrees, and the walls were flooded with an intense white light to suggest the blinding sun. Most visitors were content to peer over the half-door, flinch, and move on to the next room. Those who did enter were requested to abandon their shoes, like hope, behind them, and stride barefoot through the shifting sands. "In sand is the beginning of all life and the end," wrote the artist in the catalog. "The earth, fresh-torn from the sun, and cooling; or blasted bare and dry at the apocalypse, and hanging like a cinder in the mute firmament. Peace! . . ."

A second room was filled with large blocks of styrofoam painted in primary colors, and hanging spheres of foam rubber, gently agitated, swinging silently back and forth, colliding inevitably with the spectators.

A third room was all revolving lights and crackling electronic sounds, suggesting now the pulses of radio energy voyaging from distant stars, now the amplification of heartbeats, stroking, hammering, with the *whu-whump, whu-whump, whu-whump* rhythms of systole and diastole. Sometimes there could be heard a long, thin, piercing note—like a scream for help carried from some far corner of the galaxy.

Bolo Van Buren's room was deceptively plain. The area was a completely darkened cell—so dark you could not, literally, see your hand in front of your face. Is that all, was the usual first response; do we just *stand* here with our own thoughts? Not quite. Bolo had wired the walls so that every five minutes tiny yellow points of light in pairs and clusters erupted around the walls and in the corners and along the floor of the room. At the same time came nibbling, skittering, creaking sounds that seemed to emanate from all parts of the chamber—from behind the spectator, over his head, at his feet—most of all from between the pairs of tiny glowing eyes. So convincing was the illusion that you could almost feel the harsh prickle of fur and the rasp of claws on flesh.

"What I haven't been able to figure out," Bolo said, "is how to get everybody who comes in here bitten with real rat teeth. Wish I could get the smells pumped in, too. . . . The smell of busted sewer pipes. Stale milk and rotten cabbage and moldy potatoes. Dried piss. Gas leaks and plaster dust—cans of spit. And the blood of our abused children. . . ."

Only Elizabeth Oppenheimer's room remained enigmatic to Thatcher. The walls were calcimined and left bare. On the floor Bess threw an enormous canvas drop cloth, covered with years of dried paint. In its random profusion of color, the cloth looked like an action painting. Thatcher supposed that was what Bess was after.

"Not it," she said. "Not at all. It's going to be *me* in there."

"You mean you're going to exhibit yourself?"

"Mostly. The artist in his own environment."

"But we're open a long day, Bess. If you plan to be in there during exhibition hours, you'll be eating up a lot of your working time—seven hours a day."

"Oh, I won't be here all that time. I'll make special appearances. We can put a sign up—'Artist here from two to four'—something like that."

"I still don't see what you're after."

"What I want is a room that's going to change day to day and minute to minute. The way everything else changes, including life itself. Who cares about art that stays the same forever? I'm after the art of differences. It'll change every day, because the people will be taking part. It's got to be free-flowing, you see? If you were a woman, you'd know what I mean."

He didn't know, and he didn't press. In the end, Thatcher agreed to let Bess do what she wanted, which was to enter the room herself at selected times each day with paint cans and brushes, to become part of her own environment.

The show opened early in February. By then Thatcher was on the verge of physical exhaustion. He had lost eight pounds, Lise noticed, concerned for his health.

"Doesn't matter," he said. "I was getting flabby, anyway."

What Thatcher could not communicate to Lise, or to anyone else, was the exhilaration he felt about putting this show together. So many members of the staff, Alex Gibbs and George Trueblood among them, had doubted it could be done at all. Cooperation with a group of militant artists to stage an exhibition? Impossible. But it *had* been done, and quickly. He was dead tired; he had neglected much of his paperwork; he had refused most invitations. But now it was ready, and he felt buoyant, sanguine, almost light-headed. The rabbits had all leapt out of the hat, the doves had flown out of his sleeves. The night before the opening he slept three hours, most of it in a chair in his office. The night after, he slept for sixteen, in his own bed.

The critics were predictably cool to the show, pointing out that its concept was hardly new—new perhaps to New York art-goers, but already a cliché in Paris and, for that matter, in Spokane. And when you got right down to it, what did it mean? What was its significance?

Public reaction to the show was curious. Thatcher had thought the show would encourage in people a certain euphoria, a feeling of carefree participation. It ought to have soothed them as a pleasant escape from the difficulty of thinking about art. Instead, most viewers were reduced to silence by the rooms, and seemed more preoccupied with trying to puzzle out their meanings than they would have been in the face of more conventional art.

Thatcher stood for long periods of time watching the crowds after the opening, or circulating among them like Harun al-Rashid, unknown among his subjects. Watching people look at art fascinated him. He wished he could read lips, or better still, minds. What were they thinking about? And what were they looking for, streaming by in lines and rows, an unceasing throng snaking through the Museum from opening until closing, day after day? Was it this museum one day, the Modern the next, the Metropolitan and Guggenheim the day after? Mal Crawford had once tried out a questionnaire, but all they had learned was that 49.1 percent of the visitors came to see the permanent collections, 43.2 percent to see new exhibitions, and the balance came in because they happened to be passing by and the weather was threatening. So what did they know now? No question-naire could reach the private recesses of a human being, where motives live out their fleeting existence.

What Thatcher feared most was that people came to the Museum much as they might go to church, conditioned to believe that great art emitted an aura, a divine afflatus of some kind which would im-prove the soul by proximity, much as the stale air of a church sanctuary, the odors of moldering prayer books and hymnals, the cross hanging before a stained-glass window, are supposed to induce spiritual vibrations and leave their beholders morally elevated.

Despite the lack of obvious enthusiasm, Thatcher's new show was considered a success. People were coming in large numbers to see it.

Then, suddenly, "Dimensions" became a scandal.

It was Bess Oppenheimer's room. Bess came regularly to the room the first few days, moving among the spectators, silent for the most part, glowering now and then, flaunting a huge Women's Lib button, crouching down in a corner when she felt tired. Sometimes she would eat a salami sandwich and drink a can of beer, tossing the debris into a trash can nearby. It was reported that she had insulted a few visitors, but that was just her way of haranguing people about women's rights.

No, it wasn't Bess herself—it was her walls.

Whether she was there or not, Bess left cans of paint and brushes at hand, invitingly open to everyone who came in—friends, other artists, casual spectators.

Many responded to her invitation.

At first the graffiti were the basic inscriptions found in any subway station or nightclub lavatory: four-letter words, familiar expletives, crude drawings of sexual organs and scrawled telephone numbers along with offers of explicit sexual relief. These were objectionable enough to the squeamish. They were nothing to the profanations that began to appear on Bess's walls after the excesses of sexual hyperbole had peaked; after all, what familiar obscenity could shock these days?

It was toward the end of the first week that the graffiti began to change character. They were anti-Semitic. "GO BACK TO EGYPT, YID." "BURN DOWN YOUR NEIGHBORHOOD SYNAGOGUE TODAY." They were anti-black. "BLACK IS BESTIAL." "SUPPORT RHODESIAN INDUSTRY." No minority escaped defamation—no majority, either. "THE POPE IS A FAMILY MAN—AND A FRIEND OF FRANK SINATRA'S." "KEEP THE REDSKIN DRUNK." "EXTERMINATE WASPS." "DEPORT THE FAGGOTS TO SWEDEN." Then the legends rose in crescendo to a kind of nihilism, a dark loathing of everything human. "MOTHER HOOD." "STERILIZE EVERYBODY (BUT ME)." Every function, every aspiration, every human hope was desecrated; every prejudice pandered to. "BEATING MEAT BEATS EVERYTHING." Over and over the talismanic words. "BLOW." "KILL." "HATE." "ZERO." The pictures too became increasingly obscene: twisted bodies, deformed faces, men in a host of repellent animal poses, women giving birth to horrible insects. The walls by now seethed with corruption; they had gone entirely mad.

"Close the room," Alex Gibbs advised Thatcher.

"No."

"For God's sake, why not?"

"I gave my word."

"What difference does that make to a maniac like Elizabeth Oppenheimer? She's determined to bring us down. For all we know this is some kind of planned guerrilla action."

"Look, that room's as repulsive to me as it is to you," Thatcher said. "It's painful to think of anyone fouling her own nest so completely."

"*Our* nest."

"I want to talk to Bess before I close the room. If she agrees to have the mess painted over, I'll let it stay open."

"You're running a terrible risk, trusting that bitch."

"Well—"

"That's the best advice I can give you, Lloyd. Act soon."

As soon as Bess was scheduled for her next appearance in the room, Thatcher went downstairs to see her. She was standing just inside the door, her back to the shower of obscenities splashed against the calcimine. As Thatcher stood in the doorway, a man in a pea jacket approached the can of red paint.

"Okay with you, Bess?" he asked.

"Go right ahead, love."

He dipped the brush into the paint and began to shape crude block letters on one of the few areas of the room that remained blank. The man wore a look of rapture on a face as tightly clenched as a fist.

"MOTHER" he wrote. He stood lost in thought for some time before going on.

"MOTHER MARY:"

Again he hesitated, and then painted: "YOUR SON IS BRAIN-DAMAGED."

"Does it give you pleasure?" Thatcher asked Bess.

"I accept it," she said grimly, rather in the manner of Margaret Fuller accepting the universe.

210

"Well, then." He lifted one of the brushes from the bucket of red paint. "May I take a turn?"

Bess looked up warily. "All right."

As she watched, Thatcher jabbed the brush against the nearest wall and drew a broad obliterating swipe of paint through the words "MOTHER FUCKERS" and a return swipe through "COCK SUCKERS." He bent down to the paint can and raised the dripping brush again to the graffiti. Back and forth, back and forth, until the brush had gone dry.

"You can't take it," Bess said contemptuously.

Thatcher stopped and turned to her. "It's ugly, Bess!"

"The slums are ugly, too. The toilets of subway stations are ugly. Our streets. Manhattan is a cesspool. Why stop at bringing it into the Museum?"

"Because you haven't transformed it into art—you've just set it down. It's non-art, Bess. Anti-art."

"Who are you to decide what is and isn't art? You don't deny that collages are art, but a newspaper clipping pasted into a collage is still a newspaper clipping."

"Bess, I'm eager to see artists push their work to the limits of experimentation—even if that means going right into the heart of nothingness, where the real terror is. I'm with the artist so long as he is an artist—a maker. When it comes to playing with excrement and calling it art, I balk. It's meaningless."

"Are you so afraid to read the writing on the wall? Your artificial standards of art have to be broken down, that's all. If shit is needed to do it, then bring on the shit."

"Broken down by superior means of expression, not by throwing art away."

"Art is the point, not the expression of it. The concept, not the object. We're all suffocating under the weight of objects. This Museum is a goddam warehouse of objects."

"*You* may be surfeited. You think you speak for everybody?" A line of Auden's floated into his mind: "Without conscious artifice, we die." It had always seemed as true of art as it was of existence.

He shifted tack. "As human beings, we're capable of monstrous things, Bess, we all know that. Crimes of every kind. That's man at his worst, the way you see him in this room. But he's also capable of the supreme exercise of the imagination—in works of art as nearly immortal as anything on earth. If you want to throw all that away and go back to chaos as our first principle—"

"Yes! Back to the beginning. Back to change. Your kind of art is hopeless, Thatcher. Lifeless."

"Maybe. And maybe you say that because you're bored with making art and just don't want to try any more."

"Bored!"

"This room isn't the answer, Bess," Thatcher said gently. "Any more than imbecility is the answer to neurosis."

"It's here—whether you like it or not."

"Not for long, I'm afraid. Either we paint over these graffiti before the end of the day, or else this room will be locked and nobody allowed in it again. Not even you."

"You sanctimonious son-of-a-bitch male chauvinist—"

"Watch it, Bess."

"My being here in the first place is a rank example of tokenism—" she began.

"Now Bess, you know better."

"If you close my room, women will have no voice in this show at all."

"You're spouting nonsense."

A thick lock of gray hair had fallen across her forehead and the bridge of her nose; she was broad-nostriled, Thatcher observed, like a cat. She blew the stray lock of hair out of the way.

"I thought you were *for* us!"

"I am for you, Bess. But either the room is cleaned up, or we close it."

"That's a hell of a choice."

"It's all you have."

He headed down the corridor toward the office wing, then turned and smiled back at her.

"Unless you want to campaign for women's rights *outside* the Museum."

Close the room, Gibbs had said. This way was better.

"Close the room," Ira Garvey demanded.

Thatcher found Garvey waiting for him when he returned from the exhibition hall and his confrontation with Bess. Garvey's face was tight with anger—in part, Thatcher assumed, because he had been kept waiting longer than the statutory quarter of an hour he allowed the subordinates of this world to keep him in attendance. He had come, of course, with no warning, to issue this flat-out order.

"No, sir."

"Thatcher, I'm astonished," Garvey said, shaking his head in a schoolmasterish fashion, "that you haven't closed it already, on your own authority—"

"I have my reasons."

Garvey went right on. "—that you would wait for me to do so."

"I'm not."

"Then what in heaven's name *are* you waiting for, man?"

"For Bess Oppenheimer to agree that the room has to be restored to some sane condition. I think she will."

Garvey dismissed this with the barest wave of his hand. "Alex Gibbs said you had some odd feeling of obligation to this woman. I don't understand your toleration. Are you trying to achieve sainthood?"

"It's her room, Ira, but so far as we know, Bess hasn't put anything on the walls herself. This is all the work of other people."

"She gave them the *tabula rasa* to write these vile things. The opportunity and probably the encouragement. She must be held responsible for them."

"I want her to accept her responsibility—and I believe she will."

"That woman is a dangerous agitator. She dishonors us. Her room should be closed immediately, whether she agrees to change it or not."

"She will—I'm convinced of it. I've just talked to her, Ira. She's an artist, whatever else may be said about her, and she's hardheaded enough to want to stay in the show. Let me handle it my way. And Ira—"

"What?"

"Have you seen the room yet?"

Garvey jumped to his feet. "Seen it? No, I have not!" He turned toward the door. "I've heard enough about it—from other trustees, from friends—I've read about it in the *papers!*"

"It's a grotesque experience," Thatcher said.

"It's hideous!" said Garvey, almost shouting.

"So is much of contemporary life. And art, by its nature, reflects it." The words sounded familiar. Of course—he was echoing Bess. The ambiguity of his position distressed him, for he did not like

Bess's room, despised it, in fact. But neither did he like Garvey's vehement dismissal of it.

"Don't try to put me off with sophistry," Garvey said. "Do you think I've led a sheltered life, that I'm shocked by a handful of obscene words? There is virtually no human ugliness I haven't seen, Thatcher—and not just in books. But to set this filth into a museum and try to dignify it by calling it art—I can't accept that kind of reasoning. And I can't believe *you* do—everything I thought we believed this museum stands for. It's not just bad art, Thatcher, it's the end of art, as far as I can see. It's—it's—"

Whatever word Garvey was groping for, death or nihilism or some even darker concept of the corrupted spirit, eluded him. He looked suddenly much older to Thatcher, as though he had come face to face with some force beyond reason, a disease beyond any healing power, some failure of humanity for which his whole long and productive life had left him utterly unprepared.

He looked at Thatcher in desperation.

"Lloyd," he said quietly. "Do you know what you're doing?"

"Yes, sir."

"I wish I could understand your position—"

"I want the room closed, just as you do, Ira—but without violence, without a disagreeable clash of personalities. And I hope to avoid damaging publicity."

"Admirable, perhaps, in most situations," Garvey said. "Not in this one. *Do* you understand, though?. . ." He waved his hand in a loose arc. "All of it? The whole thing—and what it might mean?"

He did not seem to expect an answer to his question; nor did Thatcher try to give one.

He turned and walked out of Thatcher's office without a backward glance.

Within fifteen minutes, Dolan was on his direct security wire to Thatcher.

"That room is closed," he reported.

"So Bess gave in. Quicker than I expected," said Thatcher.

"Her? *She* didn't close it. Ira Garvey just posted two guards at the door of the room. No one is allowed in."

"Oh Christ," Thatcher groaned. "Where's Bess?"

"Still inside."

Thatcher dropped the phone back on its cradle. "Son-of-a-bitch," he murmured, and rubbed his eyes.

At the door of Bess's room Thatcher saw a crowd gathered in the hallway, noisy and growing rapidly in size. Pressing his way through, he reached the two guards who stood on either side of the door. Beyond them, leaning insolently against the door frame, was Bess Oppenheimer.

"You see, Thatcher?" she called out. "I'm in confinement here—a prisoner of the male power structure!"

"You can leave any time you please, Miss Oppenheimer." It was Dolan, walkie-talkie in hand, standing at the right of the guards. Next to him, and obviously giving him instructions, was Ira Garvey.

"No sir—I'm under house arrest," said Bess. "This is my room, isn't it? I'm supposed to be in here talking to people. Well, where are the people?"

"Dolan!" Thatcher called out.

"Yes, Lloyd?"

"Come over here, please."

Dolan hesitated. He looked questioningly at Garvey who nodded to him. Only then did the security officer walk over to Thatcher.

"Yes?"

"Clear the crowd away," Thatcher said. "Take one of the guards and see if you can't get people moving."

Dolan and a guard set about carrying out Thatcher's order. "Move back . . . move along now," they told the bystanders. "Nothing's going to happen. There's nothing here to see." The bystanders had moved less than ten feet.

He returned to Thatcher's side. "That's about the best we can do."

"That'll do for now," Thatcher said. "They were all too close, it wasn't safe. Dolan . . ."

"Yes, sir."

"I want you to listen carefully." Out of the corner of his eye, Thatcher saw Ira Garvey approaching them, and he raised his voice. "According to the regulations of this Museum, which you know well, the director is responsible for the safety and welfare of the Museum, its works of art, and its patrons."

"He is given these responsibilities by the board of trustees," Garvey interrupted.

"But he *is* given them, you both know it," Thatcher said. He turned to the two guards. "Step away from that door."

The guards looked at Dolan in bewilderment. Dolan turned expectantly to Garvey, but the doctor stood rigid, neither speaking nor making any gesture of confirmation or denial.

"Step away!" Thatcher repeated.

Finally the guards moved away from the door.

"Lloyd!" It was Ira Garvey's voice. "If you open that room again—"

"The room will stay open until I give the order to close it," Thatcher said. "I'm sorry, Ira, you don't have the right to give that order without my agreement."

"Stubborn and defiant!" Garvey snapped. "You are both these things, Lloyd, and a fool into the bargain, apparently."

Thatcher stared directly into the doctor's narrowed eyes. "Do you deny me the authority I have been given?"

The men held their eyes fixed on each other. Thatcher noticed the perspiration on Garvey's forehead, and then suddenly realized that he was holding his own breath. Out of the corner of his eye he could see Dolan standing nearby, frozen, his authority drained, his face a mask of indecision. And at the door of the room, watching with an air of amused condescension and contempt, Bess Oppenheimer.

A group of visitors passing by in the distance laughed loudly. The sound echoed in the narrow hall. Garvey flinched; so did Thatcher.

"No, damn you!" Garvey exploded suddenly. "I do *not* deny you your authority. It's the board's to give—but it's yours to use."

At last Thatcher took a deep breath; he could not have held back an instant longer, or kept his eyes an instant more on Garvey's.

Thatcher turned to Dolan.

"The room is not to be closed," he said, "unless I give the order for it." Then he spoke to the guards. "I want a path cleared through the crowd for Dr. Garvey so he can reach his car."

Garvey said nothing.

Both guards seemed quite terrified, torn between the orders from Thatcher and their fear of Garvey and Dolan. They shuffled up to Garvey and stood awkwardly beside him, looking back to Dolan in mute appeal.

"Are you ejecting me from this museum?" Garvey asked softly.

"I'm asking you to leave now for your own good—and ours."

"Under guard!" Garvey snorted. "I consider that I'm being ejected."

"Have it your way."

With his unwilling bodyguard scrambling clumsily after him, and then trying to keep a path cleared for him, Garvey strode out, a figure small, erect, and fierce in his wrath.

"Well now," said Dolan. He whistled softly. "This is something for the memory book."

"Let the crowd into the room," Thatcher said.

"They're already there."

And so they were. Milling about at the door of the room, too, pressing their way inside. Thatcher felt distaste rise in him—for Bess, for the people streaming into the place and staring at the obscenities on the walls.

"Our hero!" said Bess Oppenheimer in a brassy contralto which easily reached Thatcher over the dull ground-bass of the crowd. He ignored her.

First round for our side, he thought. A memorable encounter, to recast Dolan's exclamation. But the taste in his mouth was not that of victory.

23

A MARCH STORM drifted up the coast that night and folded the city in its icy shrouds. Sleet and rain pelted the windows of Thatcher's apartment with the force of a thwarted blizzard.

A glorious night to sleep, but not for Thatcher; even the Doriden tablet he took at three-thirty failed to have any effect. His imagination was fully awake, struggling to predict what Garvey would say when they next talked. Would it mean another lecture, of which he'd already had his fill—or would a simple apology from Thatcher be sufficient? After all, Bess's room had been closed at the end of the day and would be repainted in the morning before the Museum opened, so *that* issue had been defused.

At four o'clock Thatcher rose and groped his way downstairs to the bar. Helping himself to a tumbler of straight scotch, he went into his study and tried to read a mystery, but for once Lord Peter Wimsey's whimsy failed to quiet or distract him. His mind remained clear and wakeful; he sat and stared out into the waning storm and the first approach of dawn.

On the way back to his room, he paused at the entrance to Susie's room. He could see her lying rolled in her blanket across the bed, next to a huge stuffed kangaroo outlined by the light streaming from her bathroom. Around the room were distributed a whole menagerie in cloth and wool: zebra, panda, kitten, basset hound, and raccoon—the childish things she refused to put away. Walls and bookcase shelves bore the artifacts of her adolescence: peace banners,

Moratorium posters, a squash racquet and a mandolin, photographs of abandoned Korean children, and an enlarged still from Franco Zeffirelli's production of *Romeo and Juliet*. She sighed in her sleep—a lovely child—then as she turned in her bed the thick blond hair fell away from her face and she seemed transformed into a woman, with a woman's sweetly curved body.

Thatcher closed the door of the room silently. Across the hall Lorraine was snoring in a thin, fluty tenor. Since her return from Baltimore she had been preoccupied, distant, as though half-listening always for the shrill injunction of a telephone bell. The phone rang often; but the call Lorraine was awaiting still had not come.

Thatcher had not said a word to either of them about the events in the Museum that day. Why spoil their sleep as well as his own?

Garvey's summons arrived that morning, brought to Thatcher by one of the seedy-looking old men who scuttle back and forth across the city with so many of its messages.

"Expecting you at 2:10 at the Clinic," it read. "Please be prompt."

Thatcher felt somewhat relieved, although he did wonder with some amusement at Garvey's use of a messenger service instead of a simple telephone call.

Thatcher was careful to arrive at precisely nine minutes past two. He was shown in immediately. This time Garvey was hunched behind his huge oak desk, its surface clean and glowingly polished. The doctor toyed with a quartz paperweight shaped like a skull.

He nodded; there was no other greeting, though he beckoned Thatcher cordially toward a chair.

"Ira, I want you to know first that I regret what happened yesterday," Thatcher began.

"I regret it too, Lloyd—exceedingly."

Thatcher tightened his fist along his trouser legs and went on. Garvey's eyes—open, candid, thoughtful—remained fixed on his face.

"I hope you don't still believe it was out of arrogance that I acted as I did."

Garvey did not reply. Drumming his fingers lightly on the desk top he coughed—impolitely, it seemed to Thatcher.

"The Bess Oppenheimer business is over. The room was closed and redecorated. Without incident, as I said it would be."

Garvey nodded, but looked away from Thatcher.

"My position was that Bess was wrong, but that we shouldn't force the matter to a crisis. I believe that events have borne me out. However, I am sorry for any embarrassment you were put to—and I wish our dispute had not taken place. Perhaps, though, it'll serve to clear the air."

"Lloyd," said Garvey, leaning forward. "I'm sorry too. I am in sympathy with you, believe me. But this kind of thing won't do. I must ask for your written resignation, within the week, for whatever explanation strikes you as most persuasive. Shall we say—for personal reasons?"

"One week?" Thatcher did not recognize his own voice.

"By next Monday."

"For what happened yesterday? Is what we said irrevocable?"

"Every moment of life is irrevocable," Garvey replied. "And, of course, there are other reasons. The fact is, I've consulted with other members of our executive committee and we're in agreement that you are no longer the proper man to be director of this museum."

The executive committee, Thatcher thought. Ira Garvey. Dexter Llewellyn. Harry Mountjoy. Austin Vanderhanks. And Serena Lord. *Serena?*

"I should say that the Museum is prepared to be most generous, besides living up to its contractual obligations. . . ."

It was absurd, but Thatcher felt, even as he tried to sort out his reactions, that the foremost one just now was embarrassment.

"Shouldn't this all be dealt with at a board meeting?"

"A board meeting would reflect unfavorably upon you and the Museum. None of us wants that."

When Garvey rose from his desk, Thatcher was glad. He needed time to think, to react. And surely anything was preferable to prolonging this meeting.

"And, Lloyd, I want you to know, I'm—heartsick about this. I wouldn't have wanted it to happen for anything."

The surgery, so far as Garvey was concerned, was now accomplished. Was it the doctor's fault if the patient did not survive?

It was still dark when Thatcher came awake with a convulsive shudder, the echo of his own voice hanging like a scream in the overheated room, for he had cried out in his sleep.

Once again he had dreamed of Jeanne. He was traveling this time to the cemetery in Evanston where she had been buried ten years ago, down a familiar green alley thickly shaded with maple trees and a few elms that had survived the blight, out into the sun where bees swarmed over the marigolds, roses, petunias in dense clusters, all colored like a cheap Swiss art reproduction, aureoles of red and gold flickering about the heads of the flowers as though spurts of printer's ink had leaked out in the impression.

Now Thatcher was standing before the grave site in a cold sweat. There was no stone, though he had watched it laid there himself. The earth had been turned back in reddish-gray heaps—freshly turned back, for some of the soil was still damp and jeweled with bright fragments of mica. The grave was empty.

Back now to the gatehouse, confronting an elderly caretaker: *What has become of my wife?* The old man ill at ease, defensive. *No Thatcher buried here, young man.* Flipping through his ledgers again, frightened perhaps by Thatcher's desperate insistence. *Wait now, there's a Thatcher going to be buried here this afternoon—*

"No. NO!"

What the hell day was it? Monday.

A week, that was all he had. He remembered now.

What a stupid, obvious dream! The old man, of course, was Garvey, and he, Thatcher, the corpse to be buried.

Without a struggle?

Thatcher pieced together isolated fragments of his interview with Ira Garvey. Two choices: resign or be fired. The executive committee on Garvey's side. Thatcher expected to do the dignified thing, to write a graceful letter of resignation. *Without a struggle.*

Perspiring heavily, he threw off first the bed covers and then his pajama top.

And what do you think you're going to do? asked Thatcher of Thatcher in the humid darkness. *Fight back? With what weapons?*

My record at the Museum is good.

Go on.

I've worked hard.

So? It's results that count, not effort.

And I've had only six months. That's not time enough to judge results. I've only just started on my program.

That, at least, is accurate.

If I can line up support. . . .

Who? Your daughter? Your sister? Lise? The gracious Serena Lord?

Lise and Serena won't be the only ones who'll stand by me.

But are you sure you want this damned job?

What kind of question is that? I never wanted any job more than this one.

And now?

I'll admit the job is a ball-breaker. . . .

Will you admit you just can't handle it?

So maybe it's too much for any man. But if I had capable assistance, strong administrative support. . . .

Bullshit.

All right, it's gotten to be too much—trying to hold to my concept of what it should be, and also making certain all the johns flush properly . . . letting the curators spread their wings, and handling the care and feeding of trustees. It's like a machine running out of control—heading for the edge of a cliff—and I'm trying to steer it without bringing it to a stop. . . .

Now you're making some sense.

Well, maybe I can't hang on—but I can't walk off without a fight, either. Besides, with some luck, I could even—

Here we go again. . . .

Just before daylight, Thatcher finally fell into a deep sleep, his body cold and damp, his mouth set in something like a smile.

24

THATCHER BREAKFASTED with Lorraine and Susie in his usual, hurried Monday-morning fashion. The only difference was that he was playing the role of himself for all he was worth.

It helped. Somehow, after all, he was going to have to get through the week ahead of him.

At the Museum he greeted Lise warmly and asked about her weekend at Stowe.

"Only fair to middling."

"Not enough snow?"

"Not enough sun. We didn't ski much."

He would tell her today, of course, but not now. "Lise, see if you can get Austin Vanderhanks for me."

When she buzzed him a minute later, he pressed the extension button instead of the intercom: "Austin, it's Lloyd."

"Mr. Thatcher? This is Gloria."

Gloria Tronson was Austin Vanderhanks's executive assistant, and no one reached Vanderhanks save through her. Indeed, some callers never even achieved Gloria Tronson.

"Mr. Vanderhanks is on a cruise, Mr. Thatcher. He won't be back until next week."

"Have you a phone number for him? Address?"

"He's on holiday. Completely sequestered. May I help?"

"I think not, thanks. When did he leave?"

"Last Friday."

Before he could have learned of Garvey's decision, Thatcher thought, with a surge of hope.

"I'm sorry to hear that. That is—I envy him the trip."

"Don't we all?" said Gloria Tronson. "I'll tell him you called when he gets back, Mr. Thatcher. How's the Museum?"

"Fine, thank you."

"I just love that place, I wish I could get there more often. But we're so busy here, you know, especially when Mr. Van is gone."

And that was that. Thatcher didn't realize until after he'd hung up how much he'd counted on speaking to Vanderhanks. It was hard to believe Garvey would make a decision like this without discussing it with him.

And what about the other members of the executive committee?

It could hardly do much good to talk to Dexter Llewellyn. He'd seen Dexter only once since their last disastrous meeting, at the "Dimensions" opening. Llewellyn had nodded to him but kept his distance. Still, the idea of crowding Llewellyn into a corner somehow appealed to Thatcher, and he dialed Llewellyn's apartment in Kip's Bay.

Winthrop Briggs answered the phone.

"You want Dexter? Who shall I say is calling, please?"

"Lloyd Thatcher."

"Oh, I should've recognized *your* voice. Just a moment—I'll call him."

After a delay so long that Thatcher's ear ached where the receiver was pressed against it, Llewellyn came on.

"Dexter, I'm sure you know why I'm calling. I realize that our recent meetings have been—unsatisfactory—and I know you don't agree with some of my plans and methods."

Llewellyn grunted something incomprehensible.

"But may I suggest, quite respectfully, that this is a time to be calm and deliberate—not to act hastily? The feelings of the staff, the future of our program, the fund-raising campaign—all these things could suffer serious setbacks if the Museum were without a director for even a short time."

"Possibly. I'm afraid, though, there's nothing I can do for you. So far as I'm concerned, this is the best thing for you *and* the Museum."

Thatcher summoned his calmest, most reasonable tones. "All I'm asking is the opportunity to sit down and talk with the members of the executive committee. I'm sure if you made such a suggestion to Ira—"

"I've already talked to Ira. I told him exactly what I thought. Lloyd, there's simply no use discussing it further. . . ."

Thatcher hung up the receiver with both his curiosity and his sense of irony satisfied.

When he called Harry Mountjoy's office, Mountjoy's secretary gave him the broker's home number. Calling there, Thatcher got a recorded announcement which gave him twenty seconds to leave a message.

Beep.

Thatcher muffled his voice with the palm of his hand: "This is also a recording. Today's Bible verse: 'It is easier for a camel to go through the eye of a needle, than for a rich man to enter into the kingdom of God.' Dial nine-oh-one for absolution."

Now there was only Serena left. He dreaded the call. If she too had turned against him, who else could he ask for support? No, the telephone wouldn't suffice. He must do what was unforgivable in Manhattan—drop in and see her unannounced.

"I'm sorry to drop in without warning—"

"Nonsense, you mustn't be, it's a charming idea. I've often wished more people would."

So today Serena was going to be the *grande dame*. Thatcher wondered if he would be able to reach the woman he respected, under that glossy surface.

Best to plunge in, and see.

"Serena," he said. "Do you know what's been happening at the Museum lately?" A bad beginning—it sounded as though he was about to give her the exhibition schedule.

"Ira spoke to me. . . . I assume you want coffee?" She rang for her maid.

"Serena—"

"As I was saying, Ira did speak to me."

"Will you help? I hate to ask you in such a direct way, but I don't have much time."

"Ira is extremely sorry for what has happened," she said, ignoring his apology. "But Lloyd—he's made an extremely convincing case against you."

"Though I have yet to find out what it is."

"You *must* know."

225

"I'm taking nothing for granted, Serena. I want it all spelled out."

"Well, what do you expect me to do?"

"To begin with, how about insisting on a full meeting of the board to take up any charges against me?"

"Lloyd, if charges are brought against you, they could damage your whole future. Surely you can see that."

"Do you believe the charges?"

"That's not the point."

"It's important to me to know, Serena. As important as knowing just what they are."

The maid brought in the tray, and Serena poured coffee for him. Thatcher ignored the steaming cup.

"I have to know what I'm facing," he said. "Is the run-in with the artists—"

"That's part of it."

"Then my loyalty to the Museum *is* in question. . . . It wouldn't help, I suppose, to tell you how much I love the Museum—how hard I've tried to direct it well?"

"You shouldn't have to ask that question, Lloyd. In any case, you simply must be more hard-minded. To Ira intentions mean little or nothing."

"In the time I've had—"

"I'm sorry, Lloyd. You see, I love the Museum, too. I don't think you realize quite how much. I've begged money for it. I've given parties and dances, held auctions and attended meetings that bored me out of my skin, all for the Museum, and for over ten years."

"Still—"

"*And* I think that now would be the worst possible time for us to have an open fight in a board meeting—or any other public scandal."

· "Because of the fund-raising."

"Not just that. We are in jeopardy—in every way."

"So you're with Ira Garvey, then."

"With the Museum," she countered. "And I *hate* what he's doing to you. God, I wish you'd listened when I warned you about Ira."

"We were bound to clash over one issue or another. I always thought we could resolve the question of authority—whether he was going to run the Museum or I was."

"And then to turn your back on help offered to you—to reject Aaron Redburn—and me. . . ."

She flushed and bit her lip. Was it herself she mean.—tha.
moment here in her house when everything had seemed possible?

Perhaps not, but as they both stood up he knew she was remem-
bering that evening.

"There's something else," she said after a pause. "We came
awfully close, didn't we?"

"I know."

"Lloyd, it could have been any way you wanted it."

Thatcher took her arm as they walked to the foyer. "I have to be
honest with you," he said. "You're much too complex for me. Too
rich, too beautiful, too prominent. None of that might have mattered
except for one thing. So long as you were on the board, I felt helpless
to move."

She withdrew her arm, and held out a hand to Thatcher in a regal
gesture of dismissal.

Saddened and resentful, more than half in love with her, Thatcher
turned away.

That left Oscar Woods and his wife.

"How dare Ira do this without consulting the entire board?" the
professor said when Thatcher called him. "I'll go to him myself, and
if I have to, I'll go to the other board members as well."

"Many thanks—so far you're the only one who'll help."

"I am? Well, that's even more outrageous if it's true. . . . You
must understand, Lloyd, my speaking up probably won't help much.
Ira doesn't have much respect for me, you know. He thinks I'm an
ineffectual old mossback. I'm on the board because I exude a certain
appealing odor of decayed sheepskin."

"But you will try?"

"I'll make an appointment right away. In the meantime, don't
be too discouraged. There are worse things on earth than being fired
by Ira Garvey."

Tuesday. One by one, Thatcher called in the members of his personal staff and told them. He had first thought to call a meeting and
tell them all together, but that seemed too theatrical, and much too
impersonal. And so he faced them singly, ringing the changes on his
disheartening litany as gracefully as he could.

Lise first, for so many reasons. Her reaction was characteristic of
those to come.

"I don't believe it."

"I find it hard to believe too, but it's true."

She blinked. "They can't do this—who does Garvey think he is? You haven't even had a year, and that lousy rotten little man. . . ."

She ranted a while longer, and Thatcher did not try to stop her—it was rather pleasant to hear Garvey dressed down so enthusiastically. She ended by breaking down and crying shamelessly into Thatcher's pocket handkerchief, and, then, all over the shoulder of his jacket.

"One thing is sure," she said finally. "I won't stay one day longer than you do."

"Now hold on," he said. "You shouldn't make a decision like that without thinking it over."

"I just thought it over. It took exactly two seconds."

And then the parade began. One after another, they came into the office—Gibbs, George Trueblood, Homer Karp, Pat Sidney, Ted Porter. Last of all he told Mal Crawford, who kept quiet for three minutes—perhaps his longest conversational silence in years—and then shook his head in dismay. This wouldn't be an easy story to file.

Only Gibbs received the news without apparent surprise.

"I'm sorry," he said after Thatcher had finished. "When you came here, we all had such high hopes. . . ."

"So did I," Thatcher replied. "Especially in you, Alex."

"I hope you don't think I've let you down. . . ."

There was, of course, no point in going into *that*. Gibbs would never admit to any failures as an administrator; nor to any disloyalty on his part if there had been any. Somewhere there had been a breakdown of trust between them—leaving, in its wake, only platitudes.

"A lot of responsibility is going to devolve on you, Alex, until a new director can be found."

"I'll do all I can to help, of course. . . ."

At the end of the morning, Thatcher was near tears himself.

"Thank God it's over," he said to Lise. "I can't repeat this once more—not to anybody."

A few minutes later George Trueblood burst into his office.

"Look here—"

"George—*du calme*," said Thatcher. "*Je t'en prie.*"

"No French," said George. "No *phrases*. I've already met with the others—"

"What others? What are you talking about?"

"Homer, Pat and—we all feel this business is harmful to the Museum. None of us was ever consulted about it, you know."

"That's not surprising, is it?"

"You told me Garvey said you had lost the confidence of your staff. Well, that's patently untrue. *We* all want you to stay. So it's obvious that someone's been spreading rumors."

"It's possible," Thatcher said. "Though we'll probably never know for sure who it was."

"We know," said Trueblood. "And someday justice is going to be done, never fear. Ass will be kicked, good and proper. . . . Now, what we plan to do is go as a delegation, to ask Garvey to reconsider his decision. This afternoon. After all, he can't get along without *all* of us."

"George—"

"Don't try to talk us out of it."

"I wouldn't dream of it," said Thatcher.

"Ira, this is Mal."

"Yes?"

"I've heard about Lloyd Thatcher's resignation and I want you to know I'll back you up any way I can."

"Was there anything else, Crawford?"

"George Trueblood has asked us to present a solid front when we come to see you this afternoon. I just wanted you to know that—well, even though I'll be with the others, I'm on your side."

"The Museum's side, I hope you mean."

"Of course."

"Thank you. Oh, there is one other matter, since you called. All news releases on this matter are to be cleared with me before being sent out. If there are any premature leaks to the press—and I sincerely hope there won't be—direct them to me at once. Is that clear?"

And he rang off.

When the delegation went to the East River Clinic that afternoon, Thatcher learned later, they were greeted cordially and ushered into Garvey's private office. There a group of five chairs had been arranged in a semicircle facing his desk.

("We were entirely dominated by that enormous bulwark at which

Ira Garvey sits and labors," George said to Thatcher. "But we faced the fortress bravely.")

Garvey listened with polite attention to their petition. Trueblood, who had been appointed spokesman, was careful to forgo any use of his beloved rhetoric.

("I was as plain as an old ballet slipper. I asked Garvey if his decision was irreversible, and he said, 'Yes it is.'")

"I appreciate your coming," said Garvey, "but this has been no hasty decision. We are all fond of Thatcher, but he's been difficult, even refractory, for a long time—almost from the beginning. After all, we had so little chance to become acquainted with him before he came to the Museum."

"Hardly his fault," said George.

"He was hired largely on the personal recommendation of Robert Saint-Simon," Garvey said. "And I think it is highly possible that if Robert had lived he too might have changed his mind about Thatcher. Lloyd simply lacks a true leader's ability to inspire confidence."

"Surely you can see he has ours," said Homer Karp.

"Not everybody feels as you do," Garvey said. "There have been other complaints."

"Whose?"

Garvey would not be intimidated. "I cannot say without violating confidences."

"Anyone who has a valid complaint," Pat Sidney said, "should be willing to make it openly."

Garvey said nothing.

Trueblood turned to Garvey. "We think," he said, "that asking Lloyd Thatcher to resign in these circumstances will demoralize the staff. We also feel that—"

"Let me make one thing clear," Garvey said, raising one hand for silence. "I'd be reluctant to see anybody else leave the Museum in Lloyd Thatcher's wake, but if anyone in this room wishes to submit his resignation—or if *everyone* here does—the resignations will be sadly but promptly accepted. Now. Is there anything else you wanted to say?"

("So we flopped. Totally."

"It was worth a try, George," Thatcher said. "I'm grateful."

"When push came to shove, we couldn't do it. We just couldn't threaten to quit."

"That's all right, George—I never expected you to."

"Because, you see, he would have taken us up on it."

"I know he would," said Thatcher. "Believe me, I know.")

Thatcher struggled into his after-hours uniform to go to an opening at another museum, resisting the impulse to cancel. Once there, he made certain he was widely seen and heard.

He could not be sure how many people there knew of his situation; when no one he chatted with gave any indication of knowing what had happened, he began to feel more comfortable. He flagged down the cocktail waiters with increasing frequency, finally bypassing them altogether to fetch his own drinks from the bar.

So far, so good. Well, maybe he was getting loaded—but with *style*.

Mal Crawford and Winthrop Briggs appeared at his side, not quite hand in hand or arm in arm, but obviously a couple.

"Enjoying yourself?" Briggs asked.

"The most beautiful show of this or any other season," Thatcher said. "You may quote me."

"I'm the one who's used to being quoted."

"Well, what will you say about it?"

"A stale and tiresome *olla podrida*," said Briggs. "Thumbs down."

"You always were perverse, weren't you?" Thatcher regretted the words the instant they were uttered. Though he'd tried to keep them light and bantering, their spite content was too high.

"Well!" said Briggs.

"Let's go, Win," Mal said hastily.

"But I'm interested in what Mr. Thatcher has to say, Mal. After all, this may be my last opportunity to get Mr. Thatcher's opinion straight from Mr. Thatcher himself."

"You can get it from Dexter Llewellyn," Thatcher said, "or make it up yourself if you like. By the way, where *is* Dexter tonight?"

"In bed with *la grippe*."

"Who?"

"Now really, Thatcher, that's naughty of you—and not at all bright. How do you expect to find a new job if you go around *offending* people?"

"Come on, Win," said Mal. "Lloyd won't have any trouble finding a new job."

"He can always go back to the boondocks," Briggs said—and suddenly Thatcher realized, without caring, that Briggs was drunk, too. "Dexter says—"

"Oh screw Dexter," said Thatcher.

"Jealous, Lloyd?"

The air of the room was cloudy with cigarette smoke and malice; through a dark red veil of hostility, Thatcher saw Briggs as though he were standing there all alone.

"You miserable little queer," he said in a loud voice. "You can jack off in Dexter Llewellyn's best hat for all I care!" Whole groups of people turned attentively toward him. "You're an abomination as a critic. As for Dexter Llewellyn—" Thatcher stopped, suddenly encircled by hostile faces.

Briggs looked up at Thatcher, and grinned slyly, his tiny white teeth glittering. He looked pleased, even gratified, as though one of his cherished theories had been given the Q.E.D.

"You belong back in the boondocks, Thatcher," he said quietly. "I always did think so."

For Thatcher, that was the end of the party—and the evening. He could imagine easily enough what kinds of stories would spread about *this* episode. ("Museum Director Insults Art Critic"? "Nasty Exchange in Egyptian Wing"? "No Damage to Art Reported"?) Not only had he given his enemies additional ammunition, assuming they cared to use it—he was now burdened with weapons against himself. Can't control your temper any more, can you, Thatcher? Can't hold your goddam liquor, either.

He stood in front of his bathroom mirror, stripped to the waist; his eyes dull, the pupils half-hidden under the swollen lower lids. He swayed back and forth slightly, then gripped the sides of the sink with all his force.

He rummaged through his medicine cabinet, his fingers groping along the cluttered shelves, overturning medicine bottles, boxes, tubes. Where were those damn Doriden tablets? He *must* get some sleep. Found. Why not take them all? Why not, indeed—except that there were only two fat white pellets left in the vial.

He slammed the cabinet door shut. That face again—dissipated, jowly, pasty-gray—staring out of the mirror. There he was, late-twentieth-century man, existentially prepared for suicide, living among incomparably sophisticated instruments of destruction—and without so much as a bare bodkin to his name.

He laughed until his head swam, then tottered toward his bed. Later on he was quite sick in the bathroom. He returned noisily to bed, chortling softly until he fell asleep.

Wednesday—the morning after the dark night of the soul. Hangover time. An hour or so after he was supposed to be up and dressing, Lorraine found him lying in a tangle of sheets and blankets, his face turned toward the wall, his body shaped almost like a question mark.

"What is it, Lloyd?"

"Stomachache. No. Hangover."

"You're sure that's all?"

Thatcher groaned softly. "Cover me, please—I feel cold."

Returning to the kitchen, Lorraine called Lise and told her Thatcher would not be coming in.

"Has he said anything to you about the Museum?" Lise asked.

"No. What do you mean?"

"Oh . . . only that he's been under a special strain lately."

After clearing up her breakfast dishes and renewing the pot of coffee on the stove, Lorraine sat down with some mending and switched on WNYC. Toccata, Adagio, and Fugue in C: music to sew by. Massive, stately sounds pouring down from Johann Sebastian Bach in heaven. Gradually the music absorbed her attention entirely.

Thatcher had been standing in the doorway of the sitting room for several moments before she noticed him, dressed in a bulky flannel bathrobe and wavering on his feet.

"Can I get you anything—food or juice—anything at all?"

"No, thanks," he said. "Except maybe a quick burial. Lorraine—put down your sewing and turn off that radio, will you?"

"Of course."

"I want to talk to you about something that has happened to me," he said. "An accident of sorts."

And that was how Thatcher told his sister the news.

"For God's sake, why didn't you tell me before?"

"I didn't want you worrying until after I'd done everything I could."

233

"You ought to know better than that by now. And what about Susie? She's been worried about you too. Honest to Pete, you should have told us."

Lorraine was given to expressions like "Honest to Pete" and "Ye gods," awful old clinkers that sometimes irritated Thatcher. At moments like this, he found them homey and endearing.

"You'd better lie down again," she said.

Thatcher stretched out full-length on the couch, conscious of a great wooziness, as though he were becoming lighter than air, a monstrous inflated figure in Macy's parade. Lorraine leaned over and touched his forehead.

"You had a fever—it's gone now."

"Yes."

"Lloyd, what do you think you'll do?"

"I don't know yet. If I don't resign, it'll be much harder for us—understand that."

"You mean financially."

"Yes. If I go quietly, they'll be generous. If I make a fuss—"

"Well," she said. "I don't know. We've been short of money, and long on it. I suppose I can manage either way. But Lloyd, you must tell Susie, today. When she comes home from school. Don't let her find out any other way."

"I won't."

'She'll be hurt because you are, but in a way she won't be sorry. We shouldn't have come in the first place—"

"Oh Christ, Lorraine—"

"We've never been at home here, not for a moment, not Susie and me. And what good has it done *you*, after all is said? We should've stayed where we were happy—"

"Now what's the sense of that?" Thatcher said. "Maybe we were happy, and maybe it was a mistake to come here, but what the hell, here we are! It's all over and done."

It suddenly occurred to him that it all probably was.

On Thursday afternoon Thatcher finally spoke to Harry Mountjoy, the Museum's treasurer.

"Lloyd. No doubt you called to talk about the terms."

"Well, Harry. . . ."

234

"I've already spoken with Ira. He's instructed me to set it up for you as generously as possible."

"What I'd really like to know just now," Thatcher said, "is what you think of this situation."

"Well, naturally, Lloyd, I'm sorry as all hell about it. I've enjoyed working with you, and of course it's always a shame when something like this happens. Sometimes, I guess things just don't work out the way you want them to."

"All right, Harry. What am I being offered to resign?"

"One year's salary, starting from the date of formal resignation. And you can keep the apartment for a year."

"As long as I pay the rent, you mean," Thatcher said. Mountjoy chuckled. "That's fine, Harry. I'll think it over."

"You mean—you haven't resigned yet?"

"I was given a week. The week is up Monday."

Harry Mountjoy was silent, reflecting perhaps on Thatcher's peculiar desire to remain in a place where he had been told he was no longer wanted.

"Thank you, Harry, and good-bye."

"Now I hope you won't hold anything against the Museum because of this, y'hear? We're all sure you'll land on your feet. Chances are you'll find a place much better suited to you next time out."

A moment more, and Harry Mountjoy would persuade himself that Thatcher, discontented, had quit his job without warning.

Now he had made all the calls he could; there was no one left who might help. He took up a blank sheet of paper and began writing his resignation.

Dear Ira:

I regret that personal considerations make it necessary for me to submit my resignation as director of the Museum. . . .

That was how Garvey wanted it put—"personal considerations." The hypocrisy in the phrase pained him, for it was his personal considerations, above all else, which had been so systematically neglected these past six months. And for what?

He tore up the sheet of paper and began again:

Dear Ira:

In view of the complete deterioration of our working relationship at the Museum, I have no choice but to offer my resignation. However, I think it would be equally appropriate, and no less satisfactory a solution, if you were to offer yours.

Which one of us is at fault? Which of us, in the circumstances, is acting unreasonably? You, in refusing to allow me to carry out my duties without constant interference—or me, in insisting that I should be allowed to lead this Museum, as firmly and imaginatively as I can, toward the twenty-first century?

Knowing your deep faith in reason as an instrument for the solution of all human problems, I beg you to search your conscience for evidences of failure of reason in your own attitude toward my role. . . .

Once he had read his letter through, he put it aside and went t
Lise.

"Write me a letter of resignation," he said.

"Oh, please. I'd rather do anything than that."

"Do this—I know you can. Make it polite, short, and impersonal—bearing in mind that I'm resigning for personal considerations. Sa nice things about the staff, and nothing about the trustees."

When she brought the letter in for Thatcher to sign it was ever thing he had asked for—succinct, tactful, immaculate. He loathed i

"Here." He handed her the draft of his previous letter to Garve "Try this one out."

Lise read it quickly, her eyes shining.

"Oh, that's *gorgeous!* The finest piece of prose you've ever written "Send it."

"With pleasure."

"And a copy to Austin Vanderhanks," he said, as an afterthough

That evening Thatcher made one call from home.

"Martha? Lloyd Thatcher."

"Hi—what's new at the mausoleum? Haven't seen or heard fro you since that last go-round with the artists. My fault, I suppose."

"You haven't heard any rumors?"

"Should I have?"

236

Despite himself, Thatcher felt miffed. Had no one thought the news sufficiently important to leak it to Martha Crane?

"Look Martha, you may very well get a press release from the Museum any day now, announcing that I'm leaving as director—"

"Do you mean that?"

"Yes. Now, I'll be glad to tell you everything that's happened—if you'll call me when you get an official release from the Museum. *Before* you run any story. At that time, I'll give you the latest developments."

"Why me?"

"I trust you to print the truth, and I want to be sure you get it. Do we have a deal?"

"Tell me."

Thatcher launched into his recital, omitting nothing important. He was still talking when he heard the front door slam and then Susie's voice.

"Up here," he called. Quickly, he wound up his report to Martha.

"It's an awful temptation you've laid in my lap," she said. "But I'll sit on it till it hatches. Be in touch."

They hung up.

Susie came into his bedroom and sat shyly on the edge of his bed. "Daddy?"

"Yes, love?"

"I've been thinking about what you told me yesterday, and I have a suggestion to make. I thought I might drop out of Rowayton and go to public school for a while. It's a pretty expensive place to send me— and it isn't all that great—so why couldn't we economize some?"

Amused and touched, Thatcher drew Susan close to him.

"Now, Susie," he said, "we don't have to worry about money yet. We're not broke—and I don't intend to be. You just stop worrying about expenses and stay in school until we're ready to move."

"Okay. I just thought it might help. . . . Can I get you a drink?"

"Yes. A Negroni. Large glass, ice, twist."

"I remember."

"You know," he said as she headed for the door, "starting any day now we're likely to have a lot more time with each other than we've had for years."

"I'll believe that when it happens, Daddy. But I sure do like the idea."

Ira Garvey telephoned Thatcher early on Friday.

"I got your absurd letter—" he began.

"Good," Thatcher said. "Although, of course, I'm sorry you didn't find it satisfactory."

"I asked for a letter of resignation."

"And I'm asking for a special session of the board of trustees."

When he resumed speaking, Garvey's tone was deceptively gentle.

"I think," he said, "that instead of the settlement worked out with Harry Mountjoy, we'll be giving you three weeks' salary in lieu of notice. Of course, if you change your mind about the resignation. . . ."

"Do not pass Go," Thatcher said softly. "Do not collect two hundred dollars."

"What did you say?"

Thatcher raised his voice. "I don't think so, Ira. But thanks so much for calling."

On Sunday, just as the week was running out, Thatcher got another call. The connection was poor, crackling with static and occasional pops, like distant firecrackers exploding.

"Hello, Lloyd? Austin Vanderhanks."

"Yes, Austin?" He paused and listened to the echo of his words as they were transmitted.

"Miss Tronson opened your letter . . . marked Urgent and Confidential. You understand, that's her job . . . thought it important enough to telex the yacht. . . ."

God bless you, Miss Tronson.

"Lloyd?" Even with the weird sound effects, Vanderhank's voice came through charged with aristocratic indignation. "Will you tell me what the *hell* is going on back there?"

25

THE SPECIAL SESSION of the board of trustees called for the following Friday may not have been the first in the Museum's long history, but no one could remember the last one. The event swept every other consideration aside; the atmosphere was mephitic with speculation, rumor, and accusation. Thatcher had his sympathizers and his detractors—most people, however, stood by like witnesses to a street fight, waiting to see what would happen next.

Thatcher himself, at Austin Vanderhanks' suggestion, spent the first four days of the week at home, while Lise kept him up to date on what was happening.

"The guards are making book," she told him on Thursday.

"What's the morning line?"

"Six to five for dismissal."

"Not so good, is it?"

"All depends on how you look at it. Yesterday it was eight to five."

"Let's wait until it gets to be even money and then put five bucks on me to win. . . ."

On Friday morning, Thatcher got to the Patrons' Room early, following his usual custom. He sat silently with his arms folded while the others arrived, with no papers in front of him. Nor, he noticed, were there pads or pencils anywhere in view. Was this an oversight, or an attempt to keep anyone from taking notes? He would have to watch himself—he was beginning to feel paranoiac.

Not that paranoia would have been surprising in the circumstances. As the trustees came in, they all carefully avoided greeting him and, for the most part, each other. Garvey first, with his assistant Frank Henley, taking a seat opposite Thatcher. Marcus Hammer and Dexter Llewellyn, unsmiling, engaged in an inaudible conversation which they interrupted only to nod at Garvey. Barney Specker, a surprise—Thatcher had heard he was in Acapulco. Harry Mountjoy. Grace Stearnes and Mary Lawless. Professor Oscar Wood and Serena Lord. Fifteen of them, altogether—and Thatcher.

They were waiting for Austin Vanderhanks. The King of Hearts in this peculiar trial, thought Thatcher. Did that make Ira Garvey the Queen of Hearts—*Sentence first, verdict afterwards?* Thatcher smiled for the first time since he'd sat down.

The door to the room was still wide open. Lise Deering suddenly appeared there, beckoning to Thatcher. He shook his head. Stubbornly, she motioned to him again, and he followed her out into the foyer.

"I *am* sorry," she said. "This just came. Actually it was delivered to your apartment, but Susie brought it down, so I read it."

Thatcher looked down at the telegram. He read the sender's name first—Lester Hillman, University of Northern California, Walnut Creek. Chancellor Hillman.

AT LAST BOARD MEETING OF MUSEUM INTEREST EXPRESSED IN YOUR POSSIBLE RETURN TO SAN FRANCISCO. DO NOT KNOW YOUR PRESENT INCLINATIONS BUT IF YOU WOULD CONSIDER COMING BACK PLEASE ADVISE.

REGARDS. LESTER.

Thatcher lifted his eyes to Lise, and smiled again. "Thanks."

"Wonderful coincidence, isn't it?"

"Maybe not. News travels fast."

"You've got to go back in," she said. "Here comes Austin Vanderhanks. But before you do. . . ."

He touched her hair, not minding that someone might see the gesture. "When it's over I'll buy you the best dinner in town. Win or lose."

"Be bold," Lise said. "*Toujours l'audace.*"

When he sat down again, just ahead of Vanderhanks, Thatcher slipped the telegram into the inside pocket of his coat. A piece of body armor, he thought. Right over the heart.

240

"Since this meeting was called partly at my request," Vanderhanks said without preamble, "I've been asked by Ira Garvey to chair it. I assume there will be no objection?" He looked conscientiously around the table, including Thatcher in his query.

"Very well. We have only one order of business on the agenda—a motion on Ira Garvey's part that Lloyd Thatcher be relieved as director of the Museum. Your motion comes already seconded, Ira?"

"By a majority of the executive committee. Three persons voted for the motion. One was absent. One voted against it."

Serena, thought Thatcher.

"We needn't keep this such a deep secret," Dexter Llewellyn offered. "I voted for this motion, and I don't mind saying so."

"Thank you, Dexter. Now—"

"Moreover," Llewellyn went on, "I for one fail to see why a full board meeting is necessary to handle the matter. I thought the executive committee had authority enough."

"Mr. Thatcher has requested a full hearing," replied Vanderhanks, "and I believe he's entitled to it." He looked straight at Garvey as he spoke.

"No objection on my part," Garvey said.

"Then we'll get on with it. Ira, it's your motion."

"If you don't mind," Garvey said, rising, "I'll stand. Not that I consider this a formal process—it seems to me that even the word 'hearing' is rather strong. We're not a jury sitting in judgment on Lloyd Thatcher—but rather officers of the Museum bound by our responsibilities to review his performance to date."

Report card time, Thatcher thought.

"Lloyd Thatcher came here with high recommendations," Garvey said, "though many of us had only a short time—or no time at all—to become acquainted with him. We've had to get to know him through his work. He must therefore be considered—and has been so considered from the beginning—as serving the Museum subject to review."

"Do you mean," Vanderhanks asked, "that his appointment was not official?"

"Certainly it was. Still, anyone on the staff would be on approval. It's a policy of the Museum."

"I believe the trial period is three months, not eight. Did you have any reason after the first three months to ask for his dismissal?"

"No, I did not."

"All right, Ira—please go on."

"I can state the reasons for believing that Lloyd Thatcher is unequal to his position quite simply," Garvey said. "The director of this museum should have the respect and confidence of the trustees and staff. He should be a person of tact, high standards, and vision. When I say vision, I mean also that he should be clear-sighted." Garvey removed his glasses, breathed on them, buffed the lenses with his handkerchief.

"It's certainly no reflection on the sagacity of Mr. Thatcher's distinguished predecessor, who recommended him, or on Mr. Thatcher himself, if he fails to live up to these exacting qualifications. Few men in the art field could. . . ."

So that was to be the melody, Thatcher thought.

". . . It's entirely possible that none of us here might have the stamina to hold down this post." Garvey smiled tolerantly and then went on, offering his diagnosis of the situation: A common enough syndrome, ladies and gentlemen, the man and job just don't make a proper fit. Nobody's fault, really. . . . It happens. . . . "Lloyd Thatcher has undoubtedly done his best according to his lights, but. . . ."

Garvey paused for a moment to sip from a glass of water; Thatcher seized the opportunity and rose.

"Dr. Garvey still has the floor," Vanderhanks said.

"I realize that. However, I'd like to ask one question if I may."

"Please," said Garvey. "Let Mr. Thatcher put his question." He turned to Thatcher amiably. "Lloyd?"

"Dr. Garvey, I appreciate the tone of goodwill you've been showing here, but frankly I'd prefer to hear you state the specific charges against me."

Garvey flushed. "Mr. Thatcher, as I pointed out before, this is not a trial."

"It may not be for you," Thatcher said. "It is for me. My reputation is in the dock, as well as my job. After all, I've directed two major art museums with no serious complaints. Are you claiming that the principles involved in running this museum aren't the same?"

Vanderhanks intervened before Garvey could step into the trap Thatcher had set. "Is that the question you wanted to ask Dr. Garvey?"

"No, I want to ask him, plainly—what *are* his charges against me?"

Vanderhanks turned to Garvey. "Well, Ira," he said ruefully, "I'm sure you didn't have in mind to resurrect Robert for this job, and the only perfect man we have knowledge of isn't available either. Let's deal with the young man we did pick."

"All right," Garvey answered. "Here's my bill of particulars. Since Mr. Thatcher has been director, the Museum has been faced with a volley of unreasonable demands by militant artists. Lloyd Thatcher has been submissive and vacillating instead of firm and consistent. We have seen obscenities scrawled on our walls by a public virtually invited to do so. Our junior curators have expressed private dissatisfaction and, I'm informed, are in a state of almost open defiance. A valuable work of art has been destroyed as an outcome of his imprudent lending policies. In that same connection, he has threatened in effect to dismantle the Museum's collection by distributing it to other parts of the city. He has been in constant conflict with individual trustees, while we have all been disappointed by his failure to proceed vigorously with our fund-raising plans. Finally, there have been a series of unpleasant confrontations between Thatcher as director and various board members carrying out *their* responsibilities.

"Now, if I wished to be personal, I could cite one instance in which I myself found his conduct crudely offensive. Is that enough in the way of individual charges, or shall I continue? To me, the record suggests that Mr. Thatcher, despite his museum experience and background, which I admit is impressive, is fundamentally suspicious of and hostile toward the creative functions of patronage and connoisseurship. . . ."

Through the course of his speech, Garvey's voice rose steadily in power and volume, now conveying an intense conviction. Why, the man thinks I'm subversive, Thatcher thought. No wonder he wants me out—it's not a personal matter after all.

"I should think," Vanderhanks said after Garvey had finished his indictment, "that Lloyd Thatcher can best reply to these charges himself. Mr. Thatcher?"

Thatcher got up. "I hope you won't mind my beginning on a personal note," he said. "You're used to thinking of me as a westerner, and it's true I was born in California—a distinction I share with Mr. Specker, among others." The bleak suggestion of a smile passed across Barney Specker's ravaged face. "Yet a surprising amount of my life has centered on this institution. When I was a student, when I courted my wife here, when I visited Manhattan as a tourist—I was one of your resident gallery ghosts. Now, as a professional museum director, I have lost my amateur standing. But not, I hope, my standing among amateurs—I am closer to them than they can know.

"I want to say that I consider my present position the high point of my career, that I have no advantage to gain anywhere else by my performance here, and no ambition except to surpass myself if I can. . . .

"Is this museum the most difficult and demanding institution I have ever known? It is.

"Is it a Hydra, as Dr. Garvey suggests? When one problem is solved, do two others spring out in its place? It would seem so. And I may indeed be incapable of achieving real mastery over the heads of this Hydra. . . .

"I certainly do not blame all that has happened—the alienation of our young curators, the discord among the artists, the Museum's fiscal sufferings—on the trustees, or on my staff, or on the planets. But is it fair to lay the fault for these misfortunes entirely at my feet?

"What about the alienation of the younger curators Dr. Garvey cites? Their dissatisfactions, I submit, date back some while and are cumulative, not spontaneous. It is also true—is it not, Dr. Garvey?— that after the announcement of my impending resignation, a deputation of Museum curators came to ask you to reconsider your decision."

Vanderhanks looked at Garvey.

"Of course it's true, as he knows. I assumed he put them up to it."

"I did not. But if a man could order his staff to do that, and count on their doing it, surely he wouldn't have to worry about their loyalty."

"I didn't know of any such visitation," Vanderhanks said. "Quite a credit to you, Mr. Thatcher. Would you like to make any further comments?"

Oh, would I—how much time do you have to listen? Thatcher glanced quickly around the table and went on.

"I'd like to discuss Dr. Garvey's most important point—what he calls my insensitivity to the trustees, my 'hostility toward patronage and connoisseurship,' as I believe he put it. My relationships with artists also have a bearing on this subject.

"I have already suggested the degree of my personal devotion to the Museum: to the degree a man may love an institution, I love this one. As its director, I am bound in a web of responsibilities for the

244

Museum's health and survival—and I feel every one of these responsibilities as a personal obligation. How could I direct any museum without believing in the mission of every museum to collect? The museum
is the *supreme* collector—but a collector for the whole public, not the
favored few.

"It has been suggested by Dr. Garvey that I am too sympathetic to
the artists, militants, and radicals in particular. . . . The battle lines in
our lifetimes have been sharply drawn along many boundaries: youth
and age, black and white, poor and rich—artist and museum. Yes, we
too are in a battle.

"Well, it's tempting, when you're in a fight, to crouch behind the
barricades and shoot to kill whether you can see clearly or not. A practice designed to insure that enemies never become friends—and a good
way to destroy or 'radicalize' friendly neutrals who happen to find
themselves between the lines.

"I do not believe this museum should be turned into a fortress. I
do not believe that my mission is to beat back the criticisms of the
artists, or to ignore their problems. If we don't speak to them, who
will hear what they have to say to us?

"I think it is not only my job but my plain duty to try and reach
across this gulf. Nothing grows in a battle zone, nothing survives in an
atmosphere of suspicion and hostility.

"Maybe it's true that this institution as we know it is obsolete and
must give way to something different. Maybe I'm in the service of an
idea whose time has gone. I don't believe so—or I couldn't go on in
my profession—yet I do know that we must change. But with a clear
purpose and resolution, and with sensitivity to welcome the new and
the untried. . . . From which, after all, the art of the future will come."

Thatcher sat down, so abruptly that no one moved or spoke for a
moment. Austin Vanderhanks stared at Thatcher; Ira Garvey stared at
the chandelier hanging overhead.

"That's all you wish to say, Mr. Thatcher?" Vanderhanks said
finally.

Thatcher nodded.

"Very well. We are now open for other questions. Or discussion, if
you wish."

Barney Specker was the first to speak. Thatcher could not have
been more surprised—nor did he seem to be the only one caught off
balance.

245

"Seems to me," said Specker, "that when you give a man a damned hard job to do, you have to give him the authority to do it and the time he needs. Then if you're not satisfied, you get rid of him. Now, as much as I've enjoyed listening to Mr. Thatcher talk, I'd a hell of a lot rather see what the man can do."

Another hand was up.

"Mrs. Stearnes?"

"I'd like to ask Mr. Thatcher whatever happened to that painting that was attacked this fall . . . *Dallas?*"

"It has been completely restored," Thatcher said, "and we have returned it to Austin Vanderhanks. Mr. Vanderhanks has informed us that it will now be given to the National Gallery, as the artist had originally intended. It will thus be available free to anyone who wishes to see it."

"In other words, we lose the painting."

"We lose it, but the public gains. I think Mr. Vanderhanks' solution is the best under the circumstances."

Vanderhanks cleared his throat. "It was Mr. Thatcher's suggestion, not mine, but I'm glad we were able to settle the matter." He seemed embarrassed. "Mr. Thatcher," he said, "it's been suggested you've been delinquent on the fund-raising program. Would you care to comment on this?"

"Our staff is working to carry out the objectives of the program as effectively as possible. At the same time, I've raised what I think are legitimate questions about the program and about our priorities. Is this the right time to seek massive financial support? Shouldn't we perhaps be drawing back and trying to manage more frugally, using our present resources imaginatively instead of joining all the other institutions now beating the drum for large contributions? The Goodman Hart show cost almost as much to mount as an Off-Broadway musical. On the other hand, the "Dimensions" exhibition was an attempt to put on an interesting low-budget show."

Mary Lawless' heavily ringed hand moved back and forth until it caught Vanderhanks' eye.

"Mr. Thatcher," she said. "I was told people put dirty words and pictures on the wall of the Museum."

"Yes, there were graffiti in the exhibition I mentioned. They have now been removed from the walls."

"I should think so. I should certainly *think* so."

Vanderhanks turned to Garvey. "Dr. Garvey, do you have anything else to add?"

"Just one thing," said Garvey, remaining seated. "I don't want to seem unforgiving or insensitive, but I have given this whole matter a great deal of thought, and nothing Mr. Thatcher has said has altered my thinking. I will in fact speak right out and say that if Lloyd Thatcher remains as director, I don't see how I can continue to serve you effectively as president of the board. That's all."

"Then I think we should proceed to a vote," said Vanderhanks. "Mr. Thatcher, will you be willing to accept a secret ballot?"

"Certainly."

Suddenly everyone realized there was no paper, nor any pencils. A few minutes of telephoning and scurrying produced the necessities, perhaps more swiftly than paper and pencil had ever been fetched in the Museum before.

Thatcher sat and waited calmly through the silence in which ballots were filled out and turned back in. He had done what he could, said what he wanted to say. The world had seldom seemed so clearcut, so free of intrigue.

Now Vanderhanks had put on his tinted glasses and was counting the ballots, carefully entering little penciled slashes in two neat columns on his pad, shielding the operation with his cupped left hand.

Finally he raised his head and took up the tally sheet.

"The vote," he said, "is eight for the motion, and seven against."

Thatcher looked at Ira Garvey. Slumped in his chair, he was shaking his head slowly from side to side. He looked terribly tired.

"Ira?"

Garvey raised his head finally.

"Is there anything else you want to say?"

Garvey sighed. "A few minutes ago, I suggested that if Lloyd Thatcher were retained as director I would feel obligated to resign. I haven't changed my mind about his effectiveness in the position he was hired to fill. But I want to say that I can certainly see some of the justice in his position—and with a few important changes in wording, his statement of faith in the Museum might be my own. Also, I can't help being impressed by the fact that nearly half of you voted for him and against me. That fact makes me feel that maybe I don't have the board's confidence as president, not enough of it anyway." He looked up at Vanderhanks.

"Now, Ira—"

"And if I don't have the board's full backing, I'd frankly prefer to step aside."

What's he up to, Thatcher wondered. Was this an uncharacteristic bid for sympathy?

"What is it you want us to do, Ira?" Vanderhanks asked.

"Mr. Chairman, I'd like you to consider accepting my resignation."

A sudden intake of breath, which Thatcher realized was his own, and then:

"So moved!"

Both Serena Lord and Barney Specker had spoken at once; Oscar Wood chimed in behind them only because he was trying to light his pipe when the thunderclap sounded.

"Seconded," came several voices together.

"Wait!"

"Dr. Garvey," Austin Vanderhanks said, "you have the floor."

"I don't wish any discussion of this motion."

"Then we put it to a show of hands," said Vanderhanks. "All those in favor of accepting Dr. Garvey's resignation as president of the board, please raise your hands. . . . Opposed?" He turned to Garvey. "Your resignation is accepted, Ira. With our deep gratitude for your service to the board in that capacity."

Thatcher stared at the former president of the board in amazement; Ira Garvey looked across the table and shrugged. Then, sadly but with unmistakable affection, he smiled at Thatcher.

"Ira . . ."

"Yes, Austin?"

"You will, of course, remain on the board?"

"Well, now, I never had any intention of leaving the board," Garvey said. "Of course I'll stay, whether you people like it or not, and I can assure you that sometimes you're not going to like it at all."

"Lloyd," said Vanderhanks, "I believe the vote on your separation was just, if harsh. We'll be as generous as possible, and you'll be permitted to resign if you wish."

"Thank you, Austin," Thatcher said. "You'll have my resignation this afternoon."

"The way I see it then," said Austin Vanderhanks, "this meeting stands adjourned."

248

They were all as silent in leaving as they had been in coming. Serena lingered behind to talk to Thatcher.

"I'm sorry, Lloyd. I know how hurt you must feel—"

"Hurt?"

"Well, aren't you?"

Thatcher considered her question. How *did* he feel? Numb, he supposed. Tired. Even relieved. But hurt?

"Not really," he said. "In many ways I'm inclined to agree with Austin that justice has been done."

"Maybe I'm the one showing the wound then," she said. "I suppose it's too soon to ask, but do you have any idea what you'll do now?"

"Hell, I hadn't really thought much about it." He started to take the telegram out of his inside coat pocket, then pushed it back in. "I've had one offer already—I hope there'll be others. I'd like to take my time, and look around carefully. If I can, I want to find a museum that will satisfy both my requirements—and Abe Zachary's."

"Anyway—good luck."

Thatcher smiled. "Don't believe in it," he said. "But if it comes from you—if it comes at all—I'll take it."

They walked toward the elevator; wordlessly, yet without a trace of constraint.

"Lloyd?"

Ira Garvey came up alongside them as they waited for the car.

"Will you take it at face value if I tell you I'll be glad to help you in any way I can?"

"I'll take it for what it's worth," Thatcher replied. "Maybe someday I'll even feel like thanking you."

The doors slid open and they stepped into an elevator crowded with parents, children, students, the curious squeezed in beside the wary—all of them, in a manner of speaking, patrons of the arts.

RENEWALS 69

DAT

NOV 0 1

Demco, Inc. 38-293

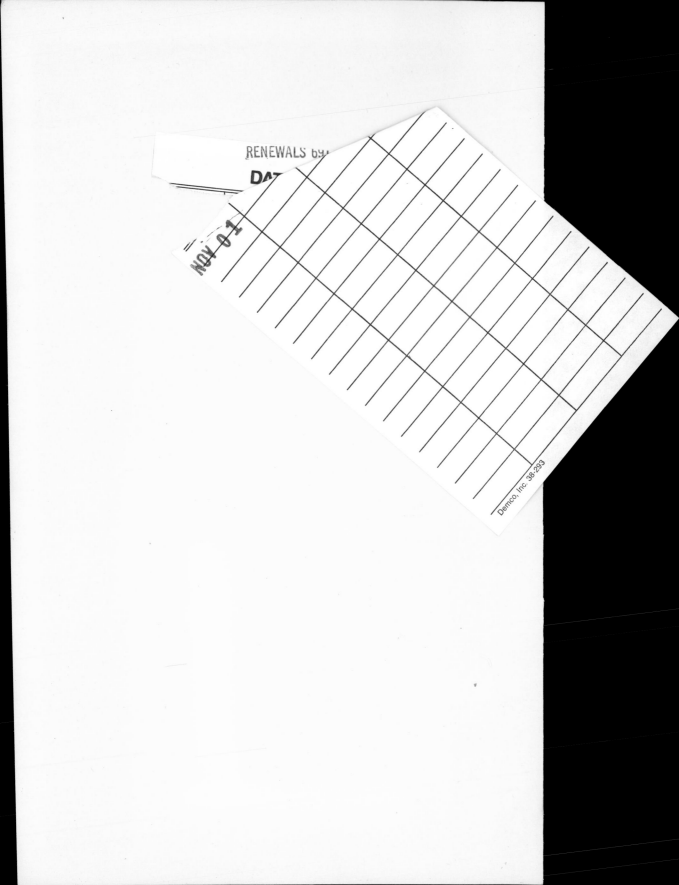